A FRENCH COUNTRY ESCAPE

JENNIFER BOHNET

Boldwood

First published in Great Britain in 2024 by Boldwood Books Ltd.

Copyright © Jennifer Bohnet, 2024

Cover Design by Debbie Clement Design

Cover Photography: Shutterstock

The moral right of Jennifer Bohnet to be identified as the author of this work has been asserted in accordance with the Copyright, Designs and Patents Act 1988.

Every effort has been made to obtain the necessary permissions with reference to copyright material, both illustrative and quoted. We apologise for any omissions in this respect and will be pleased to make the appropriate acknowledgements in any future edition.

A CIP catalogue record for this book is available from the British Library.

Paperback ISBN 978-1-80162-304-9

Large Print ISBN 978-1-80162-303-2

Hardback ISBN 978-1-80162-302-5

Ebook ISBN 978-1-80162-305-6

Kindle ISBN 978-1-80162-306-3

Audio CD ISBN 978-1-80162-297-4

MP3 CD ISBN 978-1-80162-298-1

Digital audio download ISBN 978-1-80162-300-1

Boldwood Books Ltd
23 Bowerdean Street
London SW6 3TN
www.boldwoodbooks.com

For Richard, with all my love

PROLOGUE

The Château du Cheval, its foundations dug firmly into the Brittany countryside during the dying days of Emperor Napoleon III, fits perfectly into the landscape and dominates the valley it overlooks. The picturesque and regal drive sweeps through the grounds to the curved flight of stone steps at the front entrance, the sunshine glistening off the many original windows. Holidaymakers, catching a brief glimpse of the château as they drive along the route down towards the Gulf of Morbihan, dream of winning the lottery and living their best life in such a home, deep in the French countryside.

Winds of change have swept through the château on more than one occasion but, always, it has done its best to protect those who live there, whether they were aristocrats living in the building itself, or one of the many butlers, maids, servants and stable hands residing in the attics, or in cottages scattered across the estate in years gone by. Two world wars took both the able-bodied men and women, as well as horses, from the château and its neighbouring villages. The small chapel in the grounds bears testament to the true cost of these wars. The shrinkage of the surrounding land is another testament to how things have changed.

Visitors through the years, stepping onto the marble floor of the entrance hall, often commented on how welcoming the château felt. Everyone murmured how they wished the walls could talk; the stories they would tell would surely be unforgettable. There would be tales of owners, servants, scandals, good times, bad times, and even famous horses.

Now it's the third decade of the twenty-first century, and the château senses that things are changing once again as the warm, gentle, southerly breeze nudges things awake in spring. The building has been restored and is coming back to life. Long-forgotten actions will be brought to the fore in the modern world with unexpected consequences. An uncovered secret will give a modern generation the opportunity to mend the actions of a previous generation and heal the hurt of the past. A story that began in the nineteenth century far away from the Château du Cheval will have its happy ending here in this, the twenty-first century.

1

END OF DECEMBER LAST YEAR

The day after Sasha Heath and her brother Freddie returned home from property hunting in Brittany, Northern France, Sasha made what she realised would be one of her last visits to their old family home. It was a discombobulating feeling moving between the mostly empty rooms. In the last few weeks since their mother had died, as she cleared it ready for sale, Sasha had felt the house starting to withdraw from her, becoming a part of her past life, their close connection lost. It was such a weird feeling. Distance sprang up between herself and the memories of how the rooms had once cocooned her as the house emptied and prepared itself for another family to move in, with their own problems, foibles and traditions. Already, it no longer felt like the home it had once been for both her and Freddie.

The smart red leather Chesterfield which had been her mother's pride and joy stood incongruously alone on the bare, faded floorboards of the sitting room. Thoughtfully, Sasha ran her hand along the top of the settee which she'd planned to sell, despite it being the one piece of furniture she longed to keep for herself. But the day was approaching when she would have to list it on eBay. Her one-bedroom so-called 'penthouse' flat – but in reality, an unfurnished 'attic' – was too small, and it was doubtful that the settee would even get up the long narrow flight of stairs leading to her door. Besides, there was no real point in even trying. Any day now she was expecting to be served with the official notice to quit her flat. The new property-developing landlords had planning permission to refurbish the nineteenth-century terrace of houses and were evicting everyone with the promise that they could return afterwards – if, of course, they could afford the exorbitant new rents. Which, she was pretty sure, would be out of her price range. As for where she'd go, she had no idea. One-bedroom flats in Clifton were like gold dust these days, with so many students studying at the university. She'd be lucky to be able to afford a bedsit on the outskirts of town, turning her five-minute walk to work into a long forty-minute commute. It was one of the reasons she'd agreed to at least look at property in France when Freddie had suggested it.

His argument that neither of them would ever be able to get on the property ladder here in the UK had a certain truth to it. 'But if we join forces, we could use Mum's inheritance to buy a place big enough for the two of us in France and be mortgage-free, and hopefully still have a little money left in the bank. Property over there, especially in Brittany, is so much more affordable than here – despite all the paperwork involved now because of Brexit.'

'We still have to work though,' Sasha had pointed out. 'And neither of us are fluent French speakers, which is a major stumbling block. My schoolgirl French won't get us far.'

'We'll pick it up, and maybe we can go to classes both here before we go and then when we're over there,' Freddie had said confidently. 'We'll make sure we each keep some money back to live on. I should be able to find some odd jobs, gardening and basic maintenance. I've had plenty of experience working at Riverside Residential Home.'

'Not sure what *I*'ll be able to do,' Sasha had said. 'Maybe do some gardening with you?'

Freddie had laughed. 'One word: forget-me-nots.'

'I'm never going to live that down, am I? I was ten. I wanted to surprise Mum and help her. There were so many of them all over the place I thought they just had to be weeds.' Sasha smiled nonchalantly. 'Anyway, they all grew back again – just like weeds do.'

'You'd find something to do,' Freddie had assured her. 'If we buy the right place, we can use it as a stepping stone onto the property ladder, renovate it and then sell it on. Buy something bigger and do it again, or we can each buy one. Either way, it would be a fresh start for—for both of us,' he'd added quietly, looking at his sister. 'For you after Bradley, and for me because I've got itchy feet right now and want to do something different, get out of the rut I seem to have sunk into. I think Mum would approve.'

Sasha had bitten her lip and nodded. 'Okay, but nothing that needs major renovations. Whatever we buy must have four square walls and a good roof at the very least,' Sasha had made him promise. She was a dab hand at painting and putting wallpaper up and wouldn't mind having a go at plastering, but bricklaying and roof tiling would be a step too far. Hunting out bargains in charity shops and second-hand furniture depots and upcycling them had become a favourite hobby. She loved interior design and making rooms look stylish as well as cosy and comfy. When she and Bradley had married, she'd enjoyed doing up the house they'd rented and had fond memories of the time she'd spent turning it into a home – something Bradley had turned out to have no interest in.

Owning somewhere and having a free hand to go – not mad, exactly – but to attempt something maybe a bit different, or even funky, would be great. Now, standing in the empty house she and Freddie had grown up in, Sasha wondered about the possibility of keeping the Chesterfield as she remembered that last week in France and the property they'd both fallen in love with.

Some of the so-called 'cheap' renovation properties the agent had shown them had looked more like total rebuilds. There had been a couple that Freddie had liked but Sasha had thought their location on a main road or in the depths of the countryside far from ideal. A tall four-storey house in the centre of Morlaix dating from the eighteenth century appealed to them both, but it was a registered historical building and came complete with a list of things that needed to be adhered to, which frightened both of them.

Both Sasha and Freddie were beginning to despair of ever finding something suitable when Solange, the agent who had been showing them around every day, took them to see the two Cottages du Lac.

'These were originally agricultural workers' cottages on an old French estate, the Château du Cheval,' she had explained as she drove them. 'The estate was a lot bigger until after the Second World War when lots of the land and cottages were sold off. The château and the remaining twelve hectares were sold again a couple of years ago. The new owners have been renovating it and the garden and grounds are slowly being reclaimed from the wilderness of neglect. I think you will like these cottages.'

'It's still a private estate?' Freddie had asked.

Solange had nodded as she turned the car onto a drive with a faded 'Château du Cheval. Privé' sign on the left verge and then, thirty metres or so farther along, they had gone through an open pair of imposing wrought-iron gates, before passing some brick buildings with a clock tower.

'Is that a stable block?' Sasha had asked.

Solange had nodded. 'Yes, but I don't think the Chevaliers keep horses. I understand their plan is to open the château to paying guests this summer and also to act as a wedding venue eventually. But the gates are closed every night; the owners of the cottages will of course be given an electronic key. Like a gated domain in the UK, right?'

'Not sure about that,' Freddie had muttered. 'The grounds still look like they could do with more attention.' He had turned to look at Sasha. 'Could be a job right on our own doorstep for me.'

'We haven't seen the cottages yet, stop jumping the gun,' Sasha had said, trying to stop herself thinking about the possibility of living close to stables that could be housing actual horses. It had been years since she'd ridden a horse but her teenage passion for them had never completely died.

'The château is in that direction,' Solange had said, pointing to the left. 'But we go this way.' And she'd driven carefully along a narrow track.

Sasha had peered to the left quickly, hoping to get a glimpse of the château, but a group of trees blocked the view and regretfully, she'd turned her head away just as the lake and the two cottages came into view. 'Oh, what a gorgeous setting!'

Solange had stopped the car to one side of the cottages and the three of them had got out. 'We'll start with No. 1. The cottages are quite basic. Which means you get to modernise them in your own way.' And she'd ushered them into a surpris-

ingly spacious hallway with a wooden staircase leading to the
first floor and three bedrooms. 'Sitting room on the left, with
French windows at the front and a smaller window on the side.
Lovely fireplace, don't you think? The log burner fits in well.
Next door doesn't have a wood burner. The kitchen on the right
is a fair size, with French windows on the front again, but as this
joins the wall of No. 2, there is obviously no side window.'
Solange had pointed to the door at the back of the kitchen.
'That leads into the garden. I'll show you that after we've been
upstairs,' and she had led them up to the next floor. 'Two fair-
sized rooms, a smaller one, nice landing and a bathroom –
albeit one that needs updating.'

'It's surprisingly roomy,' Sasha had said as she followed
Solange back downstairs. 'It's bigger than I expected. And No. 2
is the same?'

Solange had nodded. 'In reverse.'

'And the owners are happy to sell just the one cottage?'

Solange had stopped and turned to look at her. 'No. The two
are for sale together.'

'But surely together they are out of the price range we gave
you?' Sasha had asked, smothering a sigh. She'd thought the
cottage was too good to be true.

'It's five thousand euros over your top price,' Solange had
said. 'But it's literally two for the price of one. If you like the
cottages, make an offer. Now I will show you the garden.'

Half an hour later when Solange had driven them away,
they'd seen both cottages, the gardens with the tumbledown
sheds they each possessed, and had walked around the lake.
Sasha, to her own surprise, was already dreaming about living
here on this wonderful estate. The only trouble was she
couldn't quite gauge yet how Freddie truly felt about the place.
He'd asked all the right questions, seemed enthusiastic, but

Sasha sensed there was something bothering him. It wasn't until after Solange had dropped them back at their Airbnb that he admitted his worry.

'On the face of it, the Cottages du Lac are perfect for us. We'd each get our own place in a beautiful setting, and hopefully have money left to live on whilst we settle in and find work.' He'd given Sasha a serious look. 'I love the cottages and can see us living there, but we could have a problem with privacy. What happens when the château and the grounds are open to the public? I know the gates will be locked at night for security, but during the day people will be able to wander anywhere. Right now, anybody could walk up and peer in through the windows.'

'Did you mention this to Solange?'

'Yes. She felt sure the Chevaliers – that is such a great French name, isn't it? – would understand and find a solution. A small amount of land in front will come with the cottages for parking, so maybe a hedge or a picket fence could be put in place around that.'

'Well, that sounds okay to me,' Sasha had said. 'Lots of the houses we've seen in villages open directly onto the street, so people could peer in there too. Shall we do as Solange suggested and make an offer? One that keeps us within the price range we agreed? And see what they say.'

'Yes,' Freddie had said. 'And, for the record, I really hope they say yes.'

'So do I,' Sasha had answered, crossing her fingers for good luck and remembering the stables she'd glimpsed. 'So do I.'

2

Ingrid Chevalier was carefully washing Merlin, the marble prancing horse statue recently returned from being restored, and now standing on his plinth in the main hallway of the Château du Cheval, when the estate agent rang. Moments later, she'd closed the large heavy oak door of the château and was striding purposefully towards the overgrown Mediterranean garden where Peter, her husband, was doing his best to chainsaw his way through the various vines and other plants that had claimed it as their own over the last few years.

Gladys, their Golden Labrador bitch, heard her approaching before Peter did and ran towards her, tail wagging joyfully.

Peter glanced up, stopped the chainsaw and put it on the ground.

'It's decision time,' Ingrid said as she reached him. 'Solange, the *agent immobilier*, rang. The brother and sister who viewed the cottages earlier this week have made an offer. I've told her we'll let her know within the next twenty-four hours whether we accept it or not.'

'We can talk about it this evening,' Peter said. 'Or we could walk over there now and talk about it on site.' He gestured behind him at the tangle of overgrown plants. 'I could do with a break from this. I swear that chainsaw gets heavier every time I use it.'

'Come on, then. Let's do that.'

And the two of them, accompanied by Gladys, began to walk through the château grounds towards the cottages that, in years gone by, had been two of several around the estate.

Ingrid gave a happy sigh looking at the view as they reached the boundary of their land behind and to the west of the château itself. A century ago, a large part of the estate had been forested, a mixture of oaks, cedar, pine, beech and fir, whilst the rest of the grounds had been a mixture of fields for arable land and sheep. At one time, an earth track had circled around the property, put there by a keen owner who had raised and trained thoroughbred horses. By the time she and Peter had bought the place about eighteen months ago, sixty-eight hectares consisting mainly of fields, some woodland and a couple of derelict cottages had been sold off, leaving the château and its remaining twelve hectares surrounded by fencing overgrown with impenetrable brambles and self-seeded saplings, and an impressive pair of wrought-iron gates on the main driveway. The traditional brick-built stables with their cobbled floors and iron metalwork dividing the stalls stood a few hundred metres inside the main entrance. A two-storey general-purpose building hidden behind the stables served as a store for farm implements, hay, straw and other agricultural supplies.

'You okay?' Peter asked as he heard Ingrid sigh.

She nodded. 'I love the panoramic view we get from this side of the château – the rolling French countryside with its hills and valleys stretching away in the distance, the wind turbines visible on the high ground. There are very few signs of habitation, just the occasional house or small village with its church spire visible, and maybe a couple of tractors working the fields. I can't help but wonder how much it has truly changed in the last seventy or so years.'

'Quite a lot, I suspect,' Peter said. 'There would have been horses and people working those small fields from dawn to dusk for days and weeks on end until about the sixties or seventies, I suppose. Hi-tech tractors and combines arrived then and got the work done so much quicker with less manpower. Cottages began to be abandoned as agricultural workers were needed less and less. Hedgerows were pulled out, joining three, four, five of the smaller fields together. The gallop dirt track around the estate was a casualty of all that. The stables that housed working animals alongside the thoroughbreds changed too as the world moved on after the Second World War.'

'I'm so glad our land still consists of smaller fields and woods and copses. It's better for the wildlife.'

'Right now, I'm glad Jean-Paul is paying us rent for the use of some of those hectares.' Peter's voice was grim. 'Together with that unexpected DIY livery in the stables starting soon, it does at least mean some money coming in.' The enquiry from one of the villagers who needed somewhere to stable her horse had been a complete surprise. Neither Peter nor Ingrid had realised there would be a demand for something like that. Their long-term plan had been to turn the stable blocks into self-contained holiday accommodation.

Ingrid nodded. 'We'll see how this first one settles in and then clear the other stalls and ask around, see if anyone else would like to rent one. I still haven't decided what to do with all the horse memorabilia I found in the tack room. Horses have been such a big part of the château's history, we can't just ignore it and throw it all away. We need to display it somewhere, I think.'

The path they were on took them past the empty house currently known as *La Maison du Jardinier,* which they planned to renovate sometime in the future. Soon they were standing looking for signs of life in the small lake in front of the Cottages du Lac.

'D'you remember how last summer there were so many dragonflies, tadpole spawn and damselflies?' Ingrid said. 'I loved coming down here and watching them. Butterflies too love that buddleia by the front door of No. 2.' She was silent for a few seconds before turning to look at the cottages. 'I still think these would make two lovely gîtes. Which would be another source of income for us.'

'At the moment, we haven't got the money to do the necessary upgrade,' Peter answered. 'And we require an injection of cash right now so we can finally get the château open this summer for guests and start to get our name out there for events. The occasional wedding or maybe vintage car rally, car boot sales or...' Peter shook his head in exasperation. 'I don't know what. I do know we said we'd never break up the remaining estate, but things have changed so much in the last year, selling the cottages seems to be the only avenue open to us.'

Ingrid nodded thoughtfully. 'Everything has been so much more expensive than we expected – despite all those flow charts and spreadsheets we created.' She gave Peter a small smile. His unexpected redundancy at sixty had given them the opportunity to change their lives and they'd seized it happily. They'd both done their 'due diligence' at the time of buying the château, but they'd definitely been guilty of looking at things through rose-coloured glasses with a touch of naivety thrown in.

'This offer we have then – is it close to the asking price? Or do we have to try to negotiate for a few extra thousands?' Peter asked.

'Close enough. It's eight thousand short, but we did agree that the maximum we could drop would be ten thousand euros. So,' Ingrid shrugged, 'Solange says the couple have really fallen in love with the place and are cash buyers, so the sale should go through quickly. The man – I forget his name, Solange did say – will be looking for work and could be interested in helping with the grounds.' Ingrid hesitated. 'There's something that worries me though. What if whoever buys the cottages doesn't fit in, doesn't like living here, and in a few months they put the cottages back on the market? We'll have no say then about who they sell to.'

Peter was silent for a moment. 'We could try to put a clause in saying that if that happens, we have first refusal and the right to buy the cottages back. And then cross our fingers that if that *does* happen, it won't be until the château is established and earning its keep with guests and events. I'd rather turn them into holiday rentals too, but...' He caught hold of Ingrid's hand. 'The château rooms are ready for guests this year, and the money from the sale of these two cottages will give us enough to finish the chapel renovations so we can offer a full wedding package. We need to employ a gardener and general handyman to help me finish sorting out the grounds, ready for safe public access. And then we can start doing some proper publicising for the *chambres d'hôtes*. I know it has been a struggle getting this far.' Peter glanced at Ingrid. 'And the last year has been hard on both of us. I also know people thought we were mad at our age to take something like this on, especially in a foreign country. Do you regret taking it on? I know it was my idea to leave

England, my dream to live in France more than yours.' He hesitated. 'If you feel it's too much for us, rather than just sell the cottages, we could sell up completely. The château is in a much better state than when we bought it, so we should at least get our money back.'

Ingrid shook her head defiantly. 'No regrets.' Peter might be the one with the French ancestors, but she loved their life in France and felt completely at home there. 'I love the place, and the last year, seeing it come back to life has been worth all the hard work, and I'm longing to see it filled with guests and busy with people enjoying themselves. And don't forget Penny. She loves it here too and I'm just hoping the time will come when she...' Ingrid paused, thinking about their daughter and weighing up her words carefully, 'decides to join us and make a life for herself here in France.'

'I know you and I weren't that keen on Rory the one and only time we've met him after we moved over here,' Peter said. 'And I have to admit, I can't quite see suave Rory giving up his job to come and live in rural France. Paris maybe, but not Brittany.'

Ingrid gripped Peter's hand hard. 'They aren't even living together yet and my gut feeling is they never will. I think Penny is holding back from that commitment for some reason. Anyway, back to our current problem. I refuse to sell up and let someone else benefit from all the hard work we've already done. Selling the château will be our very last resort. I say we accept the offer on the cottages and continue with our dream.'

3

The next few weeks passed in a daze for Sasha. Since their offer on the Cottages du Lac in Finistère had been accepted, her life had been beyond busy. There was a never-ending list on her laptop of jobs to be done, people to be contacted, contracts for telephones, Netflix, internet, electricity – to name but four – to be cancelled, packing up her few possessions, her notice to be worked. Handing in her resignation had prompted Derek, her boss, to try to bribe her to stay with a pay rise. A pay rise she would gladly have accepted months ago, but now it was just too late to be told how valuable a member of the team she was and that they didn't want to lose her. She had a new life waiting for her in France and nothing they said or offered was going to delay the start of it. A life that would not include spreadsheets, if she had anything to do with it. Of course, she realised that her schoolgirl knowledge of French was going to limit her choice of jobs, especially at first, but hopefully that would change once they were living there and using the language on a daily basis.

It was in the middle of the night that the worries and the fears flooded her dreams in full Technicolor, waking her with a start and leaving her catching her breath. Were they doing the right thing? They were both aware they would have to be careful with money. Would they make friends? What were the Chevaliers like? Sasha wished that they'd had time to meet them before buying the cottages – what if they were Parisians who'd moved to Brittany for a different way of life after the pandemic? She'd been told Parisians were difficult to get on with. Full of attitude and superiority. Solange had assured them that the owners were really lovely people, but then she *would* say that, wouldn't she? However hard she tried, the worries of the unknown future she and Freddie were voluntarily leaping into wouldn't be stilled.

Since her divorce from Bradley, she'd struggled to get not only her finances back on an even keel, but also her life. Her mum had been her champion there. Sasha knew that she could have spiralled into depression if it hadn't been for her mum insisting she was not a failure and calling Bradley names, not so quietly under her breath. There hadn't been a marital home to sell, no children, no joint account to divide – just divorce lawyers to pay. Now, two years down the line, she'd recovered from the trauma of that period and was happy enough with her life, although, if pressed, she would admit to being ready for another relationship. One that this time would lead to the family she longed for. She pushed that thought way. Her top priority was settling in and sorting out her cottage, and then finding some sort of revenue.

Her savings were reasonable, but wouldn't last forever in France without being topped up with an income from something or other. She planned on trying to set aside some money by being as self-sufficient as possible when they got to France – growing their own vegetables, mainly tomatoes and lettuce in this first summer, and things like that. She figured that buying small plants and putting them in weed-free, freshly dug soil would give her a head start on recognising the weeds when they started to appear which, of course, was inevitable. Freddie was going to plant a couple of things in both the cottage gardens that they'd taken from their mum's plot. Some cuttings of a couple of the rose bushes and some roots of the ground-covering snow-on-the-mountain to edge the paths.

Asking herself how long it would take to improve her French, find a job and settle into a new culture was a proverbial unanswerable question. But Sasha hoped it wouldn't be as long as she feared it might be. She was determined to have room in this new existence of hers to have some fun, to spend time doing things she enjoyed and to make new friends.

As she packed sketch pads and paints into a box ready to leave England, she knew she wanted that side of her life back too. Before she and Bradley had got together, she'd built up an Etsy shop with her sketches and watercolours of horses, dogs and cats. Bradley had called it her 'side hustle' and made rude comments about her 'little hobby' whenever he got the chance. Although he hadn't been adverse to her spending the so-called 'pin money' on dinners out for the two of them, or on putting the petrol in a car she rarely drove. By the time they divorced, sketching and painting had virtually disappeared because of Bradley's insistence that she spend more time with him, and her Etsy shop had been down to merely ticking over. Recovering from the hurt Bradley had inflicted on her when he'd left her for Monica – the woman living two doors away from them – had taken time as she struggled to pick up the pieces of her existence again.

Best not think about that. It was in the past. *He* was in the past. And there was no way Sasha was going to let a man rule her life like that ever again. She took a deep breath, closed and sealed the last box, pushed her shoulders back and promised herself that her new start in France would be different and wonderful.

And then, like a bad smell, Bradley turned up again.

* * *

It was the week before they were due to move when an unsuspecting Sasha answered a knock on the door of her flat. Assuming it was one of her downstairs neighbours, she opened it without thinking. Struck dumb for a second or two from the shock of seeing him standing there, she tried to close the door in his face, but Bradley already had his foot in the way.

'What are you doing here? And how did you get in?' Sasha demanded.

'Hi, Sasha. How are you? I heard about your mum, and I thought the least I could do was to come and pay my respects.'

'There was no need, but thank you and goodbye,' and Sasha pushed the door again to try to close it. Bradley's foot though stayed firmly wedged in the way.

'I'd also like to say I'm sorry for the way I behaved.'

Sasha caught her breath as she gazed at him, dumbfounded.

'Please may I come in and we can talk?'

'No. There is nothing to talk about,' Sasha said. 'Just leave. I'm expecting Freddie any moment.'

'Of course you are.' Bradley gave a sceptical laugh. 'Monica and I are no longer together. I realised I'd made a mistake.'

'Still lying your way through life,' Sasha replied. The day she'd bumped into Monica in the local shop and been told the truth directly would stay in her mind for a long time. 'It was Monica who realised the whole thing was a mistake and kicked you out six months ago, which quite frankly made me laugh. A bit of karma there I think.'

Bradley shrugged. 'Doesn't matter how it happened. It's us I want to talk about. You have no one else in your life and neither do I now. We could start again, give ourselves a second chance in a home of our own. Make it work this time. What do you think?'

Sasha took a deep breath as she realised what this visit was truly about. 'What do I think? I think you are not only delusional but also a despicable human being. You heard about Mum dying, realised Freddie and I might inherit some money, and thought you'd like some of it. Now please take your foot away from my door and leave. I don't want anything to do with you ever again.'

'And to think I once thought you and I were soulmates.' Bradley gave her a contemptuous look. 'You're nothing but a selfish cow.'

'Looks like I got here just in time,' Freddie said, stepping onto the landing. 'You all right, sis? Or do I have to accidentally trip up this scumbag so he falls down the stairs?'

'I'm leaving,' Bradley huffed.

'Good decision,' Freddie said. 'I won't assist you then.' And he and Sasha both stood watching as Bradley strutted down the stairs and disappeared.

Sasha gave a deep sigh. 'Good riddance to bad rubbish. I can't wait to get to France and begin my new life in the Cottages du Lac.'

4

It was the last week of March when the cottages became theirs and Sasha and Freddie left England for France on the night ferry from Plymouth to Roscoff. Despite it being a calm crossing, Sasha couldn't sleep and spent most of the night listening to her brother gently snoring in the top bunk, and worrying about the future.

An hour and a half after they'd driven off the ferry in Roscoff, they were deep in the Brittany countryside and a few moments away from their new homes. Sasha gazed around her. 'It's as beautiful as I remember. Even better now that the sun is shining and the sky is blue,' she said laughing, remembering the grey winter sky from their original visit to view the cottages. 'And look, there are primroses in the hedge.' She turned to Freddie. 'It is going to be all right, isn't it, Freddie?' she asked tremulously. 'We are doing the right thing, aren't we?'

'Too late for second thoughts now, sis,' Freddie answered. 'We're here, so it's up to us to make it work and we will,' and he turned the car onto the château drive.

Sasha bit her lip. Knowing Freddie as well as she did, she

could tell from the tone of his voice that he was just as anxious as her. 'We *will* make it work,' she muttered to herself determinedly as Freddie pulled up to one side of the cottages, leaving room for the small removal van that had followed them from Roscoff to park alongside.

Time passed quickly as the two removal men, helped by Freddie and directed by Sasha, unloaded the van and divided the meagre contents between the two cottages. Freddie, having lived in furnished accommodation as part of his job, had little of his own – just a bed and a chair he'd bought to bring with him, a couple of rugs and a box or two of personal possessions. The plan was for him to sleep in No. 2 but to spend most of his time with Sasha in No. 1 until he'd sourced some more fittings and sorted a kitchen. Sasha's one-bedroom flat hadn't exactly been full of furniture, but she did have the basics for a bedroom, her mum's Chesterfield for the sitting room, and a cooker and fridge for the kitchen.

Sasha was indicating where the cooker should go to the removal men, when Ingrid appeared at the door with a flask of coffee and several pains au chocolat for everyone.

'Hello, I'm Ingrid Chevalier. Welcome to the Cottages du Lac,' she said, shaking Sasha's hand. 'I hope you and your brother will be very happy here.'

'I'm Natasha Heath, known as Sasha. My brother is Freddie. Thank you for this,' Sasha said, taking the basket containing the drink and the food. 'It's really kind of you. I haven't found the kettle yet.' Sasha smiled at Ingrid. 'Your accent... With your surname, we expected you to be French, but you sound English.' She gave Ingrid a quizzical look.

Ingrid laughed. 'Lots of people make that mistake before they know us. Yes, we're both English, from the West Country, but Peter does like to boast about his French ancestors from the nineteenth century.'

'If I had French relatives, I'd boast about them too,' Sasha said, relieved that Ingrid was so friendly and welcoming. 'The château looks wonderful from the outside. Solange, the estate agent, said you've been renovating – did you have a lot to do?'

'More than we expected.' Ingrid sighed. 'Thankfully, it's more or less finished now, although, of course, it will never be finished totally, there will always be maintenance – for the grounds as well as for the building itself. The grounds really need a full-time gardener, but until the place provides an income, Peter will carry on doing it as best he can with part-time help. Now, moving-in day is always fraught, but we're hoping you and Freddie will join us for a celebratory glass of champagne to welcome you, and a bite to eat tonight? I can give you a guided tour of the château then as well, if you'd like to see it.'

'Thank you,' Sasha said. 'Please. That's so lovely of you.'

'I'll leave you to it then. Please don't hesitate to come and find us if you need anything, otherwise we'll see you about seven,' and Ingrid turned to leave. 'Oh, I nearly forgot. Our apartment is at the back of the château, we personally rarely use the front entrance. Bit too grand for everyday use!'

As Sasha poured coffee for everyone and handed the pains au chocolat around, she smiled happily. Only their first day and already things were going better than she'd dared to hope. Ingrid was so welcoming with her basket of food, an invitation for supper, and the offer to give them a longed-for tour of the château. Life in France was definitely getting off to a good start.

* * *

For the next few hours, Sasha and Freddie worked together, unpacking the boxes they could, pushing into various corners in both cottages the ones with contents that had to stay packed up for the lack of cupboards or somewhere to place them. To Sasha's delight, the pantry in No. 1's kitchen had an electric socket under the marble shelf where the fridge fitted perfectly once they'd found the box with the French adapters. Freddie checked the ancient wall cupboard was fixed securely before Sasha placed her crockery inside, and the kettle and coffee machine found a home on the small pine kitchen table she'd brought with her, when it was pushed against the wall to act as a working surface for the time being.

Freddie's meagre belongings did little to fill the rooms in No. 2.

'I need to seriously find some furniture,' he said ruefully. 'Starting with a fridge and a cooker.'

'You can use mine, don't go spending money too soon. The list of things I need is growing too,' Sasha said. 'Just in here, I want a dresser, a proper kitchen table and chairs, some shelving, and that old fireplace is calling out for a modern range. Think the floor needs some new tiles too,' she added, scuffing her foot along the floor. 'And the walls need painting.'

'Better make painting the last job,' Freddie said. 'But it would be good to decorate before we fill both cottages with furniture.'

Sasha nodded. 'You're right.' She glanced at her watch. 'We'd better try to tidy ourselves up before we go to the château. I did switch on the water heater earlier, so hopefully there will be hot water.'

Twenty minutes later, when they'd both freshened up as best they could, Sasha switched the hall light on to welcome them home later, locked the front door behind them and they set off.

'I wish we had something to take with us – a box of chocolates or a bottle of wine,' she said. 'I don't like going anywhere empty-handed. It seems rude.'

'I'm sure it doesn't matter on this occasion,' Freddie said. 'They've invited us as a welcome to the cottages, so I'm sure they're not expecting us to turn up with the champagne.'

Approaching the curve in the path that led to the château, Sasha glanced back at the cottages and sighed happily as she saw the hall light shining in No. 1. She owned that cottage. Whatever happened now, she would always have a roof over her head. She squeezed Freddie's arm. 'I miss Mum so much, but if it weren't for her, we wouldn't be here. I wish we could hug her and say thank you.'

Freddie, never one to show his emotions, nodded and murmured something in agreement that sounded like, 'I'll plant those rose cuttings tomorrow.'

5

As they got closer to the château, Sasha and Freddie followed the lights that were shining out from the side and back windows onto a flagstone path. The back door, an ancient heavy oak one, was illuminated by an old-fashioned oil lamp converted to electricity. Sasha made a mental note to try to find something similar for their cottages.

Freddie reached out and lifted the ring of the antique brass door-knocker and gave a gentle tap.

There was a short bark before they heard Ingrid call out, 'It's open. Come on in.'

As Freddie turned the handle on the heavy door and ushered Sasha in to a large, beautifully fitted-out kitchen, a Golden Labrador wandered over to inspect them. Sasha immediately bent down to stroke her. 'Aren't you beautiful?'

'Hello, I'm Peter Chevalier. Welcome to the Château du Cheval from the three of us,' Peter said as he moved forward to greet them, while Ingrid poured four flutes of champagne.

'Gladys does like to inspect and greet everyone,' Ingrid said.

'We wish you every happiness in your new life in France and here in the cottages,' Peter said, handing them each a flute.

'Thank you.'

The four of them clinked glasses and took a sip before Sasha said, 'Ingrid mentioned you have French ancestors – is the château connected to your family? Is that why you bought it?'

Peter smiled as he shook his head. 'The French side of my family originated in northern France, but sadly my great-grandfather Edward Chevalier was the last of the line and by the time my grandparents had moved to England, there were no French relatives left alive – all gone by the beginning of the twentieth century. I did have one of those wonderful breathless moments when we moved in and a lady in the village introduced herself as Madame Chevalier. I almost stopped breathing with shock, thinking she was a long-lost relative I'd failed to discover.' Peter shook his head. 'Sadly, she's not. Her family have lived in the village for a couple of generations but originally came from the Loire valley. It turns out the name Chevalier is one of the most common surnames in France. But I haven't given up looking. It's finding time, at the moment.'

'So, no family connection at all to this château,' Ingrid said. 'Peter and I simply fell in love with it. What brought you two here?'

'The need for a change of scene, a bit of an adventure,' Freddie said. 'And, of course, current English house prices. Buying here together definitely gave us more for our money.'

Peter nodded in agreement before changing the subject. 'Solange said you might be looking for some work as a general handyman and gardener?'

Freddie laughed. 'No doubt about that.'

'I could certainly do with some gardening and general help; shall we have a chat about it tomorrow morning?'

'Sounds good.'

'Nine o'clock by the stables then,' Peter said.

Ingrid glanced at the large wall clock next to the dresser. 'Supper will be another twenty minutes; would you like to see around?'

Sasha immediately put her glass down. 'Definitely.'

Freddie's mobile rang at that moment. 'Sorry, but I need to answer this. I'll catch you up.'

Sasha followed Ingrid along a short corridor where she opened a modern fire door and they found themselves in the marble-floored foyer of the château, with its sweeping marble staircase in its centre reaching to the first floor and dividing left and right.

'If we stand here with our backs to the door, we can pretend we've just come up the steps and in through the main entrance,' Ingrid said. 'The property was built towards the end of the nineteenth century so is relatively "young", at only one hundred and fifty years old. We don't know a lot about its history, but we do know a family called Colbert built it and ran a horse stud here. It remained in that family until after the First World War when it was sold for the first time. Sadly, the equestrian side of things slowed down between the two world wars and had virtually finished altogether by the late sixties as the estate was divided up and sold off.'

Sasha gazed around her. 'I adore your horse statue. It's beautiful. Was it here when you bought the château?'

Ingrid laughed. 'Unfortunately, the place came with very little in the way of furniture or artefacts. Merlin here was a wonderful surprise. The stables, as they fell out of use, had become a real dumping-ground over the years for anything and everything deemed to be broken or no longer useful, and we found Merlin on his side, buried under rotting carpets and all sorts of rubbish. Restoring him was one of those additional expenses that swallowed money, and one we definitely hadn't anticipated, but once we discovered him,' Ingrid gave a wry smile, 'we couldn't not restore him,' and she gently stroked one of Merlin's raised forelegs. 'The only thing we know about him is his name. There were the remains of a metal tag screwed into the base and we could just make it out. We believe, though, that he's part of the history of the château. I like to think of him as our mascot, telling us that everything will be all right in the end.'

'Did the stables need a lot of restoring too?' Sasha said.

Ingrid sighed. 'Thankfully, the building, like the château itself, is sound. But inside – again, like the château, only worse – was – *is* – a mess. We've only recently partially cleared the stables out to make room for a DIY livery request. There's still a lot to sort out, as well as the tack room and the rooms above. Let's just say they're all on the long "when we have the time and money" to-do list.'

'But how lovely to have at least one horse again in the stables that were clearly important to the château,' Sasha said.

'Do you ride?' Ingrid said, hearing the wistful note in Sasha's voice.

'I did. Pony-mad as a young girl. Never had my own horse, though, and I haven't ridden for ages, but I love horses,' Sasha said. 'The nearest I've got to them in recent years is sketching and painting them.' Ingrid gave her a questioning look but Sasha shrugged. 'That's been pushed to one side recently too, but I'm definitely going to start painting again soon.'

Ingrid, realising Sasha wasn't going to say any more, nodded understandingly. 'Penny, our daughter, was pony-mad too;

nothing I could say would persuade her to change to ballet.'
Ingrid laughed. 'Do feel free to wander down to the stables at
some point. I'm sure Colette, who keeps her horse there now,
will be happy to chat. Maybe even let you have a ride. Now, let
me show you around,' and Ingrid led her on into the château.
'As you know, we are planning on opening this summer as a
chambres d'hôtes, so here we have the sitting room which leads
into the dining room. We are also hoping to do some small
functions in here. There is a larger room on the next floor
where we will cater for bigger groups like wedding parties. And
there is also an orangery on the side of the building, not visible
from here, which hopefully people will book for small, intimate
celebrations.'

'This is a lovely room,' Sasha said. The cream and pale
green colour scheme complemented the honey-coloured oak
panelling that lined three of the walls and was, in her eyes,
perfect. She wandered over to look at an old-fashioned portrait
hung by the huge inglenook fireplace, with a large silk flower
arrangement standing on the hearth. Two formally suited men
stood stiffly behind a beautiful young woman sitting gracefully,
her dark blue gown spread out around her, and her hand, with
a beautiful opal and diamond ring on her third finger, placed on
the head of a white dog at her feet. 'Do you know who these
people are? Or is it just a portrait you bought to furnish the
château?'

Ingrid smiled. 'It's a family heirloom. Came down through
Peter's family, together with the family bible.' She pointed to the
taller of the men. 'He's Edward Chevalier, Peter's great-grandfather, and this is his brother, Charles, and his younger sister,
Bernadette. We think it was painted about a year before the
First World War when the two of them went off to fight. Sadly,
only Edward returned; Charles was killed early on in the war.'

'And their sister?'

'Unfortunately, we have no idea what happened to her,' Ingrid said. 'Her name and date of birth, 1896, had been scratched over in the family bible.'

'Oh, that is so sad,' Sasha said. 'She looks so beautiful in that portrait.'

'Peter suspects that she probably married against her parents' wishes and was disinherited. He's been unable to unearth any leads about what happened to her at all.'

'You mentioned the family bible; do you still have it?'

Ingrid nodded. 'Yes. When we bought the château, Peter's parents thought our small library would be a fitting home for it. Let's go upstairs and I'll show you.'

Sasha followed Ingrid up to the wide landing with its huge arched window throwing light down the length of the marble staircase. Sasha stopped to take a closer look at the antique wooden rocking horse placed in front of it. She touched its worn saddle. 'I wonder how many children have sat on him through the years, dreaming of riding adventures. I always wanted one. Was this Peter's too?'

Ingrid shook her head. 'No. I found this in a second-hand shop in a nearby village and couldn't resist it.' She glanced at Sasha. 'I've never been particularly into horses, but since we bought the château, I keep finding horse memorabilia every-where. It seems to leap out at me, saying, "I belong in the Château du Cheval" and I have to buy it. It's quite strange.' She turned to show Sasha the library. 'It's a bit of a misnomer to describe this room as a library at the moment, as it only has the one barrister bookcase with a few volumes in it, but there will be more eventually. I've tried to make it inviting and calm, somewhere pleasant to sit in and lose yourself in a novel for an hour or two. At least that's how I hope guests will feel about it.'

'I want to book a holiday here just for this room,' Sasha said, gazing around. 'It's amazing. It feels so luxurious and inviting. I can just imagine curling up in here for a good read.'

The same golden oak panelling as downstairs was echoed around the room and in the parquet flooring. A marble fireplace, paper, kindling and logs were already in place, and a full log basket to the side dominated one end of the large space. A huge cream wool rug with three different flower motifs – roses, hydrangeas, oleanders – repeated in the twenty squares created across its surface, stretched from in front of the fireplace into the centre of the room. A three-seater green velvet sofa had been placed facing the fire. Four curved recesses were spaced down the wall facing the full-length windows, with their heavy green velvet drapes matching the settee. Around the sides, there were various upholstered seats, small tables, two or three brass standard lights placed strategically near chairs, and a tabletop glass chandelier on the small writing bureau in the far corner. There was even a pair of library steps ready for when the alcoves were filled with volumes.

'Is this the family bible?' Sasha asked, walking across to the barrister bookcase with its glass-fronted doors and pointing at a closed, thick, leather-bound tome with a brass clasp.

'Yes,' Ingrid said. 'We keep it closed because we don't want the sunlight fading the pages, and we decided to lock the bookcase itself to stop any guests unintentionally damaging it. I'll have to show you properly another day, I've forgotten to bring the key up with me.'

Ingrid's phone buzzed with a text and she gave it a quick glance.

'Supper is ready. We'd best get back down.'

As they walked into the kitchen, Peter was placing a round dish on the table.

'Smells delicious,' Sasha said. 'What is it?'

'It's flamiche,' Ingrid said. 'Peter's mother gave me her recipe as it's one of Peter's favourite suppers. Very French and very easy to make. Basically, it's leeks and cream in puff pastry. Hope you like it. Help yourself to salad.'

The flamiche was delicious, as was the lemon meringue cheesecake that followed.

'Does your daughter visit often?' Sasha asked, shaking her head as Peter offered her another glass of wine. 'No, thank you.'

'We'd hoped she'd move over with us,' Ingrid said quietly. 'But she's happy where she is and she's got a boyfriend, whom we suspect doesn't like the idea of her joining us.' She shrugged. 'What will be will be. We can only live our own lives.'

It was nearly ten o'clock before Sasha and Freddie thanked Ingrid and Peter for a lovely evening, said goodnight and began their walk back to their new homes under a moonlit sky.

'They're really nice aren't they, the Chevaliers? Such a shame that Peter can't trace what happened to his great-aunt Bernadette,' Sasha said.

'Sorry I missed seeing the inside of the château,' Freddie said.

'It's wonderful. I'd love to have a holiday there. Who was your call from?'

'My replacement at work. Wanted to know where a couple of things were. I left all the information in the handbook but...' Freddie shrugged. 'Takes time to settle into a new job.'

Sasha tilted her head up and turned around in a circle, looking at the sky. 'So many stars. There's no light pollution at all – and the moon is so bright.' She sighed contentedly. 'I'm so happy to be here. I'm sure we've done the right thing in moving.'

6

The next morning, the light streaming in through her uncurtained bedroom window woke Sasha early, and she lay there for several moments enjoying the dawn chorus. Last night she'd stood gazing out of the window, trying in vain to catch a glimpse of the owls she could hear screeching in the nearby woods before giving up and climbing into her bed, where she'd drifted off to sleep within moments. As the dawn chorus died away, Sasha promised herself she'd learn to recognise the calls of the various birds who greeted the beginning of the day.

Once up, she wandered into the old-fashioned bathroom with its pink, faded tiles and the shower over the bath, and lifted the lever before tentatively holding her hand under the water. To her relief, the water came through the showerhead at a good pressure and within seconds, was hot enough to stand under.

Ten minutes later, Sasha was downstairs in the kitchen, sipping a cup of coffee and making a list of the things she needed to do. Top of the list, food shopping. The question was, where? Last night, Ingrid had told them the nearest village, five hundred metres down the narrow lane that ran behind the cottages, had a small supermarket – 'more of a local corner shop, really' – a bar cum cafe, a boulangerie, a school, a doctor's office with an attached pharmacy, and a *mairie* with a *La Poste* counter. The local town, twelve kilometres away, had several big supermarkets, builders' merchants, garages, a large *Poste*, vets – everything you'd expect a large town to have.

Perhaps today she'd unpack a few boxes, wander down the lane to the village, pick up a few bits and pieces from the small supermarket and then tomorrow, she and Freddie could drive into town and stock up properly, as well as buy some paint and other stuff to make a start on decorating.

'Morning, sis,' Freddie called out as he opened the front door. 'Any coffee going?'

'Machine is on and the coffee is next to it,' Sasha said, pointing to the cups. 'There's some cereal and a dribble of milk if you're hungry. I thought I'd walk into the village via the back lane this morning and get a few things whilst you meet with Peter.'

Ingrid had explained last evening that the back lane was classified as a country 'C' road and although drivable most of the time, it was really just a dead-end lane leftover from bygone days. 'Apparently it started life as a gallop for the racehorses that were bred and trained here back in the nineteenth and twentieth centuries, when the estate was much larger. These days the *route de galop* peters out at a gate on the far end of the estate in one direction, but the other way you can drive or walk into the village, which saves going round by road.'

'You could take the car,' Freddie said.

Sasha hesitated. She'd passed her test years ago, but Bradley had persuaded her to sell her car and put the money towards a newer model that they could share. Fine in theory but in practice, a big mistake. Bradley had always insisted on driving them whenever they went out together, unless he decided he wanted a drink; then he insisted she was the designated driver because she didn't mind not drinking. The drive home was always a nerve-wracking affair as he sat alongside her emitting deep sighs and criticising her driving. Whenever she asked to use the car to go and see her mum, it was never convenient for her to have it. And that meant she hadn't driven any distance for several years while she was with Bradley, and once they split up, he kept it. Her confidence at the time had been at rock bottom and she hadn't bothered buying another one. Not that she had the money then to do so, even if she'd wanted to.

'I doubt there's much traffic between here and the village,' Freddie said. 'Quiet roads to start to get your confidence back and learn to drive on the wrong side.' He grinned at her.

Sasha nodded. She knew it was time to get back in the driving seat – either in Freddie's car, or by buying one of her own. 'I will definitely start driving again, but this morning, I'm walking.'

'Okay, but I shall make sure you do drive again. Living here, it's going to be necessary,' Freddie warned her with a look. 'Right, I'm off to talk to Peter. Fingers crossed I can help him.'

A quarter of an hour later, Sasha locked the door behind her and made her way through the cottage garden, opened the gate and stepped onto the *route de galop*. Haphazard hedges, a mixture of overgrown gorse bushes, hawthorn trees, the occasional small oak or beech tree, lined both sides of the track and grass was growing in the muddy centre. Lots of blackberry brambles were everywhere too, raising Sasha's hopes for lots of fruit later in the year for blackberry and apple crumble. Her mum had made the best blackberry and apple jam, and her recipe was in the old cookbook Sasha had kept.

The verges had the occasional primrose plant flowering, and Sasha glimpsed a few delicate violets still hiding in the undergrowth as she walked towards the village. Briefly she wondered whether there would be bluebells later as spring edged its way into early summer.

Five minutes later, as the lane joined the village road proper at a T-junction, she was on the outskirts of the village. Sasha took a deep breath. The air was so pure and fresh. The church, whose spire she'd seen in the distance as she walked, was now in full sight in front of her, its cemetery spreading out to one side, standing at the head of the village square. On the opposite side of the square, she could see the bar, with a couple of small round tables and chairs on the pavement outside, and next to it, the small supermarket Ingrid had mentioned. She took a couple of appreciative sniffs as the enticing smell of freshly baked bread drifted towards her from the boulangerie farther along. It was all so different to the suburban street she'd lived on in the UK.

Sasha gave an involuntary gasp at the unexpected sound of the church clock booming out the hour and shattering the peace of the village, and she stopped and waited for the deep chimes to stop.

As the vibrations died away, Sasha began to wander farther through the village. Past the primary school where two teachers were organising a crocodile of excited children to walk the short distance to the sports field a few metres away. Past the village's eighteenth-century *mairie*, the French flag flying over the door and the revolutionary motto '*Liberté, Égalité, Fraternité*' chiselled into the stonework above. A double yellow postbox inserted in the wall with separate openings for local post and '*Étranger*' letters. Several new houses formed a small estate along the road that ran down the hill and out of the village into the countryside.

Sasha turned and made her way back to the village square and pushed open the door of the supermarket. A young woman scanning things through the till for an elderly lady glanced up and called out '*Bonjour*' before returning her attention to her task.

'*Bonjour*,' Sasha said before quickly picking up a basket and making her way to the refrigerated section for butter, milk, cheese and ham. The shop might be small, but the variety of goods it sold didn't stop at food. Conscious that she had to carry everything back to the cottage, Sasha decided to avoid the DIY section. Even so, the basket was heavy and full by the time she returned to the counter.

The girl on the till smiled and said something in rapid French. Sasha quickly shook her head before slowly and carefully saying the phrase she had practised and practised, knowing that it was probably going to be her most used phrase over the coming weeks.

'*Je suis désolée, je ne parle qu'un peu français.*'

'*Anglaise?*'

Sasha smiled and nodded.

The girl – Chloé, according to her name badge – gave her another smile before speaking again, and this time Sasha heard the word she herself had used, '*désolée*', coupled with '*anglais*' this time, and smiled her understanding – Chloé was sorry but she didn't speak English.

After a quick detour into the boulangerie for bread and croissants, Sasha turned to make her way home and saw Ingrid in front of the church, opening the door of her parked Land Rover.

'Morning,' Ingrid said. 'Would you like a lift back?'

Sasha hesitated. It wasn't a long walk, but the small amount of shopping was proving to be heavier and more awkward to carry than she'd anticipated. 'Thank you.'

'I'm sorry, I should have mentioned last night that I was coming into the village this morning,' Ingrid said as she placed Sasha's shopping in the back of the muddy vehicle alongside a bundle of dog towels, wellingtons and waterproof coats. 'I could have given you a lift both ways.'

'I enjoyed my first walk along the *route de galop*,' Sasha smiled. 'I could almost smell and hear the ghosts of horses from long ago thundering along.'

It was a short drive back to the château and as she passed through the main gates, Ingrid glanced across at Sasha. 'Time for a coffee? Or are you in a hurry?'

'I'd love one,' Sasha said and once Ingrid had parked, she grabbed her shopping and followed her into the kitchen.

Ingrid looked out of the window as she spooned coffee into a cafetière. 'Peter seems to have got Freddie working already, by the look of it.'

'I know Freddie was hoping to get some work here at the château, so hopefully Peter is giving him a trial,' Sasha said. 'He's a good gardener and handy at maintenance too.'

'Are you going to be looking for work as well?'

'I want to get the cottage straight first, and I'd also like to do something myself rather than work for anyone, but we'll see how long my savings last,' Sasha said. 'The biggest problem to getting a job is my lack of French. Did you speak French when you came?'

Ingrid handed her a coffee. 'I have a lot of vocabulary but my grammar and accent leave a lot to be desired, I'm told. Peter, of course, is fluent, having been taught by his grandparents.'

Sasha smiled. 'I've got a couple of books with written exercises and verbs that I've been going through, but I really need the opportunity to put my school French into practice.'

'Do you read?'

Sasha nodded, surprised at the question. 'Always got something on the go on my Kindle.'

'Fancy joining the château book club? We're a mixture of French and English members, so we read novels that are available in both languages. Discussions are in a mix of English and French. We get together once a month. You'll meet people as well that way.'

'What kind of things do you read?' Sasha asked.

'All sorts, nothing too intellectual. This month's book is by the French author Antoine Laurain, *The President's Hat*, which I'm really enjoying. It's quite a short one, so you've probably still got time to read it. I'll let you know when the next meeting is, nearer the time.'

'Thanks,' Sasha said, her thoughts lifting at the thought of there being English speakers living locally, but she knew if she was going to have any chance of making a life for herself in France, learning French and actually speaking it would have to be a top priority.

Ingrid's phone rang at that moment and she gave Sasha an apologetic look as she picked it up. 'Sorry, it's Penny, my daughter. Help yourself to more coffee. Hi darling, how are things?' and Ingrid moved over to stand by the window.

Sasha, feeling awkward, wondered if she should leave but didn't want to appear rude by disappearing without saying goodbye. The conversation was very one-sided on Penny's part for a moment or two, so she wasn't exactly eavesdropping. She sipped her coffee and looked around the kitchen with its pale marble worktops, cream-coloured units and a wonderful tiled picture behind the large La Cornue cooking range. Last night with the lights on, Sasha had thought it looked wonderful and today in daylight, it was just as impressive. Perhaps the same colour scheme would work in the cottage? Obviously on a much smaller scale, both size-wise and budget-wise, with more utility furniture. Maybe there was an Ikea somewhere in Brittany?

Ingrid's vehement voice broke into her thoughts. 'Penny, you have to leave him. Thank goodness you're not married. You can simply walk away. Come home to us.'

Sasha shifted uncomfortably in her seat. The conversation between Ingrid and her daughter had definitely moved into the deeply personal now. There was a pause before Ingrid spoke again.

'Rubbish. Of course you can. Do you want your father to come and collect you?'

Another longer pause before Ingrid finally said, 'I'm certainly not going to keep this situation from your father, but I will spare him the exact details and endeavour to stop him from catching the next ferry over, providing you promise me one thing: you will end this toxic relationship asap.'

Sasha saw Ingrid's shoulder slump in defeat at hearing Penny's next words.

'I'll ring you later to make sure you're okay. Love you.'

Ingrid's eyes were swimming with tears when she turned to face Sasha.

'I expect you gathered from that one-sided conversation that Penny is in a bad relationship.'

Sasha nodded. 'I'm sorry. You must feel utterly helpless, being so far away.'

Ingrid tore a piece of kitchen paper off a nearby roll and wiped her eyes. 'It definitely adds to my worry. Penny did talk a little to me when she was here on her own at Christmas, hinting that things between her and Rory had become difficult.' Ingrid shook her head. 'She didn't say then just *how* difficult. Apparently, she thought she could handle it. Even change him.'

'I can tell you from experience that that is impossible,' Sasha said quietly.

Ingrid gave her a surprised look. 'You too?'

Sasha nodded. 'Only I was *married* to my abuser. In retrospect, though, I was lucky. After two years, he left me for another woman – but by then he'd milked my bank account and shredded my confidence to bits.' She pulled a rueful face. 'My mum was furious with me. She said it should have been me walking out, not him. She felt he'd got away on his own terms and scot-free. But I couldn't walk out.' Sasha paused. 'I was too terrified of the consequences to take the first step. The relief when Bradley left me was overwhelming. But the knowledge that I could begin to reclaim my life took a while to sink in. My mum was my rock during those difficult times.'

'I'm more than willing to be Penny's rock, but she seems desperate for me not to interfere,' Ingrid sighed. 'I just want her to get away from him.'

'Do you think she will find the strength to leave this Rory? Because unless she takes that first step – or he leaves her – you can't really do anything,' Sasha said gently.

Ingrid shrugged. 'I think – and hope, after what she's just told me – that she's had enough and wants out.'

'Once she's done that, if she's anything like me when Bradley left, she'll turn to you. The only person I could talk to was my mum,' Sasha said.

'Fingers crossed then that she sees sense and kicks him out of her life. I know Peter will be happy, he's never truly liked Rory – not that we've met him more than once.' Ingrid wiped her eyes again. 'I'm sorry, what must you think. We hardly know each other and here I am telling you my personal worries.'

Sasha smiled gently. 'Try not to worry. I'm sure things will resolve themselves soon now that Penny has told you the truth about her relationship. Telling your mum you've cocked up and made a terrible mistake is not easy.' Sasha stood up. 'Thank you for the lift and the coffee. I'd better get home and do some more unpacking.'

Sasha walked back to the cottage deep in thought. Ingrid reminded her of her mum in so many ways, but especially the way she'd talked to Penny about what she should do. She was so friendly and down-to-earth. The fact that she was of a different generation didn't seem to matter. Neither did the fact that she and Peter might have sold the cottages because they were currently strapped for cash, but they were clearly used to having more money than either Freddie or herself. But Sasha was happy to think she'd made a new friend already, although it would be nice if there were to be some people of her own age around. Perhaps joining the château book club like Ingrid had suggested would be a good start.

Once the shopping was safely stored in the old-fashioned larder and the fridge, Sasha went through to the sitting room and opened her Kindle. Before making a start on the rest of the unpacking, she'd download the book Ingrid had mentioned and see what it was like. It was only when the internet connection wouldn't open that she remembered Freddie had promised to put their new Starlink satellite dish up later today, after he'd had his chat with Peter. Rather than read on her phone, which she hated, she'd wait until the internet was up and running. Right now, though, she'd enjoy a fresh croissant and another cup of coffee, and send positive vibes to Freddie for his job trial with Peter.

7

Freddie was full of enthusiasm when he returned to the cottage at midday. Peter had offered him work for three days a week as a general handyman/gardener starting asap. 'I think he'd really like to take me on full time, but he's a bit hesitant about finances until the château is up and earning, if not its keep, at least making a contribution, which is fair enough. To be honest, I quite like the idea of a variety of jobs. Don't want to put all my eggs in one basket.'

'And don't forget our own renovations and gardens,' Sasha reminded him. 'You'll need time to work on those too.'

'I won't forget. Peter has said there's a long ladder in one of the outbuildings that I can borrow to climb up and fix the Starlink dish in the best position for our internet connection and get it working. That's my first job here.'

'Tomorrow, if you're not working, we could go into town,' Sasha said. 'We need to find a supermarket and stock up with food. Be nice to have a proper look around the town too.'

'Talking of a proper look around, fancy a walk in the grounds?'

'Oh yes,' Sasha said, jumping up. 'I'll get us some lunch when we get back.'

By mutual consent, they started walking in the opposite direction to the château and found themselves on a camellia- and hydrangea-lined track. The camellia bushes were in bloom with pink, white, red and some beautiful variegated blossoms. Too early yet for the hydrangeas, but the buds were showing, and it wouldn't be long before they too were in flower as the camellias died away. The track meandered round the estate, criss-crossing a couple of others, until eventually they found themselves approaching the old chapel to the side of the château.

'Peter wants me to give him a hand with the inside,' Freddie said.

Sasha tried the door. 'Shame, it's locked. Let me know when you're working in there; I'd like to come and have a look.'

Farther on, they passed the empty *Maison du Jardinier*.

'That would make a lovely detached home,' Sasha said. 'I wonder what Ingrid and Peter plan to do with that.'

Freddie shrugged. 'Probably turn it into a gîte – or maybe their daughter will take it on. While we're this close to the château, I think I'll go and collect the ladder for this afternoon. Okay?'

Sasha nodded. 'I'll go home and get some sandwiches ready.'

* * *

Whilst Freddie unpacked the satellite dish and read the instructions, Sasha cleared the lunch things away and went upstairs to start unpacking a few boxes. An hour later, she heard Freddie give a shout and hurried downstairs.

'The router is by the plug in the sitting room. Can you plug it in please? Once it's connected, the dish will start to locate the best angle for it to receive the signal.'

'That sounds highly technical,' Sasha said, joining Freddie.

They both watched, fascinated, as the unusual rectangular-shaped dish on the pole Freddie had fixed high up on the side of the cottage slowly moved into position, finding its own perfect location to connect to the satellite.

'We're lucky that with so many trees on the estate, there aren't any close enough to the cottages to block our direct access to the satellites up there,' Freddie said, looking at the app on his phone, which was showing him the details of the connection.

'I can't believe it's doing it all by itself,' Sasha said, staring up at the roof where Freddie had fixed the satellite pole.

'D'you want to go and switch your laptop on? You'll need to create a password, but then you should be good to go,' Freddie said.

Sasha went indoors and, opening her laptop, clicked on the internet icon. Choosing a password was easy. She'd use the phrase 'Happy2BinFrance' with a few symbols randomly placed. A few minutes later and she was online.

8

The instant Penny Chevalier had finished the call with her mother, her mobile rang. No need to look at the caller ID. With Ingrid's supportive words still ringing in her head, Penny closed her eyes, took a deep breath, accepted the call, and forced the words out in as determined a voice as she could before Rory had a chance to speak.

'It's over, Rory. Please do not contact me again.' She pressed the off button on her phone, not waiting to hear his protestations, and exhaled a shallow sigh of relief.

She'd been expecting the phone call ever since he'd stormed out of the flat last night after their latest row. Briefly, she wondered whether this argument would follow the pattern of previous ones. After the obligatory phone call to say how sorry he was and to beg her forgiveness, a contrite Rory would appear clutching flowers, chocolates, and a hangdog expression on his face, reiterating how sorry he was and assuring her it would never happen again. An assurance that no longer held a grain of truth in it for Penny – she'd heard it too many times before. She knew, though, it was not going to be simple breaking off this relationship. Rory did not like to be thwarted.

Last night's disagreement hadn't been an outright fisticuff clash – more of a one-sided verbal fight, with Rory hurling words at her; but for the first time he had gripped her by the arms and shaken her as he shouted horrible names in her face. Those names had hurt Penny as much as his tight grip on her arms. And all because she'd said she wasn't ready to have the baby he was desperate for her to provide him with. When she'd tried to point out that they didn't even live together yet, he'd retaliated with: 'That's your fault. I've been happy to move in with you for ages now, but you keep saying no. That you're not ready.'

'If I'm not ready for you to move in, I'm certainly not ready to have a baby either,' she'd snapped at him. Which was the point where he had called her more names before pushing her against the kitchen counter and storming out. And that was the moment she'd finally acknowledged that she had to stop fooling herself that this was a healthy relationship, and that she must end it.

At the beginning of their relationship when he'd occasionally been cross with her, he'd acted distant, shrugging his shoulders and being coldly indifferent towards her, but recently he'd changed tactics, becoming more demanding and shouting at her – maybe hoping to frighten her into doing what he wanted? The niggles over Rory's behaviour had been increasing in her mind for some weeks. He'd always been moody, but now his temper flared at the slightest provocation if she happened to say something or do something he didn't like, changing him, in a split second, from the happy, successful man she'd been drawn to when they had first met, to someone she was afraid of.

Recently too he'd taken to ringing her at odd times during

the day when she was at work, wanting to know what time she'd be finishing so that he could pick her up. He knew she wasn't supposed to receive private calls, but that didn't stop him. When she asked him why he did this, knowing it would cause trouble for her, he'd shrugged and said, 'I needed to hear your voice.' As if his needs overrode everything else. He seemed to want to control every aspect of her life.

Whatever the reasons were behind the change in him, she hated it and last night's altercation had been one disagreement too far. Penny knew there could be no going back from this final denouement and his contempt of her for not doing what he wanted.

In so many ways, she wished she'd gone to France with her parents when they'd first moved over. She'd only just met Rory then and had wanted to give their relationship a chance, believing he could be the one. But everything had started to change soon after her parents had left. Penny caught her breath at that thought. Was that a coincidence? Or had Rory deliberately waited until she was alone, unable to talk face to face with her mum or even to run to them about his moody, controlling behaviour to ask advice about how she should handle it?

He'd wanted her to spend Christmas with him and his mother, but for once she'd stood firm and told him there was no way – she was going to France to spend time with her parents. She deliberately kept the whole truth about her relationship away from them on that visit, knowing how upset they would be on her behalf. She knew her father in particular had found Rory difficult to like on the one occasion he'd met him. Something that was confirmed as the Christmas break came to an end. Peter had driven her to Roscoff for the ferry and after she'd checked in and he was preparing to leave her in Departures, he'd given her a tight hug before giving her a serious look.

'Your mum told me not to say anything, but she's not here, so I'm going to. Believe me when I tell you it's said out of love and not meant to hurt or upset you. Your mother and I are worried about you. Not only are you painfully thin, you've lost your joie de vivre since you've been with Rory.' Peter had paused before adding quietly, 'We think you are with the wrong man. Rory sounds far too controlling.'

Penny remembered shifting uncomfortably in his embrace as she feebly brushed his words away but inwardly accepted the truth of his words, even as she assured him she was just tired.

Her dad had given her another hard look. 'Finish with him please, Penelope, and then come and spend some time with us in France.' He'd given her a final squeeze and said, 'Time for you to go through,' before turning and leaving.

Penny had spent most of the long ferry voyage to Plymouth thinking about her dad's words and the way he called her Penelope and not Penny. A leftover from childhood when the use of her full name had been the indication that she was in serious trouble.

Realising that her parents had sensed there was something seriously wrong about her relationship with Rory from the little she'd told her mum, this made her wonder if everyone else felt the same. That was another thing she'd realised as the ferry had ploughed through the choppy water: over the last nine months or so, she'd lost contact with all her girlfriends. Rory had started organising 'date nights' for the two of them on a Friday, ignoring the fact that she liked to meet up with her pals on that evening. One by one, the girls had drifted away, her invite disappearing. Dawn, her best friend, had been the only one to keep in touch, but weeks had started to go by without her making contact.

By the time the Devonshire coastline was in sight, Penny's

decision had been made. As soon as Rory returned from his mother's, she would tell him as gently as she could that their relationship wasn't working for her and that it was over. That was the resolve and the plan.

Walking out of the ferry terminal, both had been scuppered by a smiling Rory waiting for her, clutching roses. Months later, she still hadn't managed to end it, and then last night had happened.

Phoning her mum earlier had been an impulsive decision. A hug was impossible, but she needed to at least hear her mum's voice. At least the truth about Rory was out in the open now. Listening to her mum telling her she had to leave had stiffened her resolve.

The caller ID flashed up on the phone as it rang again. Penny took one look and blocked it. She needed to get away. There was only one place she could go to and feel safe – France. The question now was how soon could she go? And how could she stop Rory from following her? She needed a plan.

Penny scrolled through her phone contacts, found the one she wanted, took a deep breath and rang it. Dawn sounded wary when she answered.

'Penny, haven't heard from you in months.'

'No, and I'm sincerely sorry about that.' She and Dawn had been friends since they'd met at a party five years ago when Penny had first moved to Bristol. 'I seem to have neglected my friends badly.'

'You have, but I forgive you. Are you okay? You still with that twat Rory?'

Penny had realised early on that Dawn disliked Rory, but

this was the first time she'd ever called him that directly to Penny.

'Sort of, that's why I've rung. I need your help.' And Penny told her about the recent row.

'You want help kicking him out of your life? It will be my pleasure,' Dawn said. 'None of us could ever fathom what you saw in him. So, what can I do?'

Quickly, Penny explained what she was planning, and Dawn willingly agreed to help while she organised things over the next few days.

'Of course I'll help, but there is one condition. You must come and stay with me. I don't think you should stay in the flat on your own. Pack a suitcase, order a taxi and come on over.'

Ending the call with Dawn, Penny let out a huge sigh. One large hurdle over. She had help to do this. Now she had to square things with work. Everyone in the catering team had recently been put onto zero-hour contracts because business was so quiet. Emma, the boss, had been apologetic but had explained that the current turndown in hospitality and outside catering meant she had no option. 'I know it will pick up, but until it does...' She'd shrugged her shoulders and hinted that if anybody wanted to look for another job, she'd understand. Penny, who loved working with Emma, had decided she could cope without a fixed income for a few weeks in the hope that the upturn in business would arrive sooner rather than later. Now though, she didn't have much choice.

Emma sighed when Penny rang her and told her she was leaving. 'You are the one person whom I hoped would manage to cling on for another month, but I understand and wish you well. Where are you going?'

'To an upmarket bistro pub in the Lake District,' Penny said. 'Sous-chef for the time being.' She took a deep breath. 'At least that's what I'd like you to tell a certain person if he comes calling.'

There was silence on the phone.

'Are you okay, Penny?' Emma asked, a concerned note in her voice. 'Has Rory been bullying you?' Emma was another one on the long list of people who hadn't taken to him.

'Yes. I know when he finds out I've left, he'll assume I've gone to France, which I plan to do, but no harm in giving him a little misdirection first.'

'Happy to misdirect him,' Emma said, laughing.

When Penny unblocked Rory's number on her phone twenty-four hours after she'd told him their relationship was over, it immediately began to fill with texts and voice messages from him, all declaring his love for her and asking for forgiveness. After reading his latest text, Penny decided it was time to reply and she typed a carefully worded message back.

> I realise you are sorry, but you frightened me the other evening. I think you know we do need to talk about our relationship, because I can't simply ignore what happened. And neither should you. I'll meet you for dinner, seven-thirty Saturday evening at Billy's Bistro. Please do not come to the flat, ring me, email me or harass me in any way in the meantime. I need space to really think things through. See you Saturday. x

Penny read the message again, wondering about deleting the kiss she'd put at the end, before deciding to leave it in place. Her texts to Rory had always ended with three kisses. If she didn't put any, it might send a signal she didn't want to give him, and she needed to keep him onside for a few more days. Putting even just one kiss would, she hoped, reassure him that he was in with a chance of saving their relationship and buy her some time.

She pressed 'Send' and turned the phone off. She'd keep it off and switch it on only when she needed to make calls and check her messages. Hopefully she now had a week to fine-tune her plan and put it into action.

9

The next few days passed in a whirl for Sasha as she finished her unpacking and settled into No. 1. She and Freddie had breakfast together before he walked up to the château to begin working for Peter. He'd also started to put out feelers in the village for some more work. One evening the two of them, Sasha armed with her tablet, had gone through the two cottages room by room, making notes and deciding what needed doing first. Freddie was upbeat and happy.

'Basically, the cottages are sound, with good roofs. They haven't stood empty for years and years like some do. Bathrooms and kitchens need updating, but we knew that when we viewed. Windows could probably do with double-glazed units, but we can leave that for a few months.'

Sitting on their mum's Chesterfield, they'd sketched out the plans for the two bathrooms, each slightly different, which Freddie was going to plumb in and then they'd help each other decorate. Freddie had also driven them into the nearby town twice. The first time, they'd explored Carhaix with its Roman remains a little before doing a large supermarket shop. The second time, they'd braved the builders' merchants, buying paint and the other DIY things they needed as well as choosing and ordering baths, shower units, sinks and toilets, all to be delivered in a couple of weeks when everything was in stock.

Today, Freddie had gone into the village to meet someone who had seen his notice in the village *tabac* offering gardening services. Sasha, itching to start turning the cottage into her own, had scraped the wallpaper off in the sitting room, rubbed the walls down and was now painting them, having pushed the settee into the centre of the room and thrown an old sheet over it. She'd chosen a pale cream paint and the three walls she'd painted so far were looking good. The last one, with its large window overlooking the garden and the *route de galop*, was next. The sky was blue, the sun was shining and Sasha hummed happily as she brushed the paint on. It was hard to believe she'd been living in the cottage for little more than a week, she felt so at home. Of course, she knew it was early days and life here wouldn't always be plain sailing, but it was a long time since she'd felt as happy as she currently did. Freddie, too, seemed a lot more relaxed, especially now he was earning some money.

Painting slowly around the window frame, a movement outside caught her eye. Sasha hesitated before carefully putting her brush down, going through to the kitchen and stepping out into the garden. Ten or fifteen sheep were nonchalantly ambling along the lane, enjoying the shoots of spring grass in the verges and down the centre of the route.

Sasha looked up and down the lane. There didn't appear to be anyone with them. She grabbed her phone out of her pocket and rang Ingrid.

'Hi, there are sheep wandering down the back lane. Are they allowed to do that?'

Sasha smiled as she heard a muffled swear word. Obviously not.

'Are they headed towards the village?' Ingrid asked.

'Yes.'

'Typical, when both Peter and Jean-Paul are out for most of the day.'

'Freddie's out somewhere too,' Sasha said.

'Okay, I'll block the lane with the Land Rover to stop them getting onto the main road,' Ingrid said. 'And then I'll try to encourage them down towards you. Could you walk down the other way and see if you can spot where they got out? If you stop a few feet the other side of the gap, we can try to persuade them to go back through it. Just remember – no quick movements or they'll panic and run in all directions.'

Sasha made sure the garden gate was closed firmly behind her as she stepped onto the *route de galop*. The sheep seemed to have edged a little farther up the lane and were grazing happily. Slowly, Sasha walked away from them, hoping that Ingrid would have blocked the lane at the road junction, whilst she searched for a break in the hedge. Eventually, she found a well-trodden muddy gap in the bank where the flock had clearly pushed through. She stopped a couple of metres farther on in front of the gate at the end of the lane and turned to wait for Ingrid.

It was a few minutes later before she saw and heard the sheep being urged in her direction by Ingrid. As the herd got closer, Sasha stepped back towards the gate to give them more space to approach. Ingrid was close behind them now and as the leader of the flock hesitated by the gap, she held out her arms in a sideways gesture and patiently waited for the first sheep to decide to step up the bank and into the field. Sasha held her breath as they both watched, and she heard Ingrid's sigh of relief as one by one the sheep followed the leader back into the field.

'Thank goodness for that,' Ingrid said. 'That was easier than I expected. Sheep can be notoriously stupid.' She pulled a round orange ball of baler twine out of her pocket. 'The hole isn't too big. Hopefully I can block it with enough twine and small branches to keep them in until Jean-Paul can fix it later today.'

And she set to work, tying the twine around the trunk of a small oak tree on one side and stretching it across the gap and wrapping it around the thin trunk of a hazelnut tree on the other. Sasha helped her criss-cross the twine several times before they collected some broken small branches to thread through the twine and pile some close to it as another deterrent.

'Not perfect,' Ingrid said, 'but it's the best we can do. I'll ring Jean-Paul and tell him. He and Peter have gone to a farm auction today near Gourin.'

Together they started to walk back up the lane.

'Good job you saw the sheep when you did,' Ingrid said. 'It would have been mayhem if they'd reached the road.'

Sasha shrugged. 'It was pure luck. Do they get out often?'

'No. The hedges and fences are all generally in good condition, but you can always trust sheep to find the most vulnerable spots – and then point them out to you by escaping.'

Sasha laughed. 'So kind of them to do that. Can I offer you a coffee today?' she asked, standing by the garden gate of the cottage.

Ingrid shook her head. 'I'd love to, but I need to move the Land Rover and then I have to phone Penny.'

'How is she now?'

'Quiet. Hasn't told me her plans yet, so I'm continuing to

apply gentle pressure. Thanks again. By the way, the book club is tomorrow evening. Seven thirty. Have you decided about coming?'

'Yes, I'd like to. Do I need to bring anything?'

'No. See you tomorrow then,' and Ingrid carried on walking up the lane.

Sasha made herself a cup of tea and stood outside drinking it as she took the first proper look at her garden. A wooden fence enclosed both cottage gardens, with a lower one down the middle dividing the two. There were well-established bushes of hydrangea plants, which Sasha knew were regarded as the emblematic flower of Brittany, forming a hedge inside the fence along the bottom of the garden bordering the lane. Clumps of daffodils, competing with the weeds in flowerbeds edged with pointed terracotta tiles, were waving their heads in the wind, and tulips with their fat leaves were pushing their way through. A large vegetable plot with several dead brassica plants was on the right-hand side near the dividing fence, a wooden shed close by.

Sasha walked a couple of paces into the garden and turned to look at the back of the cottage. The small terrace that ran the width of the building had a few neglected weed-filled pots. A large half barrel under the kitchen window had been dug over recently and Sasha saw Freddie had planted the rose cuttings from their mum's garden in there. In summer when the window was open, their perfume would fill the kitchen wonderfully.

Thoughtfully, she looked at the terrace. A table and chairs for al fresco dining here in summer needed to be added to her list. Sasha drained her tea. So much to do both inside and outside, she'd better get back and finish painting the sitting room.

10

By late afternoon, Sasha had finished painting both the walls and the skirting boards in the sitting room and was feeling pleased with herself, if a little sore and achey from all the bending and stretching. Shower time now.

A knock on the front door made her jump. Who on earth...? Freddie was back banging away at something in his cottage. Besides, he wouldn't bother knocking anyway. Sasha glanced down at her paint-splattered jeans and gave a sigh. Whoever it was would, as her mum used to say, 'just have to take her and the cottage as they found them,' and she opened the door.

A tall, fair-haired man – in his early thirties, Sasha guessed, giving him a hesitant smile – was standing there holding a bouquet.

'*Bonjour, Sasha.* I am Jean-Paul. These are for you to say *merci beaucoup* for helping with *les moutons*,' and he held the bunch of flowers out to her.

'*Merci*,' she managed to stutter as she took them before he'd turned and walked away. Even she, with her poor French, realised he'd brought them because she'd helped Ingrid with the escaped sheep. Which was really kind of him. When Ingrid had spoken of Jean-Paul, for some reason, Sasha had imagined the farmer would be about Ingrid's own age, fifty- or sixty-something. Instead, Jean-Paul was nearer her own age. And he'd brought her a thank-you present.

Closing the door, Sasha took the flowers into the kitchen and tried to find something to put them in as she didn't possess a single vase. In the end, she divided the colourful dahlia blooms between two jugs – one she left in the kitchen, and the other she took upstairs to the small landing and placed it on the low table she'd put there in front of the window. The mix of vibrant pink, white and orange colours brightened up the landing, and as Sasha made for the bathroom and the hot shower which the arrival of Jean-Paul had interrupted, she promised herself to try to always have some flowers up there.

Downstairs, fully refreshed after her shower, she slipped her phone into her pocket and set off to explore the château grounds in a different direction to the one she and Freddie had taken on their first walk. Freddie, after his three days of working in the grounds with Peter, had said they were beautiful, especially the Italian garden, which he was thrilled to be helping restore.

Without conscious thought, her feet took her in the direction of the stables. There was a small car parked outside on the stable yard and she could hear water being splashed about. Somebody was busy mucking out.

Sasha stood for a moment or two, taking in the warm smell of the stables as it drifted towards her, a mixture of horse, hay and feed. An earthy, country smell that was evoking so many memories of her teenage years. Her Saturday job at the local stables had been the highlight of her week, back then. She had begged her parents to let her go to college to do a diploma in equine management so she could work with horses, maybe even have her own stables one day. Her dad had insisted, though, that she also did a six-month online business and office management course. He wanted her to have something to fall back on should she ever need to earn more money than working with horses was likely to provide. It had been hard doing both courses and after almost three years of study, it had saddened her that she never got to follow her dream.

Shortly before she finished her diploma, their dad had died. Freddie had already left home, so there was no way she was going to move away and leave her mum alone. When a friend of the family had offered her an office job in the local town, she'd taken it. And that had been the beginning of putting her dreams on hold, never to be revisited, as life with all its commitments and duties took precedence.

But here she was in France now, starting over. A new beginning that she was determined would be different and have a certain amount of fun in it.

'*Bonjour.*'

Sasha came to with a start. A woman about her own age was standing in front of her with a smile on her face, her hands gripping a wheelbarrow piled high with muck.

'Oh. *Bonjour, je suis désolée...*' Flustered, the carefully rehearsed words to say she didn't speak French had completely deserted Sasha.

'I speak English. I am Colette. I think you must be Sasha? Ingrid told me you have bought one of the lakeside cottages.'

'Yes,' Sasha said.

'Would you like to meet Starlight, my horse?'

Sasha nodded gratefully. Ingrid had clearly told Colette about her interest in horses. 'Please, but I don't want to interrupt you or get in the way.'

'This pile of muck can wait,' and Colette rested the wheelbarrow on the ground.

Starlight was in the second stable stall with its tall iron partition sides on top of the wooden surrounds, and watched them as they approached, her head in the curve of the decorative ironwork of the door. Sasha held out her hand to the bay-coloured mare, allowing her to inspect and sniff it before gently stroking her muzzle. 'She's lovely. About sixteen hands?'

'Yes.'

'Do you compete with her? Jumping or eventing?'

'There's not a lot of opportunity locally, but there are a couple of showjumping events over the summer I try to get to. Did you have a horse in the UK?'

Sasha shook her head. 'No, never, sadly. Always my dream to have one. But I did ride a lot as a teenager. Would you mind if I took a photo of her with her head over the door?'

'Feel free.'

'I like sketching horses and Starlight is beautiful.'

'Will you show it to me when you've done it?'

'If I think it's any good, yes,' and Sasha stepped back and took several shots on her phone of Starlight's head from different angles.

Colette chatted away about how grateful she was to Ingrid and Peter for allowing her the use of the stables as she finished the mucking out. 'I wish there were more horses in here, though. I don't like the fact that Starlight is alone a lot of the time while I'm at work. Hey,' she turned to Sasha. 'You could get a horse and keep it here. Get back to riding again. We could hack out together. I know all the best rides around here.'

Sasha laughed the suggestion away. 'Once I'm settled in, maybe. Right now, I've enough things to sort out.' She closed the camera app on her phone down. 'I'll let you get on.' Turning to go, she hesitated. 'Do you work every day? I could come down and check on Starlight during the day if you'd like me to?'

'Oh please, do that whenever you've got time.'

'And, if you ever go away and need someone to look after her, just let me know,' Sasha said, giving Starlight's muzzle one last stroke.

Sasha walked back to the Cottages du Lac thinking about Starlight, the empty stables, and Colette's suggestion of her getting a horse. The timing wasn't right, but suddenly her dream of having one of her own was back, and this time maybe it wouldn't turn out to be such an impossible one.

11

Sasha, glad that Ingrid had reminded her about the book club, was looking forward to the evening. Reading on her Kindle in bed last thing at night, once Freddie had set up their internet connection, she'd managed to almost finish *The President's Hat*, enough to be able to say she'd enjoyed it, anyway. She was also looking forward to meeting some more of the villagers. She'd suggested to Freddie that he might like to join her, but he'd declined. 'You know I'm not much of a reader,' he'd said. 'Anyway, tonight I thought I'd wander down to the bar in the village.'

The sun was shining on the weeping willow on the far side of the lake in front of the Cottages du Lac as Sasha left to walk to the château. The willow's long drooping branches were bursting into life and becoming greener by the day as spring progressed. Other trees scattered around the grounds, ancient oaks and horse chestnuts, were also showing signs of responding to the warmer weather as their leaves cautiously opened, giving a green edge to the outline of their branches against the sky. Another week or so and they would be a mass of leaves.

Two or three cars were already parked down the side of the château and Sasha hoped she wasn't late. When she hesitantly pushed at the open kitchen door and peered inside, Ingrid immediately came to welcome her.

'Sasha, come on in and meet everyone. They are all in our small sitting room,' and Ingrid took her through.

Six or seven people were holding glasses of wine and helping themselves from plates of nibbles that had been placed on small tables between the chairs.

'Does Peter not come to the book club?' Sasha asked.

'When we choose something he likes,' Ingrid said, laughing. 'Tonight he is planning to try and trace some more of his family history whilst it's quiet in the kitchen.'

The first people Ingrid introduced her to were a retired teacher, Benjamin, and his wife, Suzie, from the UK, who said how nice it was to have another English member in the club as they didn't really speak French.

'What they mean is, they don't even *try* to speak the language, which is naughty of them and upsets the locals,' Ingrid muttered sotto voce as she led Sasha towards a small group of people talking quietly amongst themselves.

Sasha, surprised to see Jean-Paul, gave him a smile before Ingrid began her introductions.

'This is Madame Eliza Albertini,' she said to Sasha before turning to an elderly woman and speaking French as she introduced her to Sasha.

'*Bonjour, Madame Albertini,*' Sasha said, smiling at the petite woman with the white hair; she received a warm smile and a quiet '*Bienvenue*' in return. She reminded Sasha of the main character of one of her favourite childhood books – Mrs

Pepperpot. 'You know Jean-Paul already, and this is Lucas Briet, Eliza's grandson, who is staying with her at the moment,' Ingrid said.

Whilst Jean-Paul smiled and said a quiet *'Bonsoir, Sasha,'* Lucas gently shook her hand and stared into her eyes as he said, *'Enchanté* and welcome, *mademoiselle.'*

'Merci,' Sasha said, smiling. Lucas and Jean-Paul – both in their early thirties she guessed, and clearly friends – couldn't be more different. She noticed that Jean-Paul didn't quite roll his eyes at Lucas's exuberant greeting, but clearly found it amusing.

'You know Josette from the boulangerie,' Ingrid said, moving on to another couple. 'This is her husband, Robert.'

Before Sasha could respond, two women hurried into the sitting room. *'Désolées, tout le monde.* Sorry we're late.'

Sasha glanced across to see Colette and an older woman who had to be her mother, the likeness was so striking. Colette waved at her, mouthed 'We'll talk later,' and they both went to join Eliza and Lucas, who immediately poured them a glass of wine each.

'Time to start, I think,' Ingrid said and held up a copy of *The President's Hat.* Everyone fell silent. 'I enjoyed this. What about everyone else?' She quickly translated her words into French for the benefit of those who didn't speak English. Soon, there was a lively discussion going on in two languages, as some thought it was slow and a bit dull, whilst others had enjoyed it and were going to read the author's other novels.

As the discussion slowed down, Lucas went around the group offering more wine to those who wanted it, and talk became general as people began catching up with all the latest village news. Sasha settled back in her chair, happy to listen and absorb the scene that she wasn't quite a part of yet. She watched Jean-Paul chatting quietly with Eliza for a few moments and received a smile from him when he glanced across and caught her looking. Colette and her mother were talking to Ingrid, and Benjamin and Suzie were talking – or maybe arguing – with each other, Sasha couldn't decide.

When Lucas appeared at her side offering her a top-up of wine, she declined. '*Non, merci.*'

'*Vous parlez français?*'

'No,' Sasha said, shaking her head. 'I am going to learn, but right now I just have a few phrases from learning French at school.'

'I speak English, so it is not a problem,' Lucas said. 'You like living in France?'

'We haven't been here long, but I'm loving it so far.'

'*We?* You have a husband? He is not here tonight?'

Sasha laughed. 'No, I don't have a husband. My brother and I bought the Cottages du Lac. I live in one and he lives in the other.'

'*Très bien.*'

Knowing that '*bien*' meant good, Sasha wanted to ask why he thought it was good, but Lucas was smiling at her as he took his phone out of his pocket.

'Give me your telephone number, *s'il vous plaît*, and I send you mine. Then I can teach you French. Or help you when you need it.'

Before Sasha could hand over her phone, Colette joined them.

'Lucas, are you flirting with Sasha already?'

'*Non.* I am just offering the help,' Lucas said, slipping his phone back in his pocket.

'He can be quite useful at times actually,' Colette said. 'He's come in handy more than once,' and she flashed him a smile.

'I forget to tell you,' Lucas said. 'Grand-maman say to me

that Alice, she come home for the summer soon. Alice is my sister,' he said, turning to Sasha. 'She and Colette are great friends. You and Alice will like each other too, I think.'

Josette and Robert were the first to leave because of their early morning start at the boulangerie. Ingrid called out a general, '*Bonne nuit*, everyone, and don't forget next month's book choice is *Rebecca* by Daphne du Maurier. A real English classic.'

Sasha thanked Ingrid for inviting her, said goodbye and '*Bonne nuit*' to everyone and started to walk home, having gently refused Lucas's offer to accompany her. She smiled as she remembered that they never did exchange phone numbers. Shame. She rather liked the idea of getting to know Lucas better. With his fair hair and blue eyes that smiled at her with Gallic charm, he seemed to be full of fun, even if he was a bit of a flirt. And hadn't she decided that there would be some fun in this new life of hers?

12

'I'm going to phone Penny again this morning,' Ingrid said to Peter as they sat eating their usual breakfast of croissants and coffee in the kitchen two days later. 'I do wish she'd hurry up and let us know what's happening.'

'Maybe she's changed her mind. Decided to give Rory another chance,' Peter said, a despondent note in his voice. 'I sincerely hope that isn't the case, but...' He shrugged.

Ingrid bit her lip. She'd promised Penny she wouldn't tell Peter the whole truth about the situation with Rory, trusting Penny to do that when she was safe, and she'd simply told him that their daughter's relationship was over. 'I'm positive she's finished with him. I expect she's trying to decide what to do for the best now. She knows how much we'd love her to join us here, but maybe she wants to stay independent in the UK.'

Peter nodded. 'Sadly, we'll just have to wait and see what happens.' He finished his coffee and stood up to take his mug and plate across to the dishwasher. 'Freddie and I are going to work in the orangery this morning. He seems to think the plants in there are salvageable and is going to suggest which new ones would blend in well. Might drive down to the *pépinière* later, see if they've got some citrus trees in stock.' He gave Ingrid a serious look. 'It's early days yet, but I think Freddie's going to be a godsend to us. I think I'm going to offer him as many hours as he can manage; there is so much still to do out there.'

'Summer is coming and we already have a few guests booked in, and we're on a couple of holiday websites now, so at least we're starting to create an income, and the money from the sale of the cottages will be a cushion for several months at least,' Ingrid said. 'And there's another thing; if Penny comes, we can start to offer a dinner menu – both in the main building and in the orangery.' Ingrid stood up and gave him a hug. 'The place will start to earn its keep this summer. I know it will all come right. As for Penny, we just have to be patient. Like we are with this place.'

Peter returned her hug but didn't say anything as he turned to leave.

After tidying the kitchen, Ingrid went through the adjoining door into the château and stood by the sitting-room windows where the mobile signal was stronger; she rang Penny. The last time she'd rung, she'd had to leave a message, but this time she didn't even get that option. The phone was switched off. Something was definitely going on in her daughter's life. Ingrid could only hope and pray that Penny was sorting things out successfully, and that everything would be resolved very soon. She'd try calling again this evening. If she didn't get a reply, then she'd talk to Peter and suggest that he book a ferry ticket to England soon to go and find out what exactly the situation was with Rory.

In the meantime, she'd spend the morning in Huelgoat at the weekly market. Impulsively, she rang Sasha; maybe she'd enjoy a trip out.

* * *

Sasha had easily slipped into a routine of walking into the village early every morning to buy the breakfast croissants. Freddie had offered to do alternate mornings, but Sasha said she was more than happy to do it every day. The bakery opened at seven thirty and by eight o'clock Sasha was back home, enjoying a mug of coffee and tucking into her buttery croissant. This morning, she'd been held up a little when she'd stopped to study the 'À vendre' notices pinned up in the *tabac* window. One in particular had caught her eye and she'd taken a quick photo of it. Now, sitting at the table, she opened her phone and scrolled through, stopping to look at the photos she'd taken of Starlight, before reaching the new one. 'Des chiots colley prêts pour leur nouveau foyer.' There was a telephone number followed by a picture of three or four adorable pups cuddled together.

Sasha ate her croissant thoughtfully, her eyes focused on the photo all the time, trying to convince herself it was a bad idea – and failing. There had been a couple of dogs at home while she was growing up. Holly had been the last one and she'd died when Sasha was at college. Her mum had never had another dog and Sasha's working life since had never allowed time for her to have her own. But now she was here in France, in her own cottage, she could have a dog if she wanted. As the advert was in the local shop, presumably the puppies were nearby. She'd ask Ingrid if she recognised the telephone number or knew anything about puppies being born recently, just in case it was a puppy farm.

A text pinged into her phone. To her surprise, it was Ingrid.

I'm off to Huelgoat market in about fifteen minutes. Would you like to come with me?

Sasha quickly typed her reply.

Yes, please. Be with you in ten.

Ingrid was sitting in the Land Rover waiting for her when Sasha arrived at the front of the château, and they were soon on their way.

'How far is it to...' Sasha hesitated. 'Huelgoat?'

'About thirty-five minutes. I have to tell you, it's a very scenic route, some people get carsick. It's up hill and down dale, the route I take. But the views are good for passengers.'

It was also a narrow, single track in places, Sasha realised, as Ingrid had to reverse into a small lay-by for a yellow *La Poste* van to pass.

'Do you drive?' Ingrid asked.

'I've got a licence, but I haven't driven for several years. I'm not looking forward to driving over here, although I know I'm going to have to,' Sasha said. 'But Freddie is changing his car for a left-hand drive one soon, so once that arrives, I'll have a practice. I'm sure it will be like riding a bike once I get going.'

'Compared with other places, there's not a lot of traffic up here,' Ingrid said. 'Which definitely makes life easier. And there is so much to explore.'

'Have you heard from your daughter yet?' Sasha asked.

Ingrid shook her head. 'No, and I have to admit I'm getting worried. I just want to know she is all right. I'm almost at the stage of suggesting Peter go over to check on her, but I'm not sure how Penny would react to her father turning up and probably punching Rory on the nose!'

'I'm sure she'll be in touch soon,' Sasha said. 'She'll know you will be worrying.'

'Hope so,' Ingrid said, braking at the bottom of a steep hill and indicating left.

'Before I forget, do you know if there are any puppy farms in the village or locally?'

'I sincerely hope not,' Ingrid answered sharply. 'Why?'

'I saw an advert for collie pups in the *tabac* this morning and was thinking of going to see them and possibly getting one, but not if it's someone running a puppy farm.'

Ingrid laughed. 'I can tell you now that if you go to see them, you will end up with one. There's nothing quite so sweet as a collie puppy. I think maybe one of the local farm bitches has had a litter and the farmer doesn't want to keep them all. That's the usual thing around here. Jean-Paul will probably know.'

'Thanks. There wouldn't be a problem, would there, with us having a puppy on the estate?' Sasha asked. 'I'd make sure it was trained and everything.'

'Not a problem,' Ingrid said. 'I'm almost tempted myself. Gladys is getting on now, though not sure how she'd react to a puppy in the house.'

Sasha's first impression of Huelgoat was one of delight. The water in the huge man-made lake at the bottom of the town glistened in the sunshine as they drove past. The black and white Breton flag was flying above the foyer of the large hotel on the right-hand side as Ingrid took the one-way system up the hill before turning left into the bustling atmosphere of the market in the High Street.

'What a pretty town centre,' Sasha said, looking at the granite buildings lining either side of the street, the marketplace itself with its cherry trees full of pink blossom and filled with stall after stall.

'It is, and the legendary magical forest behind the town is a wonderful place.'

Sasha glanced at her. 'Magical forest?'

'Ancient folklore links it to King Arthur; there are huge boulders, a fairy pond, a Devil's Cave, and a very special atmosphere everywhere. We won't have time to visit it today, but another day,' Ingrid said.

Once Ingrid had found a parking space, the two of them wandered through the market for almost an hour, looking at all the different stalls. Flowers, plants, vegetables, jewellery, early-season strawberries, cheese, roast meat, buttons, pottery, clothes, handbags, books, home-made cakes, umbrellas and, tucked away at the end of the market, Sasha discovered a stall selling baskets of all shapes and sizes. The 'Oh So French' handmade, straw shopping tote with its flat leather handles was hers from the moment she set eyes on it. Now she lived in France, she should have one. Try to look as if she belonged even if she couldn't speak the language fluently yet. The tote, a perfect size for shopping in the village, made her feel she was a part of the local scene swirling around her the moment she slipped the handles over her shoulders.

They wandered on down through the town and stood on the bridge by the lake. 'May I treat you to a coffee?' Sasha said, looking along the road where there were several pavement cafes.

'That would be lovely,' Ingrid said. 'The next cafe along does good coffee and cakes.'

Sitting there watching the swans on the lake as well as the world go by, Sasha smiled happily. 'Thank you for bringing me today,' she said, just as they both heard Ingrid's phone in her bag ping with a text message.

Ingrid quickly pulled it out and read out loud:

> Sorry I've missed your calls. Busy tying things up here. I'm planning on coming over very soon, waiting on something before I can finalise the date. Love to you both. Penny.

Ingrid looked at Sasha. 'What the hell does "waiting on something" mean?'

Sasha could only shake her head. 'I don't know. At least she is planning on coming over soon. You'll just have to hang on to that thought.'

13

Sasha declined Ingrid's offer of lunch when they got back to the château and instead, enjoyed the fresh baguette she'd bought in Huelgoat market filled with cheese, ham and salad. She ate it accompanied by a glass of rosé, sitting out on the terrace and watching the birds flitting to and fro in the garden. Mentally, she added bird table and bird bath to her ever-growing 'wanted for the cottage' list.

Sasha gave a happy sigh. The countryside was so quiet here. Not having to work nine to five was wonderful. She could just sit and live in the moment. Such a long time since she'd been able to do that. It couldn't last forever, of course, but she was determined to enjoy it for as long as possible. Maybe even try to find a way of earning an income in a different way. The recurring question '*Why don't you reactivate your Etsy shop?*' flashed into her mind again.

Could she? Spend her days drawing and painting? Sell enough for it to become her main income? Work from home? Lots of people did these days. In theory, all you needed was an internet connection, which she now had, and something to sell of course. Deep in thought, Sasha sipped her rosé. She had her savings and there was still some of her mum's money left over. If she was careful about how much she spent renovating the cottage, she could probably survive for a year on the money she had. But was she brave enough to risk it?

She finished her drink, put the glass and plate in the sink, and went upstairs to the small third bedroom where she'd placed several unopened boxes. Boxes that contained not only her paints and sketchbooks, but also the remains of her Etsy shop. Stock that could possibly kick-start her 'side hustle' into a thriving business.

Sasha looked around, trying to visualise this turned into her studio cum workshop. It was an adequate size for a single bedroom, but would it really be big enough for all the necessary paraphernalia that she knew would inevitably be needed for a successful Etsy business? Thoughtfully, she wandered into the empty second bedroom and then into the one she'd chosen to use for herself. Too big, she decided, but the empty one was a perfect size. Standing there, she could see her easel to the side of the window next to a drawing table, another table for her computer and printer and shelves to contain paper, paints, frames, envelopes and all the other artistic things that she would need. With the walls painted white and the large window, it would be a lovely, bright space to work in.

But giving up a decent-sized bedroom would mean that she would have a problem if she ever had a couple of guests. Sasha gave a mental shrug. Having guests was a long way away; the small bedroom would be fine for a single person, and she could always give up her bed and sleep in there if she needed to. Determinedly, she started to move boxes from the small room to the middle of the floor in the larger one. She was going to do this.

Sasha had just pulled the largest of the boxes along the landing to the space she already thought of as her studio when Ingrid phoned.

'You okay? You sound breathless,' Ingrid said when she answered.

'I'm fine. Just been moving boxes.'

'I made a couple of phone calls and I've found your puppies. It's a local farmer's dog on the other side of the village. Definitely not a puppy farm. Bruno, the farmer, is well regarded in the village. There are only two of the litter left. I can take you to see them this evening, if you'd like me to? I know Bruno and he doesn't speak English, so I can interpret for you.'

'Thank you so much.'

'See you about five o'clock then.'

Sasha smiled to herself. Ingrid was turning into a real friend despite the difference in their ages. To think she'd been worried about the Chevaliers being stand-offish; nothing could be further from the truth, they were so friendly and helpful. She was looking forward to meeting Penny if and when she arrived, hoping that she too would turn out to be a new friend.

Hearing a car parking outside the cottages and knowing Freddie wasn't around, she quickly ran downstairs to see who it was. As she opened the cottage door, Sasha was surprised to see Freddie stepping out of a silver-grey van, a happy smile on his face.

'What d'you think?' he said. 'Traded in the old right-hand drive for this. It's a Renault Diesel. Reckon it'll be more useful to us than an ordinary car. It's automatic, which you'll soon get used to. Fancy a drive?' And Freddie held the driver's door open for her.

Sasha went to shake her head and say no but stopped herself. She knew that driving again was one of the things she had to do, had promised to do, and taking the first step was always going to be difficult. 'Okay,' she said hesitantly. 'Just here on the estate, okay?'

Freddie stood watching as she slid into the driver's seat and then he leant in and pointed out the things she needed to know. Finally, he said, 'Tuck your left leg out of the way and just take it easy. Off you go.'

'Aren't you coming with me?'

Freddie shook his head. 'No. You know how to drive, you've passed your test, just do it. Me sitting next to you would probably unsettle you. You're not going on the road so...' He shrugged, closed the door and walked into his cottage.

Sasha started the engine, put her foot lightly on the accelerator pedal, released the handbrake and moved off, gripping the steering wheel tightly. She drove slowly down towards the main gates where the drive was wide enough to allow her to simply go around without doing a three-point turn. When she got back to the cottages, she reversed and did the same again, a little quicker this time, and actually enjoyed the feeling of being back behind the wheel; the light steering and the automatic gearbox made things easy. However sitting on the left-hand seat did feel as if she were in the wrong place in the vehicle, but she guessed she'd get used to that in time. How she would feel out on the road though, she wasn't sure. But she'd taken the first step.

A few moments later, Sasha had made a pot of tea, opened a packet of biscuits, and she and Freddie were sitting out on the terrace catching up with each other's news. Freddie, as well as working with Peter on the estate, had taken on two gardens in the village. 'It's enough for now, I just need to keep some money coming in to help pay for paint and other stuff to renovate this place.'

'I'm going to turn my second bedroom into a workroom and

reopen my Etsy shop,' Sasha said quietly. 'See if I can earn enough working from home. I'll have to do it on their main site rather than the UK one because of Brexit and import duties, and pray that I can attract some French and European customers.'

'Good idea,' Freddie said. 'Your stuff always did well until Bradley came into your life.'

Sasha nodded ruefully. 'Yep. Before I forget, Ingrid is taking me to look at a puppy this evening. Do you want to come?'

Freddie shook his head. 'I plan to brave the bar in the village again tonight. Big football match on and they have a huge screen.'

'You and your football. You don't mind me getting a dog, do you?'

Freddie shook his head. 'Why would I? You know how much I love dogs.'

'With the cottages being so close, if I get one, it'll probably treat both cottages as its own.'

'Okay by me.'

'I'd better go and meet Ingrid. I shouldn't be long. I'll get supper organised when I get back.'

'I'll get supper before I go out tonight,' Freddie said. 'So take your time.'

* * *

'How did Peter react to Penny's message?' Sasha asked as Ingrid drove them out through the gates.

'Like you. We have to wait and see what happens, but at least she's coming home.' Ingrid sighed. 'I can't help worrying though.' She glanced across at Sasha. 'Did I see you driving a van down the drive earlier?'

'Yes. Freddie's newly acquired transport. The first time in ages I've actually sat behind a wheel. And the first time I've ever driven an automatic. Not to mention sitting on the left.'

'I like automatics, not having to worry about changing gear is wonderfully liberating,' Ingrid said. 'You'll soon be bombing around all over the place.'

'Hope so, I need to suss out some things for the cottage. Which reminds me, are there any second-hand furniture places around? Or even good charity shops?'

'France doesn't really get the idea of charity shops,' Ingrid said. 'But there are a couple around: the best one is an animal charity about forty minutes away in Poullaouen. There is a big second-hand outlet in Carhaix – you can furnish a house from top to bottom with stuff from there. Some of it's old-fashioned, but good quality. I bought a couple of tables and Breton bedframes and wardrobes for the château from there. And then there is Emmaüs in Pontivy, about an hour and a half away.'

'Great. I'll check out the more local ones first,' Sasha said. 'I've decided to reopen my Etsy store, but I need some shelves, a desk and a table to turn one of the bedrooms into a workroom.'

'What do you sell?' Ingrid asked as she indicated to turn down a farm track.

'Prints, stationery, birthday cards, paintings of whatever catches my eye or are commissioned – mainly horses, dogs or a countryside theme. Occasionally, I take a commission to do people portraits. I also used to design brochures, bookmarks, logos and things for a couple of businesses in the UK.'

'I think Peter and I need to talk to you about a logo for the Château du Cheval when you're ready. Right, let's have a look at these pups,' and Ingrid pulled to a stop outside the farmhouse.

Almost immediately, the front door opened.

'*Bonjour, Bruno*,' and Ingrid introduced Sasha. After the

obligatory handshakes, Bruno said something in rapid French before indicating they should follow him. 'The puppies are in the barn,' Ingrid translated.

Bruno pushed open the door of a nearby outbuilding and as they walked in, they were greeted by a friendly long-haired sheepdog.

'Meg, the mother,' Ingrid said.

Bales of straw and hay were piled high, and sheep with lambs at heel were bleating gently in several pens. Sasha smiled, spying a duck sitting high up on a bale, and then she saw the pups, curled up sleeping together in one of the open pens.

Sasha dropped to her knees in front of them, as their mother appeared at her side. Tentatively, Sasha held out her hand for the bitch to sniff before gently stroking her head. The sleeping puppies soon awoke and moved inquisitively towards her; within minutes, they were clambering all over her.

'Oh, aren't they adorable. Can you ask him if they have names?' she asked Ingrid. 'How old are they? Have they been inoculated? And how much are they?' She was gently tickling the tummy of one who had rolled onto her back. As she concentrated on playing with the puppies, she was dimly aware of Ingrid and Bruno talking quietly behind her. One of the dogs, who'd seemed a little more hesitant in the beginning than the other one, nudged her free hand and rolled onto her back for a tummy tickle too. Sasha smothered a sigh. They were both adorable. How on earth could she choose between them?

'They're female collies, but neither of the parents is registered as such. They are three months old, weaned, inoculated, but neither have names,' Ingrid said behind her. 'The other four in the litter have sold for seventy-five euros each – basically covering food costs, inoculations, but not chipping. These two bonded almost from the moment they were born, and he'd really like them to stay together. He's willing to let you have them both for one hundred and twenty euros.'

'Tell him yes. I was struggling to decide which one to have, but now I don't have to,' Sasha said happily. 'Freddie and I can have one each.'

'Are you sure?' Ingrid said, taken aback by her instant decision.

'Yes. Freddie will be thrilled. Can I pay for them now but pick them up tomorrow? I need to buy a few things! Get organised. Oh, can you ask him which brand of dog food they are used to, please?'

With Ingrid's help, the formalities were completed and Sasha gave the puppies one last cuddle. 'See you both tomorrow.'

'I've got a small cage at home that I'll put in the car for them tomorrow,' Ingrid said as she drove back up the farm lane. 'We got it for vet visits for the cats we no longer have, but it's big enough for the pups for such a short distance.' Ingrid laughed. 'You are going to have your hands full with those two.'

'I know, but aren't they adorable? Freddie and I will manage between us.'

'Do you need anything from the village shop as we go through?' Ingrid asked. 'I need to pick something up for supper.'

'I'll come in with you and check out their pet supplies,' Sasha said.

Once Ingrid had parked outside the village shop, they both went in and Sasha made a beeline for the pet corner, which was surprisingly well stocked. She picked up a bag of the dog food Bruno had said he was using, a couple of plastic feeding bowls, water bowls, collars and leads. The pet beds were all cat-size, so not big enough for two puppies to share, but she had plenty of blankets and towels at home to make them comfy. With no one else in the shop, they paid for their purchases and were soon turning onto the château driveway.

Ingrid had parked the Land Rover in its usual place when she sighed unexpectedly and turned to look at Sasha. 'I know I'm probably being irrational, but our first guests are due soon and I'm getting more and more nervous about the whole thing of having paying guests. What do I know about running a place like this?' She gestured towards the château. 'The answer is, I know nothing. Nothing. I know if I try to talk to Peter about this, he won't really understand. What if they don't like it when they get here? What if my standards aren't high enough for them? What if they are expecting... oh I don't know, something more upmarket?'

Shocked, Sasha looked at her. 'I can't believe you're seriously doubting yourself and the beautiful place you've created here.'

'It's so important that I— we, make this place work,' Ingrid said. 'I know Peter would hate it if it failed and we had to sell up. Not yet knowing what is happening with Penny is stressing me out too.'

Sasha took a deep breath. 'I guess worrying about Penny isn't helping, and starting any new job or venture is bound to be stressful. But honestly, I don't think you should waste your time fretting about how people are going to react to the château. You've made it beautiful inside. And you might not realise it, but you do know something about hotels and guest houses. In the past, how many have you stayed in? Lots, I'm sure. I bet you remember the ones where you were made to feel genuinely welcome and looked after, over and above all the others?'

Ingrid nodded. 'That's true.'

'Well, that's how you treat your guests – make them feel you personally care about their stay in this beautiful place, without being too obsequious of course. Some people will always come with an attitude. You and Peter are naturally hospitable and friendly. I'm sure neither of you wanted to sell the Cottages du Lac, but you've made us both feel so welcome and helped in many ways, without showing any resentment you could have felt towards having strangers living on your private estate.'

'Thank you,' Ingrid said, releasing her seat belt. 'I feel better for having talked to you and you're right, of course. I shall become known for the magnificent breakfasts I serve. I might be a novice in the hospitality business, but I do know how I like to be treated, and I will make sure my guests are made to feel good during their stay – unless they are absolute horrors of course, in which case I shall politely tell them to leave the château.'

Ingrid, giving a small laugh at that thought, turned to get out, and Sasha watched in horror as she caught her foot in the dangling seat belt and fell out of the Land Rover, landing in a heap on the ground.

14

Sasha gave a long blast on the Land Rover horn in the hope that Peter would hear it and come out. It wasn't that Ingrid was fat or anything, but she was taller and heavier than Sasha, and she knew she'd struggle to pick Ingrid up on her own.

'Where do you hurt?' she asked gently as she crouched down by Ingrid.

'Just my wrist and my ankle,' Ingrid said. 'So stupid of me. I've been so careful with that seat belt recently, the bloody thing has been twisted and not rolling back in for a week or two. Tonight, I just completely forgot about it. And I haven't made up the beds for the guests.'

'Don't worry about that right now,' Sasha said. 'I can do them for you.'

Peter came running at that moment. 'Are you okay? Do I need to phone for an ambulance? Shall I drive you to *Urgences* in Carhaix?'

'Neither,' Ingrid said emphatically. 'I'm pretty shaken, but I'm fairly certain it's just a twisted ankle and possibly a sprained wrist.'

'Come on then, let's get you in and put cold compresses on everywhere that hurts.'

Between them, Peter and Sasha helped Ingrid onto her good foot and, with Peter on one side and Sasha on the other holding her up, she hopped her way into the kitchen and collapsed onto a chair. Peter gave her a worried look as he wrapped an ice-cold tea towel around her ankle before elevating her leg onto another chair and wrapping another tea towel around her right wrist.

Sasha put the kettle on as Ingrid told her where to find everything, and made a pot of tea. Handing Ingrid a full mug with plenty of sugar in it, she shook her head.

'I'm so sorry. If you hadn't taken me to see the puppies, this wouldn't have happened. I feel so guilty.'

'Don't be silly,' said Ingrid. 'My own fault for not remembering about the seat belt. At least it happened here on home ground. I wasn't stranded on my own in town, unable to drive home. The worst part of it is, I have so many last-minute things to do for the first two guests arriving the day after tomorrow.'

'I'll come up tomorrow and help. I can make up the bed and make sure everything is ready for when they arrive. You can sit and direct me as to what else needs doing. And I'll come and cook the breakfasts while they are here too. Okay? So stop worrying,' Sasha said.

'Thank you. I'm sure I'll be fine in a day or two,' Ingrid said. 'I'll get a crutch and at least I'll be able to get around.'

'I think you'll have to rest that ankle, not aggravate it by trying to hobble around,' Sasha said. Looking at the swelling and the psychedelic colouring on the ankle already, she was pretty certain it was going to be more than a day or two before Ingrid was fully mobile again. 'Right, I'd better get home.

Freddie is cooking supper tonight. I'll see you in the morning. I hope the ankle and wrist feel better tomorrow.'

* * *

Back in the cottage, Freddie had prepared a salad and was waiting for her before he cooked the cheese omelettes. As he beat the eggs before pouring them into the hot pan, he looked at the two feed bowls, the two water bowls, the two collars and the bag of dog food that Sasha had dropped in the corner of the kitchen. 'Two of everything? We're having two puppies? Where are they?'

'Bruno wanted them to stay together, and I couldn't possibly have chosen between the two anyway. So I thought we'd have one each.'

'Brilliant idea,' Freddie said.

'We're collecting them tomorrow. At least, that was the plan, but Ingrid fell out of the Land Rover when we got back and hurt herself.' Sasha sat down with a sigh. 'I feel so guilty. Ingrid has been so kind and now because she was doing me a favour, she's injured and she's got the first guests coming to the château in about forty-eight hours.'

'I'm sure she doesn't blame you,' Freddie said. 'These things happen.'

'Doesn't stop me feeling guilty though. Can you take me to pick up the puppies?' Sasha asked hopefully.

'Sure, but it will have to be about eight o'clock tomorrow evening. I'm working all day.'

'It's a bit late. There won't be much time to settle them in, but at least we'd have them. Okay, thanks. I'll ask Ingrid to ring Bruno tomorrow for me and let him know I'll be later than planned to pick up the pups.'

After supper, Sasha went up to her soon-to-be studio room and studied the boxes before emptying the biggest one and leaving the contents in a pile on the floor. She took it downstairs and placed it in the corner of the kitchen. Freddie cut it down to the size she thought it should be, whilst she went to find a couple of small blankets to make it comfy. She'd buy a proper bed for the two of them when she went into town next.

'Right, I'm off to the bar to watch the football. You could come if you wanted to?' Freddie suggested.

'No thanks. I might download a copy of *Rebecca* and start to re-read it, ready for the next book club meeting. I know I read it at school, but that was sometime ago.'

15

Sasha was almost at the château early the next morning when she saw the Land Rover with Peter at the wheel and Ingrid in the passenger seat about to drive away. Peter wound down his window. 'On our way to the doctor. Hopefully we won't be too long.'

'Waste of everyone's time. I know it's just a sprain,' Ingrid grumbled from the passenger seat. 'I've done it often enough in the past.'

Peter ignored her. 'Will you pop in when we get back?' he asked Sasha.

'Of course. I'll come and make the bed up for the guests later too,' Sasha said. 'And do anything else Ingrid wants done.'

As Peter drove away, Sasha followed him down the drive towards the stables, thinking she'd give Starlight a stroke or two. Being around horses in the past had always lifted her spirits. She hesitated when she saw that the car parked on the fore-court wasn't Colette's usual one, but then she heard a man's voice talking gently to Starlight as he mucked out her stall. A man's voice she recognised.

'Lucas. Why are you here? Is Colette all right?'

'*Bien sûr*,' Lucas said. 'She ask me for the muck out today because she had the early rendezvous in Quimper.' He laid the shovel and fork he'd been using across the full wheelbarrow. 'I get rid of,' and he grabbed the handles and trundled it outside.

Sasha stroked Starlight's muzzle before giving her a piece of carrot and going outside.

Lucas, washing his hands with a nearby hose, looked at her. 'Why you look sad?'

Startled, Sasha smiled. 'I'm not really sad. Just a bit down. You have heard about Ingrid's accident?'

When Lucas shook his head and gave a worried '*Non*,' she explained, and said how guilty she felt about it.

'Freddie will take me to collect the puppies but not until this evening, which is a little late to get them settled.'

'I take you to pick up the puppies after lunch, okay? About two o'clock. Today it is good for me. My sister Alice, she arrive on the ferry one day this week.' Lucas shrugged. 'I have to collect her but she not tell me which day yet.'

'Are you sure? That would be great. Thank you.'

'See, I said you need my phone number. We do it now.' Lucas took his phone out of his pocket, and waited expectantly as Sasha told him the number. 'I ring you and then you have the number to save.' On cue, the phone in her hand rang.

'Thank you,' Sasha said, saving the number in her contacts.

'*Bon*. Now we get together when we like,' Lucas said, giving her a cheeky grin.

* * *

Leaving the stables, Sasha walked back to the cottage. She ran lightly up the stairs, found her sketchbook and several pencils, and went back down to the kitchen. Opening her phone, she found a picture of Starlight, studied it for a few moments before tentatively starting to move the pencil across the paper. It was so long since she'd drawn anything, maybe she'd forgotten how to do it.

Five minutes later and her pencil was starting to shade the outline of Starlight's head. Her fingers automatically applying pressure where she instinctively knew the lines needed to be stronger, relaxing her grip of the pencil where a feather-light touch was needed. It felt so good to be drawing again.

Holding the sketchbook away from her, she studied her work critically. Okay, it wasn't perfect, but it wasn't too bad either. It wouldn't take too much practice to get back to a saleable standard.

Sasha closed the book. Time to go up to the château and see if Ingrid was back from the doctor's, and to make up the bed for the guests.

Ingrid and Peter were in the kitchen when Sasha pushed open the back door which was, as usual, unlatched.

'What did the doc say?' Sasha asked.

'Nothing broken, but bad sprains on both ankle and wrist,' Ingrid replied. 'I'm not to put any weight on the foot for at least a week and need to sit with it up on a stool. He's given me a pair of crutches to use.' Ingrid sighed. 'Peter is making coffee, would you like one?'

Sasha shook her head. 'Maybe when I've done the bed. Just the double to do in the one room?'

'Please. I'd put all the bedding in there ready. It's the first bedroom upstairs on the right. And if you could check the en suite, please.'

Sasha walked through the foyer of the château, giving Merlin a stroke as she passed, and climbed the marble stairs slowly. This place was just the right size, in her opinion. Grand, but not too grand. She'd love to stay here for a romantic weekend with someone special, it had such a lovely, intimate atmosphere.

The bedroom with its toile de Jouy curtains and bedspread, thick cream carpet, the oval antique gold-leaf mirror with its bevelling on the wall above the dressing table – it was a perfect room.

After she'd made up the bed and checked the en suite, Sasha returned downstairs. 'It's all looking lovely up there,' she said to Ingrid. 'Lucas has offered to take me to collect the puppies this afternoon. Can I still borrow the cage you mentioned please?'

'Of course, it's in the utility room.' Ingrid pointed to a door at the end of the kitchen.

Sasha laughed when she opened the door. 'Your utility room is bigger than my kitchen.'

'What do you expect? This is a château you know, *dahling*, bigger and better,' Ingrid said in a plummy voice, looking at Sasha before they both burst out laughing.

'You sound like that character in *Absolutely Fabulous* – you know, the ditzy one, Patsy. Thanks for this,' Sasha said, finding the folded-up cage against the far wall. 'I'll see you tomorrow after the guests have arrived.'

Back at the cottage, Sasha opened up the cage, put some newspaper in the bottom of it, and left it outside the front door, ready for when Lucas arrived. She sent Freddie a text.

> Not to worry, puppy collection has been sorted for this afternoon.

Lucas arrived promptly and within minutes, they were driving through the village and turning onto the farm track.

Bruno had shut Meg, the mother, away in the farmhouse so she wouldn't get distressed as the last of her puppies left home. The pups themselves were happily inquisitive, sniffing the air and making small squeaky, murmuring noises as Sasha carried one and Lucas the other out to the car and placed them in the cage.

Back at the cottage, Lucas carried the cage into the kitchen and carefully set it down on the floor and unhooked the side flap, while Sasha closed the kitchen door.

'Cup of coffee?' Sasha said.

'*Merci*,' Lucas replied. 'It is strange being here with you in Grand-maman's kitchen. It is different. There was a grand... I'm not sure what you call it in English. High with shelves and cupboards?'

'Dresser. We call it a dresser. I'm hoping to get one,' Sasha said, looking at him startled. 'Eliza lived in this cottage?'

'*Oui*, for many years. She and Grand-papa. Alice and I spent every summer here with them. Our parents—' he paused '— they prefer to holiday without their children. No, that's not fair. Since I grow up, I realise it was Dad who prefer to leave us here. And Mum accept it for an easy life. She always the one who came for our concerts, parent evenings and sports days.' He gave Sasha a nonchalant shrug. 'It was fine. *Nous préférons* – adore – the time here. We never tell them – *peut-être* they stop us coming.'

Sasha shook her head as she handed him a coffee. 'That is so sad your parents didn't want to spend time with you. Make childhood holiday memories.'

'They live in the US now. Mum come over when she can. Usually about three times a year. Dad less. Look, the puppies, they come out to explore.'

'Does Eliza miss living here in the grounds of the château?'

'*Peut-être* she did first when she had to move out, but now with Grand-papa gone, I think she like village life. It is not so lonely. She see people every day.'

'When I've finished decorating and have some more furniture, perhaps she'd like to come and see the place again?'

'I bring her when you tell me. If you look for furniture next week, the village have its big annual *vide-grenier* – you would say car boot sale, I think. People come from all over to sell things. It take over the main street and most of the village. Lots of stuff offered – these days it more of a *brocante* than a simple *vide-grenier,* with hundred of different things for sale. Furniture to baby clothes.'

'I'll pass on the baby clothes this time, but furniture, definitely have to take a look,' Sasha said.

'See you there then, if I don't see you before. You meet Alice then too.' Lucas gave each of the pups a final stroke and was gone.

Putting food in the bowls for the puppies, Sasha thought about what Lucas had said about his childhood. She and Freddie had enjoyed a far happier one than him it would seem, although having the château grounds to play in every summer must have been some consolation for him and his sister Alice, and Eliza presumably adored them both.

Sasha put the bowls of food down on the floor and as the pups started to feed, she thought about names. They both had the typical white tips at the end of their tails and whilst one had a white splodge on two paws rather like misshapen mittens, the other had a blaze of white on her chest – reminding her of a pony she'd ridden years ago called Mimi. Sasha laughed out loud. There were her names. Mimi and Mitzi. Perfect. Although as one was going to be Freddie's, she'd have to let him have the final say on one of the names.

Both the puppies were in the box sleeping when Freddie arrived home later that evening. 'How are they?'

'Lovely. Great time-wasters, though. I've been playing with them most of the afternoon,' Sasha confessed, watching Freddie drop to his knees in front of the box. The one Sasha thought of as Mitzi rolled slowly over and waited for him to scratch her tummy.

'What are we going to call them?' Freddie asked.

'How do you feel about Mitzi for that one?' Sasha pointed to the puppy with the white paws and then to the other one. 'And Mimi for this one,' she said, scooping her up and cuddling her. 'Which one do you want to be yours?'

Freddie tried out the names. 'Mimi. Mitzi. Yep, they work. I've been thinking too. They'll be happier staying together rather than me having one and you having one – they can simply be ours. We'll duplicate beds and food bowls in each cottage and they can have the run of both places. I'll pop into town tomorrow and pick up two proper dog beds.'

16

Sasha was up early after a sleepless night worrying about Mimi and Mitzi being all right on their own without their mum. They'd seemed settled in their box when she'd left them and she'd only heard the occasional short bark during the night. Downstairs, she cautiously opened the kitchen door and the two pups, awake and busy exploring the kitchen, rushed over to greet her.

Opening the back door, she shooed them both out into the garden and picked up the newspapers the puppies had weed on and threw them away before replacing them with fresh ones. The morning was warm enough to leave the kitchen door open while she planned her day as she made and drank a coffee. Staying close to the puppies for most of their first twenty-four hours seemed like a good idea, so Sasha decided to tidy the terrace. That way, she could have the kitchen door open, and the puppies could come and go between the garden and the kitchen.

It took her longer than she'd anticipated to weed all the old tubs and sweep the terrace clean in between playing with the pups. It was mid-afternoon when Sasha left Mimi and Mitzi curled up sleeping together in their box bed, shut the kitchen door so they couldn't wander into the rest of the cottage, and walked up to the château to see how Ingrid was, and to check the guests had arrived and were happy.

Ingrid and Peter were in the small sitting room when she got there. Ingrid had her foot, grossly swollen still, and a psychedelic mix of reds and purples, up on a stool. She was trying to read, a crutch balanced against her chair, and Peter was leafing through a file of papers.

'Are the guests here?' Sasha asked. 'Happy?'

'Very happy. So a certain person who was worrying unnecessarily has now relaxed,' and Peter glanced affectionately across at Ingrid.

'What time would you like me to come in the morning to sort the breakfasts?' Sasha asked.

'Lovely of you to offer, but they've said they'd like a simple French breakfast – croissants, pastries and coffee. Which means a quick trip to the village boulangerie in the morning,' Peter said. 'And I can make coffee no problem.'

'Would you like me to come up again once they've gone out for the day and make the bed, tidy up the bedroom and en suite?' Sasha asked.

'That would be great if you could,' Ingrid said. 'Thank you.'

'See you both sometime tomorrow morning then,' Sasha said. 'I'd better get back to the cottage and check Mimi and Mitzi are behaving themselves.'

'Love those names,' Ingrid said. 'How are they settling in?'

'Fine. They're adorable. I'm not getting a lot done though.'

* * *

After Sasha had left, Ingrid and Peter stayed in the sitting room for a while, until Peter went through to the kitchen to make them each a toasted sandwich for supper. Ingrid, leaning heavily on her crutches, took her time to follow him and sank gratefully onto a kitchen chair just as her phone rang.

'It's Rory. Do I answer?' she said, anxiously looking at Peter.

'Yes, put it on speaker.'

'Hello, Rory,' Ingrid said.

'I want to speak to Penny and her phone is switched off. Could you fetch her?'

'Maybe she doesn't want to speak to you, if she's switched her phone off. Why do you think she's here?'

'She stood me up last night. Promised to meet me but didn't turn up. Emma has given me some cock-and-bull story about her going to the Lake District for a new job. When we both know France is where she'd run to. Look, just give her the phone.'

'But she's not here.'

'Don't lie to me,' Rory shouted down the phone.

'I'm not.' Ingrid looked at Peter helplessly and mouthed 'What do I do? Shall I cut him off?'

'If she's not with you, I bet you bloody well *do* know where she is, so *tell me now*.'

Peter took the phone from Ingrid and held up his hand before she could respond. 'Rory, do not speak to any of my family like that ever again. Penny is not here and we don't know where she is. But guessing from your attitude, she has finally left you – something we've been urging her to do for weeks. So even if she had told us her plans, we certainly wouldn't tell you. Emma saying she has gone to the Lake District may or may not be true, but for your sake, you'd better hope Penny is okay because if she's not, I shall hold you entirely responsible. Do not phone here again – and stay away from our daughter in the future.'

Peter ended the call, put the phone down on the table and worriedly rubbed his face as Ingrid looked at him.

'Where the hell is she?'

17

Penny knew she would be forever grateful to Dawn for insisting she move in with her whilst she rearranged her life without Rory. She'd packed a suitcase and moved out of her own place the day Dawn had told her to. Rory had no idea of Dawn's address, or even the area of town she lived in. The relief as she'd locked her flat door behind her was almost palpable and once she was safely ensconced at Dawn's, her head cleared, and she was able to think straight for the first time since she'd told Rory they were over. Having Dawn repeatedly telling her 'You are doing the right thing getting away' was infinitely reassuring.

But as it got closer and closer to the time she'd told Rory she'd meet him – a meeting that she'd never had any intention of keeping – Penny began to feel a little mean. It wasn't in her nature to lie, but she'd known that if she'd told Rory over the phone that there was zero chance of them getting back together, he would have piled on the pressure and harassed her more than ever. She knew that by telling him she would meet to discuss things, he'd believe that he would be in with a chance of talking her round, as he had done in the past.

When she mentioned to Dawn she was feeling mean about standing him up, and maybe she ought to at least phone him and cancel the meeting, Dawn's reply was a robust 'Penelope Chevalier, you are out of your mind. You will do no such thing. After the way he's treated you, you could have done far worse, *far worse*, than lying to him about a face-to-face meeting. Not turning up tonight is not even a minor offence on your part.'

So last night, whilst Rory was expecting her to join him in Billy's Bistro, Dawn, as planned, had driven Penny to the station to catch a train to Plymouth. She'd booked a hotel room close to the port and downloaded a foot passenger ticket for the early morning ferry to Roscoff on her phone. Once she was settled in her seat and the train was eating up the miles to Plymouth, Penny had taken out her phone and sent her parents a message.

> Coming to stay for a bit. Will message you a definite arrival time soon. Love Penny. xxx

* * *

It was gone ten thirty the next morning when Sasha made her way up to the château, hoping the guests had gone out for the day. Ingrid was on her own and pleased to see her.

'Where's Peter?'

'Freddie needed some help in the orangery this morning, so he's down there giving him a hand,' Ingrid said.

'Guests okay?' Sasha asked.

'They're driving down to the coast to spend the day in Concarneau. Look, are you sure you don't mind acting as the château chambermaid today and tomorrow?'

'Of course not. I wouldn't have offered if I'd minded,' Sasha said. 'I'll go straight up and sort anything that needs sorting.'

The guests had left everything neat and tidy, so there was very little for Sasha to do other than plump the pillows and straighten out the bed. Even the bathroom only needed the damp towels to be rearranged on the heated towel rail.

Back downstairs, she made them both a cup of coffee. 'Have you heard from Penny?'

'We had a text yesterday evening. She's coming to stay for a while, but she didn't give a definite date. We've also had a phone call from Rory demanding to talk to her, calling us liars when we said she wasn't here. So it sounds as if she has left him, but we have no idea where she is.'

'She's still got her phone switched off?'

'Yes.'

'Perhaps she's travelling – on her way here even as we speak,' Sasha said.

Ingrid held up her crossed fingers before taking a sip of her coffee. 'Wouldn't that be good?'

Sasha left after coffee to take the pups for their first walk on a lead. She'd decided to take them along the *route de galop* towards the gate at the far end. Clipping their leads onto the collars of two hyperexcited puppies proved to be easier said than done. Mitzi was the first to stand still long enough for Sasha to clip the lead in place, but trying to grab Mimi and attach her lead whilst holding on to Mitzi, who wanted to wind her lead around Sasha's legs, ended with Sasha sitting on the floor laughing. Which proved to be the answer, as both puppies immediately tried to climb all over her, and she could finally clip the lead onto Mimi's collar and grab hold of Mitzi's trailing lead.

Sasha was still laughing as she opened the garden gate and went down the lane, pulled along by two pups eager to explore this wonderful new world. The gate at the end was open and a tractor drove out of the field and stopped in the lane. Jean-Paul waved a hand in greeting as he climbed out to shut the gate. Gate secure, he turned to wait for her to join him.

'*Bonjour*,' Sasha said smiling, hanging on grimly to Mimi and Mitzi who were determined that Jean-Paul was their new best friend.

Jean-Paul laughed, gave a short whistle, and a collie dog jumped out of the tractor and stood at his feet looking up expectantly. '*Ça va?*' Jean-Paul said before he pointed to the puppies. '*Les chiots de Bruno?*'

Sasha nodded. '*Oui.*'

Jean-Paul's dog began to walk towards them. 'Viking, *assis.*'

Viking sat immediately and, to Sasha's astonishment, the puppies followed suit and sat in front of her for all of four seconds before they were up again. Viking watched them disdainfully without moving.

'That's amazing,' Sasha said, frantically trying to think of some French. '*Il est sage.* So good.'

Jean-Paul smiled and nodded. 'I can help you train the puppies if you like?'

'Would you? That's so kind of you. If you have time.'

'I make the time soon. *Au revoir,*' and Jean-Paul and Viking jumped up into the tractor and slowly moved off. The puppies barked their farewells and Sasha echoed, '*Au revoir.*'

Why did all the French phrases she knew like *Ça va?* and *Comment allez-vous?* always desert her when she had the opportunity to use them?

18

Penny stood on the deck of the Pont-Aven ferry, watching the Devonshire coastline recede as the boat powered its way out into the English Channel. A strong wind was blowing and the sea was rough but right at that moment, Penny didn't care. She was finally on her way to France. It was time to tell her mum and dad that she was free and coming to see them. That she had broken away. She'd phone them and then go and find a coffee, and come back out here to drink it. Taking her mobile out of her bag, she went to open WhatsApp when a voice said, 'Penny Chevalier, what an unexpected surprise.'

Penny turned a smile on her face. 'Alice Briet.' She and Alice had met fleetingly a couple of times since Ingrid and Peter had bought the château, but never for long. Once when they'd all gone to the same restaurant in the next village for Sunday lunch, and Alice had been there with her grand-maman, and Ingrid had introduced them. The second time had been a few months later when they'd bumped into each other in the local shop, and they'd gone for a drink together in the village cafe. Penny knew that Alice had a busy job somewhere in the West Country and like herself, rarely got to France for a break.

'I'm going to Grand-maman's for the summer,' Alice said. 'Are you going to be around for a bit? Or is this a flying visit? Be nice to finally get to know each other properly.'

'Not sure about the whole summer, but definitely a few weeks,' Penny said.

'Great. I'm going to treat myself to breakfast in the restaurant. Join me?'

'I need to phone home and arrange for them to meet me at Roscoff. They don't know I'm on this ferry. It's a rather—um—unexpected visit,' Penny said, pulling a face.

'You don't need to phone. Lucas is meeting me, so we can take you home. Come on, let's get some food – whilst we eat you can tell me all about why you're going home unexpectedly. And afterwards, I'll tell you my tale of woe.'

'Are you sure Lucas won't mind me cadging a lift?'

'No, course not. You know how laid-back my young brother is.'

Penny shook her head. 'No, I don't. I've never met him. He's always been away working when I've been home. I've hardly been back in the past year anyway.'

'Well, you'll meet him this afternoon.'

Once they had trays of food – a full English for Alice, croissants for Penny and coffee for both of them – they found a window table and settled down.

'So, come on, tell me all,' Alice said as she cut into her eggs and bacon. 'I'm guessing a man is at the root of it, they usually are.'

Penny sighed ruefully. 'You're right. I'd realised for some time that Rory wasn't the right one for me, and if I was in any doubt, my dad told me to get out of the relationship a couple of months ago; he could see I wasn't happy. Anyway, to cut a long story short, it all came to a head last week when he lost his temper with me and became abusive. A really strong signal that it was time to leave. Dawn, my best friend, helped me and here I am on my way to France.' Penny took a drink of her coffee. 'What happens next though, I have no idea.' She shook her head despairingly at Alice.

'I'm in the same situation,' Alice said. 'Not because of a man, but because my job literally went up in a cloud of smoke. I was the events manager for a large historical house – think Chatsworth size. My accommodation, one of the perks, came with the job until one night, an electrical fault caused a terrible fire. Not on the scale of the one in Windsor Castle years ago but devastating all the same, so much was destroyed. Luckily no one was hurt but...' Alice gave a deep sigh before putting on a faux-sympathetic voice: *'Rebuilding is going to take a year or two, here's your redundancy pay, thank you for your service and goodbye.'* She put her knife and fork down on her plate. 'Not their fault but...' She shrugged. 'Life goes on. Something will turn up I'm sure – for you and me.'

For the next four or five hours, the two of them divided their time between going out on deck for fresh air until the wind drove them back inside, and to the lounge with its comfortable seats, and cups of hot chocolate from the cafe. The duty-free shop killed the last half hour of the journey as they browsed the shelves. Alice bought a box of her grand-maman's favourite biscuits, and Penny decided a bottle of champagne drunk with her parents would celebrate her freedom nicely.

Queuing to pay, Penny looked at Alice. 'I know you're French, but you speak English very well.'

'That's because of living in the UK for my job for the last few years; I've had to use it all the time.'

'Is Lucas the same? Or does he only speak French? My French is a bit rusty to say the least.'

Alice laughed. 'Lucas, he gets by with Franglais, although, mind you, I think he speaks English better than he lets on. He's a typical Frenchman in that respect! You'll see what I mean soon. Another ten minutes or so and we'll be docking in Roscoff.'

* * *

Penny and Alice were quickly through customs and out into the arrivals foyer. Alice said a rude word when she couldn't see her brother. 'He'll either be waiting, parked where he shouldn't be, or in the cafe. Come on, let's look outside.'

They didn't have to go very far, as two sharp toots on a car horn got their attention immediately. Lucas waved and came across to greet them. 'Alice, my favourite sister,' and he hugged her tight before giving her a kiss on the cheek.

'Idiot, I'm your *only* sister – at least as far as we know, so there's always a chance of another one turning up, I suppose. This is Penny, Ingrid's and Peter's daughter. She needs a lift home.'

Lucas smiled as he held out his hand. '*Bonjour* and welcome.' Penny smiled at him and quickly retrieved her fingers before he could completely crush them. The unexpected warm and fuzzy feeling that had flooded through her body as Lucas had held her hand was impossible to ignore, though. Where on earth had *that* come from? She could only hope that Lucas hadn't noticed her reaction to his touch.

Once the suitcases were stowed in the boot, they were off. Penny sat in the back and zoned out for the next half hour or so as Alice and Lucas chatted in French about their grand-maman and other people in the village she hadn't yet met. It wasn't until she heard Lucas mention the new owners of the Cottages du Lac that she began to listen and try to translate the French.

'I think they are about our ages, so new friends all round. Sasha has just taken the last two of Bruno's pups. She's been helping Ingrid at the château since the accident.'

Penny was instantly on the alert at Lucas's words. 'What accident?'

Lucas glanced at her in the rear-view mirror. 'I'm sorry. You didn't know? Nothing is broken. Your maman fell out of the Land Rover. A badly twisted ankle.'

Penny exhaled. 'My mother does tend to be a bit accident-prone at times and it's always her ankles that take the brunt.'

'I'm sure having you home will aid her recovery,' Lucas said. Five minutes later, he turned onto the driveway of the Château du Cheval.

'Even after two years, it's strange coming in through these gates. I always feel I should be going down the *route de galop* to the Cottages du Lac and Grand-maman,' Alice said.

'*Plus ça change, plus c'est la même chose*,' Lucas said. 'The more things change, the more they stay the same.'

19

Ingrid was in the small sitting room when she heard the kitchen door open.

'Anyone home?'

'In the sitting room,' Ingrid answered, not daring to believe it was who she thought it was.

'Hello, Mum,' Penny said, standing in the doorway.

'Oh, thank God you're here. Come and let me give you a hug.'

Penny gave a happy sigh as Ingrid squeezed her tightly. 'I'm so glad to be here.'

'How did you manage without calling us for a lift?'

'Alice and Lucas Briet.'

'We've both been so worried. I kept ringing, but you had your phone switched off all the time. Why didn't you at least let us know where you were? That you were okay? That last text was such a relief.'

'I'm truly sorry, Mum, but I didn't want to involve you in case things got nasty.'

'We thought you might be on your way to the Lake District.'

Penny moved away and looked at her. 'How did you...?'

'Rory phoned. Not a happy man.'

'He's spoken to Emma then. If he phones again, just tell him that's where I am. I don't want him showing his face here.'

'I doubt that he'll come here,' Ingrid said. 'Your dad made it plain that he's not welcome. Where have you been, anyway?'

'Dawn insisted I stay with her for a few days while I sorted everything.' Penny looked at Ingrid's leg resting on the chair. 'That looks a bit violent – all those reds, blues and purples.'

'I've got a matching wrist this time,' Ingrid said, showing her.

'How are you managing with the guests?'

'Sasha stepped up and made sure the room was ready, Dad's sorted breakfasts and pushed the vacuum around. They leave tomorrow and we don't have any more bookings this month. I must ring Sasha and tell her you're here – if you're happy to be tomorrow's chambermaid?'

'Of course I am. I can do whatever you want me to. Who is Sasha?'

'She and her brother Freddie are the new owners of the Cottages du Lac,' Ingrid answered before asking, 'How long are you planning on staying?'

Penny shrugged. 'A few weeks? No idea really. I've got my flat in Bristol to sort out at some point, and I've got some serious thinking to do about the future. Where's Dad anyway?' Penny said, deciding that a change of subject was needed.

'I think he and Freddie are doing some maintenance work on the old chapel this afternoon,' Ingrid said. 'Why don't you wander down there and surprise your dad?'

'I'll do that, and then I'll come back and organise dinner for us all.'

Ingrid sent up a silent prayer of thanks as Penny left. She

was finally home in surprisingly good spirits, and here for an indefinite period. Hopefully the serious thinking she'd mentioned would lead her to the decision Ingrid and Peter were hoping she'd make. But only time would tell on that.

Sasha was sitting at the kitchen table putting the final touches to the sketch she'd done of Starlight when Ingrid rang to tell her the good news about Penny being home, and to thank Sasha again for all her help. Sasha sighed as the call ended. Of course she was happy for Ingrid that her daughter was home, but she'd enjoyed helping out at the château, it was such a beautiful place to spend time. She'd miss the excuse to visit, to chat with Ingrid, but the truth was, she should be concentrating on getting her own life in France sorted.

Apart from painting a few walls, she'd barely started on the renovations she wanted to do in the cottage, like upgrading the kitchen and getting her workroom organised; this had come to a grinding halt because of her inability to source some furniture. There was also the garden to sort; and training and playing with Mimi and Mitzi took up more time than she'd truly anticipated. As for improving her schoolgirl French, she'd done nothing about that either, despite downloading a 'Learn French Quickly' app, as well as an up-to-date translation dictionary. She wanted to be able to talk to Jean-Paul – and other people obviously – but she sensed he knew a lot about training dogs from the way Viking behaved, and she hoped he'd advise her soon about the pups.

Sasha picked up the finished sketch of Starlight and care-fully slotted it into a cardboard photo frame. She'd walk Mimi and Mitzi down to the stables later and give it to Colette.

A gentle knock at the front door, followed by, '*Hello, anyone there*?' had the puppies racing from the kitchen where they'd been happily play-fighting each other, barking excitedly.

'Gosh, aren't you two adorable.'

'Mimi. Mitzi. *Assis* – sit,' Sasha said as sternly as she could. 'If you can ignore them and come through to the kitchen, they'll follow and I can shut them in the garden,' Sasha said desperately.

A few minutes later, calm was restored indoors as the dogs cavorted outside.

'I'm guessing you must be Ingrid's daughter, Penny? It's lovely to meet you,' Sasha said. 'Sorry about the puppy shambles.'

'No worries. They're adorable. I've just been talking to Dad and your brother in the old chapel. He suggested I come over and introduce myself.'

'I haven't seen inside the old chapel yet,' Sasha confessed. 'Freddie has said it's lovely inside.'

'Oh, you must go and take a look. He and Dad are doing a great job. I know Mum is hoping to hold the occasional wedding ceremony there.'

'Ingrid is so pleased to have you home,' Sasha said. 'Are you staying long?'

Penny shrugged. 'Not sure, but definitely for a couple of weeks. That's lovely,' Penny said, looking at the picture of Starlight on the table. 'Did you draw that?'

Sasha nodded. 'Yes. I was about to walk the puppies down to the stables to give it to Colette if she's there.'

'I'll wander down with you. I've met Colette before but not seen her horse yet.'

Sasha quickly put the sketch in a paper bag to protect it before calling the pups in and attaching their leads.

'Shall I take one?' Penny offered. 'It must be difficult managing two.'

'Thanks. If you could take Mitzi, she's a little calmer than Mimi most of the time. Jean-Paul has offered to help train them but so far, we haven't managed to get together.'

As they walked through the grounds towards the stables, Penny looked around her. 'It's so beautiful here, I can see why Mum and Dad fell in love with the château.'

'Freddie and I did the same when we found the cottages. It's such a special place. Life here is a million miles away from my old life in the UK,' Sasha said. 'I do worry a bit in case things like earning money and learning the language don't work out as planned and I have to leave. Freddie will always be able to pick up work, but me...' Sasha shrugged. 'I'm hoping my Etsy shop will be enough. It's my language skills – or rather the lack of them – that bother me. Your mum's French is very good. Do you speak French well?'

'It's very rusty,' Penny admitted. 'But hopefully a few weeks here will resurrect it.' She glanced mischievously at Sasha. 'You know what they say: if you want to learn French, take a lover.'

Sasha laughed. 'Now that's an idea. I'll bear it in mind.'

Colette had just finished grooming Starlight when they arrived, and she came out to greet them. 'Hi, Sasha. Penny, it's great to see you here again. Alice told me you travelled over together.'

Sasha held out the paper bag. 'This is for you. I hope you like it.'

Colette carefully opened the bag, took the sketch out and squealed with delight. 'That is so good of Starlight. You've totally captured her. Thank you so much. This is going to take pride of place at home.'

Sasha smiled and gave an inward sigh of relief. Watching

people's reactions to her sketches and paintings was always difficult; she much preferred not being there when they were viewed for the first time, in case their disappointment showed on their face.

'Hey, Alice and I are going for a drink tonight in the village bar – why don't the two of you join us?'

Penny answered first. 'Love to. What time?'

'About eight o'clock. Sasha?'

'Thanks. Shall we walk down together, Penny?' The thought of walking into the village bar for the first time on her own was frightening. Freddie had been on a couple of occasions and said everybody had made him feel welcome, but Sasha would appreciate the reassurance of someone alongside her the first time she braved the bar.

'Good idea. I'll come to the cottage at about a quarter to eight.'

20

Ingrid and Peter were in the sitting room when Penny arrived back at the château, paperwork and a monthly planner open in front of them. Both looking thoughtful and stressed.

'What's up?' she asked.

'We've each had a phone call this afternoon,' Ingrid said. 'Mine was from a woman who wants to hold a wedding reception for approximately thirty people here after their civil marriage in the *mairie*. I told her I'd get back to her; I didn't feel I could turn her away instantly.'

'Mine was from the chairman of the church fundraising committee,' Peter said. 'Would we hold a village fete in the grounds later this year when the tourists are around, to help raise some much-needed money. I said yes, no problem, but your mum thinks there could be.'

'I don't see the problem with either of those two events,' Penny said, looking at them. 'You're planning on doing wedding receptions, so you've got your first booking.'

'The problem with this particular booking is that it is in two and a bit weeks. We are simply not ready. We don't have half the equipment we need. And with me not being able to even move properly, it's out of the question.' Ingrid gave a deep sigh. 'But your father can't see that. He says we should just say yes and get on with it.'

'Why is it such short notice? Shotgun wedding?'

'Apparently the venue they wanted to use has had a major flood in both the room booked for the reception and in the kitchen. It's going to be at least a month before they're up and running again. The bride doesn't want to have to cancel guests or move the wedding date.'

'Okay. And why is the village fete a problem later in the year?' Penny asked.

'The committee want us to arrange the fete on their behalf,' Ingrid said. 'If they were doing all the organising and just wanted to use the grounds, it would be fine. But a) we know nothing about running an outdoor event in France, and you can be sure there will be mountains of bureaucracy to deal with. And b) we have no contacts for fete entertainment like... like, oh I don't know, a bouncy castle for the children, or ice cream vendors, balloon sellers, or anybody in fact,' and Ingrid threw her arms up in despair. 'And yet, knowing all of this, your father stubbornly refuses to ring the chairman back and say sorry, no can do.'

Penny took a deep breath. 'Right. Here's what I think. You, Mum, ring the woman back and confirm you will let them have the wedding reception here. She will need to come and talk to you – us – within twenty-four hours about the menu and how they would like the room decorated, and anything else they would like to make the day special. Also tell her she will need to pay us a non-refundable deposit when she comes. Once we know whether it's a sit-down meal or a buffet, we can start to organise things.'

'We? I hope you're saying what I think you're saying?' Ingrid looked hopefully at her daughter.

'I'm here and will stay for long enough to cook and help you sort out everything for the wedding. Happy?'

'Deliriously so,' Ingrid said, sniffing and trying to surreptitiously wipe a tear away. 'Does this mean you might stay on longer afterwards?'

'Mum, I have no idea what I'm doing long term yet. Let's just deal with the wedding first. As for running the village fete,' Penny said, 'think of the brownie points you'd earn from locals, so I think you should do it. I have an idea, but I need to talk to someone first, but I'm fairly hopeful you won't have to ring and say no can do, Dad. Give me twenty-four hours, okay?'

Peter gave her a thumbs up. 'Thanks, love.'

'Right, hope you don't mind, but I'm going out tonight. I know it's my first night home, but Colette has invited Sasha and me to join her and Alice for a drink in the village bar. I did promise to cook dinner, so I'd better get to the kitchen.'

'Don't worry, I'd planned a simple meal for tonight. New potatoes, fresh asparagus and salmon steaks,' Peter said.

'Want me to make a hollandaise sauce?' Penny asked.

'Yes please,' Ingrid said. 'Love your hollandaise sauce. And we can have a glass of the champagne you brought before you go out. We need to celebrate you being here.'

* * *

When Penny and Sasha walked into the busy bar later that evening, Alice and Colette were already there with a bottle of red wine and four glasses on a table tucked away in the corner. Lucas, standing at the bar with Jean-Paul and another couple of men, gave them both a cheery wave. Jean-Paul smiled and nodded, and Sasha smiled back.

Colette introduced Alice to Sasha before pouring the wine. '*Santé! À nos nouveaux amis.*' They all clicked glasses and took sips.

'Mum loved that sketch of Starlight. She was wondering whether she could commission you to do a painting for her?' Colette looked questioningly at Sasha.

'Yes, of course, but I need a couple of weeks to get my studio up and running. If she looks at my Etsy shop, she'll get an idea of the things I can do.'

Alice turned to Penny. 'Your mum recovered from the shock of you turning up unexpectedly?'

'Think so. She and Dad got a couple of phone calls this afternoon that diverted attention from me instantly,' Penny said. 'The chairman of the church-fund committee rang Dad, asking him to organise a fete in the château grounds sometime this summer. Which he agreed to do.'

'Growing up, there was always a fete in the château on the first Saturday in August,' Alice said. 'Would be good to see the tradition started again. Why are you looking at me like that?'

'The thing is, as Mum pointed out to Dad after he'd agreed, they want him to sort out everything on their behalf. She says he has to ring them back and tell them no because they've never run an event like that in their lives before and have no French contacts. So, before he rings and cancels and the village hate us forever, I thought I'd see if you, as an experienced events plan...' Penny's voice trailed away as a wide-eyed Alice looked at her. 'But I... I guess not. Forget I mentioned It. It was just a thought.'

'No, it's fine. I'll help your dad with the paperwork and the organising. I'll quite enjoy it. Grand-maman will more than likely have some contacts from the old days.'

'Are you sure? You looked terrified at the prospect.'

'Not terrified, but I've never planned an event in France before either,' Alice said. 'And the other thing is I can't promise to still be here for the actual event. I have to start job-hunting at some stage. Depends on whether the traditional Saturday date is chosen or not.'

'Shall I get Dad to ring you? Or will you wander up and have a chat with him?'

'I'll wander up,' Alice said. 'I haven't been up to the château since Grand-maman moved out of her cottage. I'll enjoy seeing what your parents have done around the place.'

'You said Ingrid received a phone call too,' Sasha reminded Penny.

'This one is definitely going to keep the three of us busy. An intimate wedding reception for thirty people. The woman is coming to the château tomorrow to discuss what they want. Doing a reception is not a problem; the short notice, though, could be. The wedding is just under three weeks away.'

'Crikey, you're going to have your work cut out,' Sasha said. 'If I can do anything to help, don't hesitate to ask.'

Both Alice and Colette offered their help, Colette with the proviso that she was at work most days in Quimper.

'Thanks,' Penny said. 'I might take you all up on that. How are you at waiting on tables?'

21

The next morning, Penny and Ingrid sat in the kitchen making a list of every question they needed to ask Madame Richard, and also decided on the answers to questions she was likely to ask.

'Thirty people isn't that many,' Penny said, biting the end of her pencil. 'Should we offer the orangery as an intimate alternative to the larger rooms here in the château? It could be really romantic.'

'Not sure the orangery is ready,' Ingrid said.

'Not a lot to do to it. I had a quick look after breakfast,' Penny said. 'One of the important things we must get straight from the very beginning is the drinks they want served. I did a little research last night and there could be a minor hiccup in that there is no way we can sell alcohol without a licence, and we won't get one in the next two weeks. You or Dad have to go for a training session before they will grant you one. You have got *chambres d'hôte* and restaurant permits, haven't you?'

Ingrid nodded. 'Yes. And we *do* have an alcohol licence. Dad did his three-day training session a few weeks ago.'

'He did? That's brilliant,' Penny said. 'Now, have you bought anything catering-related for the *chambres d'hôte* side of the business and the weddings you plan to do eventually? And what about kitchen equipment?'

'I did buy crockery, glasses and cutlery for the dining room. Otherwise, I was waiting until we were closer to starting before buying more. I want the crockery and glasses for weddings to be special and I haven't actually seen any I like yet.'

'How many place settings did you buy?'

'Fourteen, because with six bedrooms, we're never going to have more than twelve guests, and the two extra were for breakages.'

Penny scribbled on the notepad in front of her. 'Kitchen equipment?'

'You know what I had in my kitchen at home,' Ingrid said. 'But I did think ahead when we were planning the kitchen. We do have two ovens, the fridge is a big new double one, and there is another one and a wine fridge in the utility room, a small convection oven and a large freezer.'

'Right. We can always hire crockery, glasses and cutlery if we can't find anything we like in time. Depending on the menu I have to cook, I'll buy some catering trays and dishes.'

Ingrid sighed. 'I'm not convinced we're doing the right thing, agreeing to do this wedding. It's going to cost us. We're just not ready.'

'We *are* doing the right thing. Okay, we're not going to make a fortune, even if we end up charging fifty euros a head, but it means we'll be up and ready by the summer.'

'How much a head?' Ingrid said, looking at Penny in amazement. 'I don't think we can charge that much for a last-minute booking we're not even ready for.'

'Yes we can, it might even be higher.' But before Penny could say more, there was a knock on the door and Sasha called out, 'Good morning!'

'Door is open, Sasha, come on in,' Ingrid answered.

'Sorry, are you busy?' Sasha said, looking at the paperwork on the table. 'I don't want to interrupt and I can't stay long. I only came up to see how you are.'

'The swelling on my foot is going down and it's not as painful as it was, but I'm still immobile, to all intents and purposes,' Ingrid said.

'Good that the swelling has gone down, just don't try to do too much too soon,' Sasha said. 'I'll leave you to it. I have to get back to the cottage, apparently the bathrooms are being delivered today.'

* * *

Madame Richard arrived promptly at two o'clock and, abandoning her white mud-splattered sports car in the driveway, immediately launched into a torrent of French as Penny walked down the steps to meet the flamboyant woman with blue hair wearing a shocking pink trouser suit. Whatever else this woman turned out to be, it would definitely not be shy.

Penny smiled, tried to interrupt the flow of words to introduce herself, and took her into the château through the main entrance to meet Ingrid who was waiting, leg propped up, in the main dining room.

'This is Madame Richard,' Penny said.

'*Je vous en prie, appelez-moi Stella*,' Madame Richard replied. 'The château is beautiful. I am so pleased you can help with my catastrophe. I have brought the menu we agree with the now not available hotel, and also the deposit.'

'Madame Richard – Stella, we have to discuss things first.

We hope we can help, but before we can agree to host the reception, we need to know more details of your requirements,' Ingrid said, her French slow and deliberate, hoping to avoid any misunderstandings.

'First I'd like to show you the rooms available,' Penny said. 'This is one of them, upstairs there is another larger reception salon and there is also the orangery, which would be a smaller, more intimate venue.'

'The orangery sound *parfait*,' Stella enthused. 'Show me.'

'It's through here.' Penny said, opening a door at the back of the room and ushering Stella through. 'We would dress it up, of course, put some fairy lights around, mirrors, possibly candles, give it an intimate, romantic atmosphere.'

Stella stood enthralled in the middle of the orangery. 'So beautiful. I don't need to see the other room. This is the one I want. We go back and organise.'

Back in the château dining room, Penny offered Stella a drink. 'Coffee, wine?'

Stella shook her head. '*Non, merci*.' She reached into her large tote and pulled out a folder. 'This is the menu we want. Here is the deposit the hotel return, five thousand euros.'

'Thank you,' Penny said faintly. 'I'll give you a receipt when I've told you a bit more about what we can provide, and you've answered a few questions and we've agreed.'

'Okay!'

'What time is the wedding?'

'Five o'clock in the afternoon. I think we be here about a quarter to six.'

'Welcoming glass of champagne or a soft drink for everyone?'

'Of course.'

Penny glanced at the menu.

'Definitely a sit-down meal? Not a buffet?'

Stella nodded.

'One long head table? Or one just for the bridal family and several smaller round ones?'

'Oh, round ones – six people on the head table, and about five or six on the others. Informal, fun atmosphere.'

'So, no formal seating arrangement – apart from the bride and groom on the head table obviously – no place names, a "sit where you like" for the guests?'

'Yes.'

'Wedding cake?'

'Will be delivered on the day.'

'*D'accord,*' Penny said. 'Now we must discuss the main problem we have. Alcohol. We do have a licence, but we do not currently have a stock of drinks in the cellar as we have not officially opened.'

Stella looked at her aghast. 'But we must have champagne and wine with the meal and for the party afterwards.'

'I realise that,' Penny said, making a mental note to ask about the party. 'We are happy to buy in a large enough quantity of champagne and wines for the wedding meal and simply charge you for what you use. But I hadn't realised you were planning on having a party afterwards, and there is no extensive cellar or bar here.'

Stella nodded thoughtfully. 'So how do we do party drinks?'

'You could bring all the drinks you want for that and we'd serve them for you.'

'You have somewhere to store them? And an extra fridge?'

'Yes,' Penny replied.

'I bring them in the week before the wedding,' Stella said.

'How long do you expect the party to go on?'

Stella shrugged. 'Until it finish? Can you do some finger food for that?'

'Yes, I can do that,' Penny nodded and made a note. 'But the party, by law, cannot go on past one o'clock.'

'That's fine,' Stella said. 'There is an extra something I would like to arrange in addition to the reception. Do you by any chance have a four-poster bed in one of your guest room?'

'Yes,' Ingrid said.

'I hope it is free on the night of the wedding. I like to reserve it.' And Stella placed a five-hundred-euro note on top of the other notes.

'Wouldn't you like to see it first?'

Stella shook her head. '*Non*. It will be a wonderful surprise, I think.'

'I'll write you a receipt for the deposit.' Penny pulled a piece of paper towards her and quickly wrote one and gave it to Stella, who casually thrust it into her jacket pocket. 'I will send you a quotation when I've priced everything. I will need your acceptance in writing,' Penny said.

'I accept whatever it is. I know it will be expensive, but...' Stella shrugged. 'It's a very special day and I want the best. Now I must go. I leave the folder with you. My address is there for you to send the quotation. I see you again the week of the wedding with the party drinks.'

Penny followed Stella out to her car and held the door open for her as she got in. 'Thank you for entrusting us with your daughter's special day. We will do our best to make it truly special.'

Stella gave a loud hoot of laughter. 'I don't have a daughter. *C'est moi*. I'm the bride. I finally met the love of my life and I'm getting married at the age of seventy-two for the first time.' And churning up a spray of gravel, Stella drove away, cheerily waving her hand out of the window as she went.

22

'What a character,' Ingrid said when Penny rejoined her in the sitting room. 'What on earth have we agreed to? A wedding reception is one thing, but a party afterwards?'

'We can still back out,' Penny said. 'Tell her we have had to reconsider, it's too short notice. She might think twice when I send her the quote anyway. It's not going to be a cheap wedding reception.'

'I think you could quote Stella a six-figure sum and she'd wave it away as if it were nothing,' Ingrid said. 'She must love her daughter very much.'

Penny laughed. 'She doesn't have a daughter. It's *her* wedding – her first at seventy-two. And she's very happy and excited about it.'

'Gosh, I wasn't expecting that. I look forward to meeting the bridegroom,' Ingrid said.

Penny gathered together her own paperwork and the folder Stella had left. 'I'm going to be busy for the next couple of hours trying to work out the cost of everything and also the things we need to buy.' She glanced at Ingrid. 'How's the bank balance currently? I know you sold the cottages to free up some cash, but we're going to need a lot of stuff for this wedding. Buying in the champagne and wine is going to be expensive for a start. Then there are tables, chairs, crockery and glasses, to name but four. We could always hire, but that won't be cheap. I think buying for this and future weddings would make more sense.'

Ingrid nodded. 'I know you're right, but we need to find things that fit in with the spirit of the château. I don't want to buy stuff just because it's all we can find. I was hoping to eventually source some art deco crockery, but we're unlikely to find that in a hurry.'

'True, and we probably wouldn't be able to hire anything that specific,' Penny said. 'How about a compromise on crockery of delicate, plain white porcelain? If we find some art deco vintage later, we can always keep it in reserve.'

'That would work for me,' Ingrid said, reaching for her crutch and carefully pulling herself onto her feet. 'I'll make a list of things I know we're going to need and start doing some research on the internet while you work out the figures for Stella. The money from the cottages is still mostly intact so, as long as we don't go mad, we can definitely buy good quality.' Ingrid began to make her way slowly through to the kitchen. 'Before I forget. Could you please collect a box from the tack room for me sometime in the next few days? It's under the saddle racks at the far end.'

* * *

Now that the new bathroom fittings had arrived, Sasha was starting to prepare the bathroom for its makeover. Freddie was hoping to plumb the new shower in one evening this week, and to do the bath and sink at the weekend. Once he'd done her bathroom, he'd leave her to the decorating and make a start on his own. The sun was shining and she would have preferred to be out in the garden, but had decided she could do that later this evening and hopefully avoid all the midges. She was busy rubbing the window frames down when her phone pinged with a text message from Jean-Paul.

> I come to walk and train the dogs at four o'clock. D'accord?

Sasha glanced at the time. Quarter past three.

> Merci. A bientôt.

She was ready and waiting at four o'clock, having showered, dried her hair, dressed in a more respectable pair of jeans than the pair she was wearing earlier, and pulled on a clean T-shirt. A light foundation with sunblock smoothed over her face and she was ready. It wasn't a date, after all. It was simply a friend helping with training the pups – and also maybe helping her to improve her French as well.

Jean-Paul surprised her by driving down the *route de galop* and parking his tractor by the garden entrance. Mitzi and Mimi gave both him and Viking an enthusiastic, noisy welcome. Before they set off, Sasha put a couple of dog biscuits in her pocket to use as treats and to encourage the pups to do as they were told. After Sasha had clipped them onto their leads, she closed the cottage door behind them and they started to walk through the château grounds. Jean-Paul had taken Mitzi while Sasha had Mimi. Viking, who was off the lead, trotted happily alongside Jean-Paul as they walked.

Jean-Paul took his phone out of his pocket. 'I have a little English but now I have an app also.'

'I have an app too,' Sasha said, taking out her own phone. They both smiled, happy at the thought that communication between the two of them would be easier from now on.

'You like living here?' Jean-Paul asked.

Sasha gave an enthusiastic '*Oui!* I love it. I can't quite believe I live here in my own cottage in France. It's beautiful. I wish...' She stopped, not wanting to embarrass Jean-Paul with her own sadness.

'*Vous* wish...' Jean-Paul prompted.

'Mum's inheritance made it possible for us to buy the cottages and it makes me sad that she's not around to see us living here,' Sasha said slowly before shaking her head. '*Désolée.* It's the way life works, we wouldn't be here without losing her, but she's left a big hole in my life.'

'*C'est naturel,*' Jean-Paul said. 'My parents, they both still live. But I see them only sometime. My sister, she live in Bordeaux and they join her last year. They help with the *petits-enfants.*'

'You are an uncle!' Sasha said, smiling, silently wondering whether she and Freddie would ever elevate each other to the status of auntie and uncle. She could only hope that sometime in the future they would both meet someone special.

'We do some puppy training,' Jean-Paul said. 'Before we forget and the walk is finish. It is important to sound firm.' He stopped walking. 'Viking, *attends.*' The dog stopped and looked at him. '*Assis.*' Viking sat instantly, almost before Jean-Paul had said the word. To Sasha's amusement, both Mimi and Mitzi were also sitting, their tails swishing the ground, watching Viking. 'We walk a little bit more and then you give the commands,' Jean-Paul said.

'Okay.'

Having moved on a little way, it was now Sasha's turn.

'Mimi, Mitzi. Viking. *Attends.*' Viking stopped and the pups followed a second later. '*Assis,*' Sasha said. And all three dogs sat.

'The pups they are intelligent. It not take long for them to learn,' Jean-Paul said. 'You practise each time you walk them. Now I think we return to your house.'

Once back at the cottage, Sasha thanked Jean-Paul for his help and his company. He simply smiled, kissed her on the cheek and said '*À bientôt*' before leaping into his tractor with Viking and leaving. Sasha waved goodbye and smiling happily, she turned to go indoors. Downloading a translation app just to be able to talk to her must mean he liked her and wanted to get to know her.

23

'Is this the box you wanted brought up from the tack room?' Penny asked, two afternoons later, pushing open the kitchen door with her hip, and carrying a cardboard box into the kitchen.

'Yes, thank you. That's the one.'

'Where shall I put it?'

'Somewhere out of sight in the sitting room. I want to show the contents to Eliza and Lucas after the book club tonight; to Alice too of course, if she comes,' Ingrid said. 'It's most of the things I found in the tack room when I cleared it out for Colette to use. Some of it goes back to the thirties and even earlier, when the château was heavily involved in the French trotter-horse racing world. There are rosettes, photos, weigh-in slips, as well as programmes from then, but also from the sixties when William, Eliza's husband, was working as a groom here. His name is mentioned several times on race programmes. I thought she might be interested to see them and maybe tell us a little bit about that time. There's a small silver cup in there too.'

'What are you going to do with it all after you've shown it to Eliza?'

'I was thinking maybe a small display cabinet of some of the best stuff in the foyer alongside Merlin, a collage perhaps as well. Sasha would know about doing one of those. And of course if Eliza wants any of it, she can take it.'

'What time is the book club tonight?'

'Usual time – seven thirty for eight,' Ingrid said. 'Are you going to join us? I'm sure you've read *Rebecca* at school.'

'I'm one of those philistines who, whilst admitting it's brilliantly written and liking du Maurier's other books, didn't get on with it. Be interesting to see what our French friends make of it. Are you having coffee or wine tonight?'

'I always offer both. It's rarely more than one bottle.'

'I'll get the glasses out ready,' Penny said.

* * *

Two hours later and the small sitting room was crowded. Penny greeted everyone as Ingrid was trapped in her chair because of her leg. Peter made coffees and Penny poured the wine.

Once everyone had a drink and had caught up with the latest gossip, Ingrid tapped her glass and opened the discussion. 'How did you all get on with *Rebecca*?'

Everybody seemed to have something to say and there was a lively discussion before people gave their final thoughts about it.

'Didn't finish it,' Benjamin said. 'Not my sort of book at all. But Suzie liked it, didn't you?'

'Yes, I liked the psychological thriller element to it,' Suzie said.

Jean-Paul thought that Maxim de Winter was a bully and

hadn't enjoyed the book at all. Sasha loved the way he shyly apologised to 'les Anglais' for not liking it.

Eliza said something in French, which made Josette laugh.

'The rough translation is that Eliza is glad that the English people she has met no longer have the same attitudes. Mostly!' Ingrid said laughing. 'Now, the next book on our list is *Tender is the Night* by F. Scott Fitzgerald. Everyone happy with that?'

Murmurs of assent were heard before Benjamin and Suzie stood up and apologised for leaving early, but they'd agreed to meet a friend at a new pizza restaurant in the next village. Josette and Robert took the opportunity to leave early as well, once again blaming their early morning start at the boulangerie. As the door closed behind them, Ingrid turned to Eliza.

'I cleared out the tack room recently for Colette to use, and I have a box of miscellaneous things from when the stables were well-known in the horse world. I would love to learn more of the history of the château from someone who has lived here a long time. I know they were renowned for years, decades, for their race-winning French trotting horses. I don't want to upset you, but may I show you what I've found?'

Eliza gave her a sad smile. 'I would like to see. William threw out so much when the horses were taken from him and sold.'

Penny pulled the box out of the corner and placed it in front of Eliza on the coffee table. She carefully pulled open the flaps, as everyone crowded round.

'If there is anything in here you'd like, please feel free to say. It is a real hotchpotch of things. Here's a racing programme from the early 1930s. Several rosettes, a jockey's weigh-in book – oh, that's from the sixties. A poster from the twenties. A race-card – there are a few of those from various decades.'

'The one you're holding is one of William's, I think,' Eliza said, holding her hand out. 'Yes. It was when he was riding for the Ermotte family who stabled their trotting horses here.'

'I didn't know Grand-papa was a jockey!' Alice said, astonished. 'I knew he was the head groom and trained the horses, but not that he actually raced those dangerous chariot-like contraptions.'

Eliza shook her head. 'No, no. He didn't race a sulky. He thought they were dangerous too. But French trotters are a breed that are equally good ridden or driven in harness. He rode them in several races on the flat. Won a few times too. But the Ermottes left when they sold the château at the end of the sixties, taking their horses with them. They wanted William and me to go with them to Ireland, but your mother was tiny and...' Eliza shrugged. 'William didn't really want to leave Brittany. So we stayed and he worked for the new owners. That's when he became head groom and helped to train the trotters, because they concentrated totally on the harness racing.' Eliza sighed. 'He loved his horses. As long as he could work with them, he was happy.' She glanced across at Ingrid and Peter. 'He would have been so happy to see horses back on the estate.'

'Just the one so far,' Ingrid said. 'But I'm sure there will be more in time. Eliza, I have to ask: your surname, Albertini, is very Italian-sounding; was William Italian?'

'Half Italian from his father, but his mother came from Caen, here in France. William, like me, was born in Caen and his mother stayed when World War II broke out. William's father was called up to fight in the Italian army. Sadly, he was killed in the last few months of the war.'

'I'm sorry to hear that,' Ingrid said softly.

Lucas, who had been rummaging in the box, held up a black and white photograph. 'Do you know who these people are, Grand-maman?'

Eliza studied the photo intently for several seconds before giving a broad smile. 'It's Grand-papa William holding the bridle of his favourite horse after winning a big race on him. I can't remember the name of the race. The couple on the other side are the Ermottes. They were so proud of that stallion that they had a marble statue made of it. Used to stand at the top of the driveway. Often wonder what happened to it. It simply disappeared. Probably sold on for a lot of money.'

Ingrid gave Peter a startled look. 'Eliza, do you remember the name of the horse?'

'Its stable name was something like "Grey Owl out of Lady Anne", but William nicknamed him Merlin because he always said he was magical. A ride on him was wonderful every time,' Eliza said, still studying the photograph. She looked at Ingrid. '*C'est possible* for me to have this – or *peut-être* a copy?'

'Of course,' Ingrid said. 'I'll have a copy made and you can have the original.'

Peter stood up. 'Eliza, you haven't been in the château since we've lived here, have you? Would you like to come with me? There's something I'd like to show you.'

Eliza looked surprised at the unexpected invitation but happily got to her feet. 'I'd love to see what you've done to the place.'

Peter opened the connecting fire door and took her through.

'I've never spent much time here in the actual château,' Eliza said. 'I used to help William in the stables occasionally but...' She stopped as she saw the statue in the foyer. 'Merlin,' Eliza whispered as she turned excitedly to Peter. '*C'est incroyable.*'

'We found him in the stables and sent him off to be restored, he was in a bad way. He's only been back a couple of months.'

'He looks perfect in here, better than being outside,' Eliza said.

'The strange thing is the name plaque, although damaged, was still attached, so we've always known he was called Merlin, we just didn't know his history,' Peter said.

'I'm sure he'll thank you for his restoration and work the magic that William always insisted Merlin the real horse had,' Eliza said, her voice cracking with emotion as she moved closer to gently stroke the statue. 'It broke William's heart when the Ermottes took him to Ireland and he had to say goodbye to him.'

_____

24

Sasha was still thinking about Eliza the next morning as she walked Mimi and Mitzi along one of the paths she'd discovered in the château grounds. Eliza had been quite emotional when she had returned from seeing Merlin, and had left soon afterwards, with Alice and Lucas hovering protectively at her side. Ingrid had asked Sasha before she left if she would think about how the contents of the box could be displayed in the château entrance hall.

Some of the racecards, the photo of William and Merlin and also the poster could be framed and hung on the wall, Sasha decided. Rosettes and some of the more fragile weigh-in cards and racecards could be displayed in a locked glass-topped cabinet beneath them. The photo and the other items would need mounting in cardboard before framing them – something she could easily do in her workroom once it was operational.

Sasha gave a frustrated sigh. So far, she'd painted the walls and that was it. Until she got a working desk, some shelves and a cupboard, and could empty the boxes piled on the floor, it was impossible to do any work in there. She was hoping to find a few things she needed at the upcoming village *vide-grenier*. It wasn't that she was desperate to start earning money right away, but she really wanted to get back into sketching and painting. It had been out of her life for far too long.

Freddie, on the other hand, was getting more and more work. He had two regular customers in the village and another three in the next village, as well as working for Peter several days a week now on the estate. He was grumbling the other morning as he'd joined Sasha for breakfast, about not having the time to do much to the cottages. 'The weather's so good, everyone wants their garden sorted for summer instantly.'

'There will probably be rainy days when you can't work outside,' Sasha had said. 'So make the best of it.'

Today Freddie was working with Peter, finishing the cleaning of the fountains in the Italian garden. Three of them, all with old granite horse statues and small ponds, had been built into the rock at the beginning of the twentieth century and were apparently fed by a natural spring from higher up the valley. Peter was desperate to see them working now they'd been cleared of all the self-seeded small trees and weeds.

The path Sasha was following petered out by a small wood of hawthorne and ash trees, brambles and a holly bush. A few metres away on the far side of the copse, a white wooden pole and rail fence stopped access onto the field directly ahead. Mimi and Mitzi, desperate to explore this new exciting playground, tugged on their leads.

'No,' Sasha said firmly. Shortening both leads and pulling the pups to heel, she started to walk home.

Back at the cottage, both the pups flopped onto their bed as if totally exhausted, which Sasha knew was not true. They would be up and bouncy in an instant, ready for another walk if one were to be offered.

Sitting out on the terrace with a piece of toast and a cup of tea, Sasha thought about her day. She needed a few things from the village shop and then she'd walk up to the château to see how Ingrid and Penny were. Ask whether they needed any help with anything.

Putting her mug and plate in the sink to deal with later, she saw the van keys hanging from the hook by the door. Sasha took a deep breath before taking them off the hook, picking up her purse and grabbing her tote from the back of the kitchen door before closing it. She was going to drive to the village, like she'd been promising herself for weeks she was going to do. The main thing was to stop thinking about it and just do it.

Sitting behind the steering wheel, Sasha carefully adjusted the seat and the mirror before ignoring her shaking hand and slipping the key into the ignition and turning the engine on. 'I can always turn back at the main gates,' she told herself.

But she didn't, and a few minutes later she was parking by the church in the village.

Pulling on the handbrake and turning off the engine, Sasha mentally gave herself a high five. She'd get what she needed in the shop and then she'd go to the boulangerie and buy a gooey cake or two to celebrate.

* * *

Both Ingrid and Penny had set their laptops up on the kitchen table after breakfast and spread the paperwork they'd already accumulated for the 'wedding of the year', as Ingrid had christened it, over the rest of the table.

'I sent the quote last night, so hopefully Stella will email her acceptance this morning,' Penny said. 'I also suggested the minimum number of bottles of wine she needs to buy for the after-party – hopefully she'll know how much her friends drink. Did you make a list of what you found on the internet? I've done one for cooking trays, extra bowls and serving things.'

'Mine's mainly crockery, glasses, cutlery, tablecloths, ornaments, fairy lights, candles,' Ingrid said. 'I was thinking about tables and chairs – we haven't any guests that weekend so we could use the dining room furniture, d'you think?'

'Good idea,' Penny agreed. 'If they're not too big and heavy.' She glanced at her laptop as an email pinged in. 'Stella is happy with the quote and the small changes to the menu I suggested. Phew. Right. We've got two weeks now to sort everything. It's going to be tight, but we'll do it. I think we'll order the bread rolls and baguettes from the boulangerie. I can make them, but even with two domestic ovens and everything else that needs to be cooked, making enough could prove difficult. We'll get the cheese from the village shop too. Spread the business locally. Could do with someone trustworthy to delegate a few things to.'

'Why not take Sasha up on her offer to help?' Ingrid said.

'I'm here, ready and able,' Sasha called as she walked into the kitchen. 'So long as you don't want me to cook – although I don't mind preparing veg or washing up.' She placed the box of cakes on the kitchen table. 'But first, have a celebratory cake,' and she opened the box with its strawberry and cream tartlets. 'I drove to the village this morning,' she said, a big smile on her face. 'So no more excuses about driving, although I'm not sure about driving to Carhaix yet.'

Penny got up and put some plates on the table. 'Well done. I'll make some coffee.'

As they drank coffee and ate the tarts, Penny told Sasha what she needed help with. 'Menus to go on tables – need about thirty-five, one for each place setting and a couple of spares, but what I'd ideally like is for there to be a faint outline of the château visible with the menu overwritten, and on fairly stiff paper or thin cardboard.'

'I can do that. Next,' Sasha said.

'The orangery needs to be made as romantic-looking as possible on a small budget.'

'I'll need to see the orangery,' Sasha said. 'To get an idea of size and what plants are in there.'

'No time like the present,' Penny said, jumping up. 'Come on, it's this way. Won't be long, Mum.'

Sasha sighed as she saw the orangery for the first time. 'What a beautiful space. I love those arched windows with the French doors beneath. They need some floaty muslin curtains. We could do with a couple of taller, bushier plants; a big decorative bamboo would look good in the corner against the wall, and another bigger lemon or orange tree.'

'Freddie did warn Dad the orangery would take time to re-establish, but time is something we haven't got before this wedding,' Penny said ruefully.

Sasha walked over to the back wall. 'A fresh coat of white paint would be good. How do you feel about creating an optical illusion? A *trompe l'œil* rather than a simple mural the length of the wall would look wonderful, I think. I could do three *trompe l'œils* here – three windows spaced to face the real ones, tropical birds and flowers maybe... No, I think swallows would be better, and either hydrangeas or camellias, they seem to be everywhere in Brittany. Maybe a horse, too, as they are part of the château's history.' She tried to rein in her mounting excitement at the thought of painting three scenes in such a wonderful space.

'We'll need to find a few second-hand things and shabby-chic them for decoration. Things like mirrors and birdcages with candles. What about overhead lighting? Have you got a spare chandelier or two anywhere? There are two ceiling sockets. They would look brilliant in here at night.' Sasha could feel herself almost babbling with enthusiasm and turned to look at Penny. 'What d'you think?'

'I'll ask Freddie to paint the back wall and then you can have a free hand with your idea of *trompe l'œils*, they sound brilliant. As do all the rest of your ideas. You think you can do all that in a fortnight? – it's a lot.' Penny gave her a worried look.

Sasha nodded confidently. 'Doing three *trompe l'œils* should make it easier than spreading a big one the whole length of the wall.'

'Let's get back and tell Mum it's all systems go on the orangery,' Penny said. 'We will of course pay you.'

'We'll talk about that later – you might not like what I do,' Sasha said. She hated the thought of charging Ingrid anything, but on the other hand she couldn't afford to work for nothing either. Maybe she'd just charge for the materials and add a nominal sum. She'd worry about it when it was all done.

Peter and Alice had joined Ingrid in the kitchen when Penny and Sasha walked back in.

'I'd better get off,' Sasha said. 'Lots to think about and puppies to sort.'

'See you in the village tonight? Eight o'clock? Sasha? Penny?' Alice said.

'I don't suppose I'll get much chance to socialise for the next couple of weeks,' Penny said. 'So yes, I'll see you there.'

'Walk down together?' Sasha said. 'Look forward to it. Bye for now, everyone.'

'Before I forget, we've decided on 14 July for the fete,' Peter said. 'Seems like a good day to have a party.'

25

Back at the cottage, Sasha, excited at the thought of painting such a large commission but anxious at the same time, opened her sketchbook. It was a big project, the biggest she'd ever undertaken, and whilst she was confident she could do it, she knew it would take meticulous attention to detail. She'd have to measure everything out precisely on the wall, to make sure it was in proportion with the front windows of the orangery that she was reflecting in the optical illusion. The middle *trompe l'œil* would be the *pièce de résistance*, unique and special, she decided, whilst the ones on either side would be simpler open views of the château grounds.

Sasha lost herself in sketching out possible *trompe l'œil* scenes and the kitchen table was covered with discarded sheets of paper when Freddie returned at lunchtime.

'Bread and cheese for lunch?' Sasha said, closing the sketchbook and pulling all the loose sheets towards her. 'I've lost all sense of time, sorry. You'll never guess what happened this morning. Ingrid and Penny have asked me to do *trompe l'œils* on the orangery wall in time for this wedding reception they've got booked. I'm so excited, even if I am shaking like a leaf at the thought.'

'Brilliant news,' Freddie said, walking over to the sink and washing his hands.

'I'm also going to be helping on the wedding day itself.' Placing the cheese and baguettes on the table, she glanced at Freddie. 'You okay?'

Freddie nodded. 'Yes. Just tired. Getting the fountains to work has been... let's say... interesting. This afternoon, I'm going to do some twenty-first century plumbing and get your new shower in.'

'I didn't think the day could get any better, but you saying that, it just did,' Sasha said. 'I can't believe we've been here for less than two months. Our old life in England almost seems like a dream that happened to different people.'

* * *

Lucas and Jean-Paul were already in the bar when Penny and Sasha walked down to the village that evening.

'Where's Alice?' Penny asked, looking around.

'She arrive late,' Lucas answered, moving forward to greet them both with cheek kisses.

Jean-Paul, to Sasha's surprise, followed suit and she murmured a quiet '*Bonjour*' as his lips brushed her cheek.

'We have been ask to keep you company until Alice arrive,' Lucas said. 'Now, what you want to drink?'

'A glass of the local Muscadet for me,' Penny said. 'Thanks.'

'Rosé for me please,' Sasha said.

Sasha, catching Penny gazing after Lucas, said, 'Lucas is lovely, isn't he? I get the feeling he likes you too.'

Penny nodded thoughtfully. 'Yes. But I'm not ready for another relationship yet.'

'Doesn't have to be a relationship. You can be friends.'

Penny looked at her. 'How long after your marriage broke up did it take for you to "make friends" with someone new?'

Sasha pulled a face and gave a sigh. 'You've got me there. I haven't yet. Sorry. I know it's not easy, but on the other hand, you've come to France to get over Rory, so you are meeting new people. Me, I stayed put in the rut I'd created for myself. It's only now that I'm actually making new friends. So my advice would be: don't leave it as long as I have.'

'Are you going to get to know Jean-Paul better then?' Penny asked wickedly, glad of the chance to divert the conversation away from herself. She was barely out of a bad relationship, and she had no plans to head back into another one any time soon. That pull of attraction she'd felt when she and Lucas had met in Roscoff and every time since was definitely not being acted upon. She knew nothing about him, and she was going to learn as much as she could about any man before she entered into anything other than a casual friendship. But he was Alice's young brother so he couldn't be anything other than a good person, could he? Maybe she could get to know him as a friend.

A blushing Sasha answering her question brought Penny out of her daydream. 'Jean-Paul seems to be a genuinely kind man and I haven't met many of those recently so, yes, I would like to get to know him better.'

Lucas and Jean-Paul returned at that moment with the drinks and Penny asked, 'How is Eliza today after last evening's emotional events?'

'She talk happily during the breakfast about all the memories the box make come up. And Merlin was a lot in her conversation,' Lucas said. 'Seeing that Merlin he was restored and was in the château mean so much to her because of the association with Grand-papa.'

When Lucas and Penny started discussing something in rapid French, Sasha sat back and tried to think of something she could say to Jean-Paul, who was typing a message on his phone. Sasha smothered a giggle when he flashed her a smile as her phone pinged with a text. She quickly read his message and typed a sentence into the translation app on her phone before holding it out for Jean-Paul to read. 'Isn't technology a wonderful thing?' Sasha typed. 'If you put it on mute for now, we can talk to each other silently like this. Yes?'

'Yes. How are Mimi and Mitzi?'

'Getting bigger. Your training is making a huge difference.'

'I come and show you some more commands one day this week, yes?'

'I'm going to be painting *trompe l'œils* in the orangery for this wedding reception Penny is organising, but yes please.'

Penny's phone pinged with a text and she broke off her conversation with Lucas to read it. She frowned as she read it. 'Alice is sorry but she can't make it after all.' She glanced across at Lucas. 'She is all right, isn't she?'

Lucas nodded. 'Yes. I think she really feel she should stay with Grand-maman this evening. She has a nostalgic mood and Alice think it will be good for her to talk.'

'I can understand that,' Penny said. 'Seeing Merlin again must have opened up the memory floodgates for her.'

* * *

Alice and Eliza were sitting out in the small back garden of Eliza's terraced cottage in the village enjoying a nightcap and watching the bats flitting around in the gathering dusk. Eliza took a sip of her drink and gave a quiet sigh.

'I miss William so much, but I'm glad he never had to leave the Cottage du Lac to live here in the village. Leaving the estate would truly have broken his heart. And he would have hated being hemmed in by all the houses.'

'I thought you were happy living here in the village, in the heart of everything.'

'I am. It was a little lonely living in the château grounds after William died. Here, I see people every day and have most things I need, but it can't help being a different sort of life. And not necessarily one that I ever wanted.'

'Do you miss your old cottage?' Alice asked gently. 'You've got this one lovely and cosy.'

'Yes, I do miss it. We moved in directly after we married in 1960 and for the next sixty years, it was home. There's a lifetime of my memories in that cottage.'

'I love how you and Grand-papa were childhood sweet-hearts,' Alice said.

Eliza laughed quietly. 'We were. Neither of us ever wanted anyone else.' Eliza's eyes misted over. 'I miss him so much. Seeing Merlin in the château brought so many memories back.' She glanced at Alice. 'If you don't hurry up, you'll never get a fifty-year anniversary with anyone.' Eliza gave Alice a serious look. 'I do worry about you, and Lucas too. You've both concentrated on careers rather than sorting out your personal lives. And now look at the pair of you, both of you are jobless and no sign of a "significant other", as you young ones put it, for either of you.'

'My job went because of the fire,' Alice protested. 'And I am still looking for that significant other.'

'Look harder,' Eliza said. 'It's about time the two of you

settled down and had your own families. I can't hang around forever you know, waiting for great-grandchildren.'

Alice reached for her hand and squeezed it. 'I know.'

The two of them sat quietly, both deep in their own thoughts for a minute or two before Alice spoke.

'Have you heard from Mum recently?'

Eliza nodded. 'Since I moved here, she's rung every Sunday evening to check that I'm all right.'

'Any chance of a visit?'

'She's talking of later in the year,' Eliza said. 'Will you and Lucas still be here then?'

Alice shrugged. 'I can't answer for Lucas. I'm helping Peter organise this fete on 14 July, but at some stage I need to find a new job.'

'I am enjoying your company, so you can both stay for as long as you like,' Eliza said. 'And selfishly I hope you do, but you need to work on finding more than just a new job. You need that special person in your life. I'll stop nagging you for now,' Eliza said, smiling. 'But remember, I'm on your case.'

26

The morning of the *vide-grenier*, Sasha and Freddie took the pups for an early walk on their leads. Freddie was giving them their 'sit' and 'stay' commands and they were so good. They certainly responded to their names, but Sasha didn't feel they were ready yet to be let off their leads in the château grounds.

Once back at the cottages, Freddie fed the pups a small breakfast whilst Sasha made the coffee. Freddie was going to paint the orangery wall that afternoon.

'I'm looking forward to starting in there asap,' Sasha said. 'I've done rough sketches for each of the three *trompe l'œils*. I just hope the Chevaliers like it when it's finished. It will be too late to change it before the wedding anyway.'

'Honestly, sis, you know they are going to love what you do. You've never given your art much of a chance before. Now you've got the opportunity to do a Banksy and show everyone how good you are.'

'Hope so,' Sasha said. 'Have to admit I'm excited. I'll get on designing the menus Penny wants while you're painting the wall this afternoon.'

'Come on, let's get to the *vide-grenier* before all the good stuff is sold,' Freddie said. After shutting the pups in the kitchen, Sasha and Freddie left for the village. It was easier to walk there than to take the van and have difficulty parking with so many more people around.

It was barely nine o'clock, but already the village was teeming with stalls and crowds. 'I don't know where to begin,' Sasha said. 'I didn't expect there to be so many stands. Oh, they're down the side streets as well.'

Freddie found a stall selling second-hand gardening equipment and other tools, so Sasha left him to it and strolled slowly along the main street. Getting her studio up and running was still high on her to-do list, but downgraded from number one to two after the orangery.

There were lots of tables full of stuff she wasn't remotely interested in, and she was beginning to feel a little despondent. Most seemed to be full of either baby clothes or toddler's toys, DVDs, kitchen equipment from the dark ages and lots of mocha coffee pots. About to turn and walk up the other side of the road, she saw something that she was definitely interested in. A rusty, round, white wrought-iron table and four chairs that once rubbed down and repainted, would be perfect for the cottage terrace.

Sasha saw the stallholder looking at her and pointing to the table. '*Cinquante euros pour tout*,' he said, including the chairs in a gesture.

'Tell him forty euros,' Lucas whispered in her ear, suddenly appearing at her side.

'*Cinquante* is fifty, isn't it?' Sasha said, turning to look at him. 'I think fifty is a fair price.'

Lucas nodded. 'But forty-five would be better. You have to play the game and bargain,' Lucas said, turning to the man.

'*Quarante euros.*'

'*Quarante-cinq,*' was the man's immediate response.

'*D'accord,*' Lucas said, and held out his hand to shake on the price.

Sasha watched, bemused at what had just happened.

'Now you have five euros for the sandpaper and paint,' Lucas said.

'True,' Sasha said as she handed the money over. 'Can you tell him I'll collect them later this afternoon please?'

Lucas wandered with her up the other side of the main street, where she found a small cupboard that would be perfect for lots of her craft things. Afterwards, she headed down a small side street on her own that was mainly full of people selling clothes, ornaments and crockery. And birdcages. Three rusty round hanging ones that would be perfect in the orangery, sprayed gold and hung with some greenery draped around and LED candles inside, or even a model bird. As she was standing there debating how many to buy, the woman selling came over. Sasha pointed at one and said, '*S'il vous plaît – combien?*'

'Twenty euros.'

'Fifty for the three?'

'Okay. You have a bag? *Non?* I'll put them in a box.'

Wandering through the crowds clutching an awkward box and trying to look on various stands as she walked by was not easy, and Sasha was pleased when she bumped into Lucas again. Especially when he instantly took the box from her.

'Shall I take this into Eliza's cottage for you to collect after? It's over there,' and he pointed to a terraced cottage on the other side of the road.

'Brilliant. Thank you.'

'Alice and Penny are down there,' he said, pointing to another side street with yet more *brocante* for sale.

Sasha wandered on down through the village dodging the crowds, and met up with Alice and Penny by a table full of crockery. Penny was trying to contain her excitement. 'Oh, I wish Mum had been up to coming. She'd have loved all this vintage stuff.'

Alice pointed out some white porcelain plates with a gold rim at the back of the stand. 'Have you seen those?'

Sensing their interest, the female stallholder handed Penny one of the plates. 'I have *trente-six* plates of the dinner size, and the same of smaller size. From a Quimper restaurant,' she shrugged her shoulders. 'It closes.'

Penny pointed at a box of beautiful art deco plates of various sizes. 'I am also interested in that box. How much for the two lots all together?'

The woman named a price that Penny knew was a bargain but hesitated before agreeing. It was still a lot. 'No chips or cracks in any of it?'

'*Non*. Good condition.'

Penny smiled at her. 'Okay. I'll take the two lots please.'

While Penny and Alice waited for the crockery to be boxed up securely, Sasha wandered off to look at a table on the opposite side. Rolls of material, curtains of all sizes, remnants of material in a jumble in a box, and tablecloths. A pile of curtains caught her eye. Cream with a green toile de Jouy design. Opening one out, she saw that it was very faded in patches. The vendor opened another one out and held it up, just managing to keep it from dragging on the ground, to show the length. Again, it was faded in patches. Sasha counted the number of curtains there were – five.

Alice appeared at her side at that moment. 'Penny and Lucas have taken the crockery to Eliza's. Safer than carrying it around. It was a bit heavy too. What's with the curtains?'

'It's not just these curtains. There's a roll of lightweight muslin over there, perfect for the orangery,' Sasha said. 'But there's enough material in these curtains with some careful cutting out of the faded parts to make dozens of really lovely idiosyncratic serviettes – the design is a traditional countryside one with horses and châteaux. And the material is really good quality. I'm not sure I have the time to do them though.'

'Grand-maman has. And she has a sewing machine,' Alice said. 'I remember her making lots of things in the past. She's a bit down at the moment, missing Grand-papa. Making curtains and serviettes for the orangery would be a perfect occupation.'

Penny and Lucas joined them as Sasha was attempting to get a grip on the roll of muslin while Alice took the curtains. 'Look like I am your personal errand boy today,' Lucas said. 'I take those over to Eliza as well, yes?'

'You really are a star, thank you,' Penny said. 'Can you manage the curtains or shall I bring them?'

'Good idea.'

Penny took the curtains from Alice with a smile and followed Lucas.

'I think my little brother likes Penny,' Alice said, smiling as she watched the two of them joking together. 'Do you think she likes him? Or is it too soon after her break-up with Rory?'

'I know she finds him attractive,' Sasha said. 'But I think probably it is a bit soon, although she seems happy and relaxed in his company.'

* * *

The four of them were joined by Freddie and Jean-Paul as they abandoned their hunt for bargains and headed for the catering van selling coffee, crêpes and galettes.

'I can't believe it's only eleven o'clock and we've found so much stuff. It's been brilliant,' Sasha said, looking at her watch. 'Not quite sure how we are going to get everything back to the cottage, though. Some of the furniture won't go in the van, that's for sure. Does anybody know somebody who can deliver?'

Lucas pointed at Jean-Paul. 'He already offer. Late this afternoon when it quiet down, he come back with a tractor and trailer and pick up everything. Just have to tell him which stalls. I come with him too.'

Sasha gave Jean-Paul a relieved smile. '*Merci beaucoup.*'

'I've bought a small settee and a fireside chair and a strimmer,' Freddie said. 'Please can you pick them up as well? I'm working this afternoon, but I'll be at the cottage to help unload and get it all indoors.'

Lucas gave Jean-Paul a rapid translation and he nodded.

'Thanks,' Freddie said, finishing his coffee. 'Sasha, have you got five minutes before I head off? There's something I'd like your opin— I'd like to show you.'

'Sure.' Sasha stood up. 'I'll catch up with everyone in a bit.'

Sasha followed Freddie down the main street, wondering what he wanted her to see. He stopped at a stand selling a mixture of home-made sweets and jams, children's toys and books, and a few clothes on a rail. There was a little girl sitting on a chair colouring a picture in a book, and a young woman standing behind the stall. The small girl's face lit up with a smile when she saw Freddie. 'Hi, Mister Freddie.'

'Sasha, this is Maddie and her daughter Jade.'

'*Bonjour.* Nice to meet you, Maddie, and you, Jade,' Sasha said, smiling down at the little girl who must have been about five or six.

'Hello. Freddie's told me all about how you and he came to live in France,' Maddie said.

'You're English,' Sasha said, surprised, wishing Freddie had told her about Maddie and Jade before introducing them.

Maddie nodded. 'Been over here seven years now.'

'Do you live in the village?'

'My mother lives in one of the newer houses on the edge of the village. We live in the next one over. How do you like living here?'

'We both love it, don't we?' Sasha said enthusiastically, turning to her brother.

'Best thing we could have done,' Freddie answered. He glanced at his watch. 'Sorry this is such a short meeting, but I've got to get back to paint the orangery this afternoon.'

'And I've got a couple of puppies at home to sort out,' Sasha explained.

'Freddie said I could come and see the puppies one day,' Jade said, looking up hopefully.

'If Freddie said that, then I'm sure he'll arrange it,' Sasha replied.

'Not today?' Jade pulled a miserable face.

'We will make a definite date soon,' Freddie promised.

'Okay,' Jade nodded happily.

'Maddie, I'll give you a ring and arrange it, okay?'

'Bye then, Maddie, Jade. I hope to see you both again soon,' Sasha said as she and Freddie turned to leave. She gave her brother a questioning look. 'Maddie seems nice. Any particular reason you wanted me to meet her?'

'No. I had no idea she was going to be here today. I've wanted you to meet Maddie for a few weeks now, so I grabbed the opportunity to introduce the two of you.'

'And now I have?'

'I thought maybe we could invite her and Jade for tea or

something?' Freddie ran his hand through his in-need-of-a-haircut hair. 'Anyway, can we talk later? I've got some painting to do.'

27

It was early evening when Jean-Paul arrived at the Cottages du Lac, the large trailer behind his tractor piled high with everything Sasha and Freddie had bought. Freddie, hearing the noise, came running down from the château as Lucas drove in with the things from Eliza's cottage in his car. Quickly, Sasha put Mimi and Mitzi in the garden out of the way and the three men began unloading the trailer.

The wrought-iron table and four chairs were placed straight on the terrace. The small cupboard and the worktable were carried upstairs to the workroom. Freddie's settee and matching armchair were quickly placed in his sitting room. Sasha's final purchase, a large office desk with eight drawers which she'd spotted as she was leaving the *vide-grenier*, was the last thing to be unloaded.

Lucas took the box of birdcages out of the car and said he'd take the crockery and everything else up to the château. Freddie jumped into the empty passenger seat and went with him to carry on painting the orangery.

Sasha and Jean-Paul, left alone, looked at each other. '*Café?*'

Sasha asked, picking up her phone from the kitchen table and opening the translation app, ready to use it.

'*Merci*,' Jean-Paul said, pulling his own phone out of a pocket. They both left the volume turned on this time. It wasn't perfect, but at least they were communicating.

Sitting out in the garden with their coffee and Mimi and Mitzi at their feet begging for attention, Sasha felt a flash of boldness. 'Would you like to come to supper one evening *après* the wedding. A thank you for all your help – today and with the terrible two,' she said, laughing at the pups chasing their tails.

'Thank you. I would like that,' Jean-Paul said hesitantly in English, without first translating it from the French.

'Brilliant. You said that perfectly,' Sasha said.

'We do some more puppy training soon. They know "sit" and "stay" now. We need to make sure they come when you call and to heel.'

'That would be good,' Sasha nodded.

'I leave now because—' and this time he typed something into the translator before reading it out, '—I have to check the sheep and feed them. *À bientôt*.' And with a gentle cheek kiss, he left.

Disappointed that he hadn't stayed for longer, Sasha covered the wrought-iron table with cardboard and newspaper and wire-brushed each of the three birdcages. She'd seen some tins of spray paint in the DIY section of the village shop. She'd pick up some cans tomorrow when she went for the breakfast croissants.

Looking at the table and chairs on the terrace, Sasha began to dream of the day when she'd invite friends to supper and they'd sit there, good food on the table and a glass of wine in hand, watching the sunset.

The slam of a door told her Freddie was back and Sasha's

thoughts switched to him and Maddie. It was so long since Freddie had had a serious girlfriend. Had he finally met someone whom he wanted to be with?

As she prepared a supper of ham salad with jacket potatoes, Sasha broached the subject. 'Maddie seems nice. Where did the two of you meet?'

'Her parents are one of my gardening clients in the village. She was there one afternoon and her mum introduced us. We clicked straight away.' Freddie opened the fridge. 'I fancy a beer with supper. Do you want a glass of wine?'

'No thanks, I'll have a glass of water. Is Jade's dad not around?'

'No, never has been apparently. Didn't want the responsibility. His loss. Jade's a great kid.'

Sasha gave Freddie a worried look. 'You don't think you're getting involved too soon with them both? Particularly Jade. Children can be hurt and upset when things don't work out.'

'Don't worry, I'm taking it slowly. Honestly, I'm so busy and Maddie is too, we don't have the time to see each other more than occasionally, but Maddie knows I like her.'

'Taking things slowly is good,' Sasha said.

'Is that what you're doing with Jean-Paul?' Freddie asked, grinning at her.

'We're just friends getting to know each other,' Sasha said. 'And he's helping me train the pups.' She moved across to the fridge and opened the door. 'Local strawberries and cream for dessert?'

'Sounds good,' Freddie said before taking a swig of his beer. 'Maybe moving to France is going to be even better than we hoped for both of us.'

* * *

Penny was on her own in the château kitchen when Lucas knocked on the door. 'I bring the crockery and the box of vintage stuff. Alice say leave the muslin and the curtains at Grand-maman, so I hope that was right.'

'Yes, Eliza has agreed to make the curtains and serviettes for us, which is so lovely. You don't think it's too much work for her, do you?'

'No, I think she'll love helping you and the château. I fetch the crockery first from the car.'

'I can carry the box of vintage plates. I'm longing to see Mum's face when I show her what I found.'

'Ingrid and Peter not here?'

'Dad's taken Mum to visit some friends down on the coast somewhere. They did tell me where, but I'm not sure I can remember the name well enough to pronounce it.'

Once both the boxes were safely on the kitchen table, Penny started to take the art deco plates out.

'These are beautiful, Mum is going to be so thrilled. I think there's enough to mix and match for the wedding. Big problem now is to find some lovely glasses.' She looked up at Lucas. 'Would you like a coffee or a beer? Sorry, I should have offered before.'

'No thanks, but I would like you to have dinner with me one evening,' Lucas said quietly.

Penny's hands, lifting some more plates out of the box, stilled. She glanced up at him. 'That sounds lovely, but I'm going to have to say no. I'm not going to have a lot of free time until after this wedding.'

'How about after?'

'Maybe afterwards if you want to ask me again.'

'I do want to ask you again. I am going to keep asking you

until you say yes,' Lucas said, looking at her, a mischievous glint in his eyes.

Penny smiled and carried on unpacking the last of the vintage plates.

28

The next few days flew by for everyone, as wedding preparations took precedence over everything else.

Sasha took all her equipment up to the orangery. The wall had dried well and she measured out the size of the three panels she had planned for each of the *trompe l'œils*, lightly pencilling in key features before starting to paint the first one.

Over the next day or two, Sasha slipped into a new routine. She took Mitzi and Mimi on her early morning walk to the village for breakfast croissants. She'd discovered there was a hitch ring in the wall by the boulangerie, and the two pups soon learnt to sit and stay quiet while she collected her baguette and croissants. Walking home down the *route de galop* with its dead end, she let the two of them off their leads and they had a chase and a play back and forth down the lane and by the time they were at the cottage, they were happy to flop on their bed and enjoy a chew.

Sasha was up at the orangery by nine o'clock and lost herself in her painting for the next hour or two. Penny had arrived just before noon the first day she was there, with a small stepladder and a tape measure.

'I need to let Eliza know the measurements for the muslin curtains. She's nearly finished making the serviettes. Oh, I like those,' she'd said, spotting the birdcages.

'Yes, I meant to ask you – can you add a reasonable-sized trailing ivy plant, an owl or some other bird, and a large church candle to your shopping list?'

'Mum and I are going to Carrefour in Brest tomorrow for a big shop, so I'll do my best. If not, a local Point Vert store should have something suitable. Must remember to get some fairy lights too.'

'How are Ingrid's ankle and wrist?'

'Her ankle swelling has gone down, bruising is not quite so colourful, and she's trying to use her crutches less. Her wrist, I'm not so sure about. She's started to strap it up, which means it's hurting.'

'That's not good,' Sasha had said.

'No,' Penny had agreed with a sigh. 'Right, I'm off to take these measurements to Eliza. The electrician might call by sometime to look at the ceiling light sockets. I found a couple of lovely chandeliers on eBay that look to be the perfect size for in here. Fingers crossed they arrive in time for the wedding.'

The days passed in a blur for Sasha, she was so busy. After working in the orangery for several hours and walking Mimi and Mitzi twice a day, she spent the evenings trying to sort out things at the cottage. Freddie was busy working all hours too and they didn't see much of each other. He'd recently bought an oven and a microwave and was now more independent for food. Occasionally, Sasha heard him standing in the garden talking on his phone. As far as she knew, Maddie hadn't been to the cottage.

With the weather seemingly settled into full-time summer mode with blue skies and sunshine, Sasha was determined to have the terrace looking good for all the al fresco lunches and suppers she was planning to have. Every evening after a short puppy walk and a quick supper, she was out in the garden wire-brushing the wrought-iron table and chairs before finally painting them white. As she painted, Sasha couldn't stop her thoughts drifting to Jean-Paul. Life was definitely conspiring to make sure she did take things slowly with this new friendship, which was maybe for the best, but so frustrating. Once the wedding was over though, not only would dog training begin again, but she had their supper date to look forward to.

With just a week left before the wedding, Sasha finished the two end *trompe l'œils* and was hoping Penny would pop in and see them and tell her they were acceptable. She hadn't seen Penny for a couple of days and guessed she was probably even busier than she was. Sasha stepped back and regarded the paintings critically. Framed like an open window, both were countryside scenes with trees and a cottage in the distance, a graceful willow tree by a lake and a hydrangea bush in full flower.

'Wow, they look amazing,' Penny said, coming in through the open French doors and appearing unexpectedly at her side.

'You sure? I can always paint over them if you don't think they're very good.'

'Sasha, they are great. I take it the third one is going to be different?'

Sasha nodded. 'Yes. If you look closely, you'll be able to make out the very light sketch of the key points.'

Penny stepped up close to the wall. 'Oh, that is going to make so many people happy,' she said. 'I can't wait to see it finished. We'll have to have a glass of champagne to celebrate the orangery when it's completed.'

'I'm hoping to finish it at least a day or two before the wedding,' Sasha said. 'This third painting is going to be a little more difficult to get right than the other two, so fingers crossed it all goes to plan.'

'I'm sure it will,' Penny said. 'I've brought the serviettes and the first three muslin curtains,' and she indicated the things she was carrying. 'Dad is coming over later to hang them. And the electrician has promised to show up within the next two days, which is cutting it a bit fine, I think.' She shrugged. 'I guess we were lucky to find an electrician at such short notice.'

'If he lets you down, I'm sure Freddie could connect the chandeliers. He's promised to put three hooks up for the birdcages.'

'That will be plan B then,' Penny said, smiling. 'Right, better get back to the château. Stella is bringing the drinks this morning. See you later.'

Once Penny had left, Sasha began on the third painting and was soon lost in a world of her own.

* * *

Back in the château, as Penny chatted to Ingrid and checked through her to-do lists, they both heard a van pull up on the driveway. As Penny went out to see who it was, the driver jumped out and opened the back.

'Stella asked me to drop this lot off,' he said. 'Any chance of a hand unloading?'

Penny looked at the bottles of red and white wine, spirits, several cases of mixer drinks and beer, and wondered if Stella had misread the amounts she'd suggested. Penny quickly messaged Peter, whom she knew was working with Freddie somewhere on the estate.

> Could do with some manpower to unload Stella's drinks!

The reply came back instantly.

> On our way!

As Peter and Freddie started to help the driver, Penny's phone rang.

'The drinks come this morning,' Stella said. 'Could you tell me if I order enough? I have time to order more.'

'They arrived just now. Think you've got more than enough,' Penny said. 'In fact, I think you've probably gone over the top and I sincerely hope you've got it on sale or return.'

'It will keep. We plan to move house soon, so we save it for the house-warming. Everything is ready at the château and the orangery?'

'Everything is under control, but I'm glad you rang. I wanted to check that none of your guests are vegetarian or vegan, because the menu you've chosen caters for neither. And do any of them have allergies? Do you want me to have some meatless and plant-based dishes in reserve?'

Stella gave a burst of laughter. '*Non*. All my guests are French. Not many French people understand the concept of "do not eat meat". They cannot imagine why people would do that.'

'So long as you're sure,' Penny said, mentally deciding to buy some tofu and chickpeas just in case, and to use recipes without nuts for the desserts she intended to make.

* * *

Sasha put her paintbrush down with a thankful sigh. The middle *trompe l'œil* was finished and there were still almost two days to go before the wedding. Stepping back, she regarded her artwork critically before taking a photo of the completed *trompe l'œil* wall for her website. And then she took a separate photo of the middle one. She was thrilled with the way the whole thing had turned out, but the middle *trompe l'œil* looked to be as special as she had hoped.

A quick glance at her watch told her she had time to get home, grab the dogs and walk into the village, and buy a bottle of crémant and a large frozen pizza for supper before the shop closed. She quickly sent Penny a message.

> Fancy pizza and wine this evening at the cottage? I'm celebrating. About eight o'clock? If you're too busy I understand.

The reply came back almost instantly.

> Might be a bit late but yes. See you then.

Once back from the village with the wine in the fridge and the large pizza ready to go in the oven, a green salad quickly made, Sasha played with Mimi and Mitzi before jumping under her new power shower and revelling once again in the force of the water.

Freddie appeared in his garden as Sasha was tidying up the terrace and putting some cushions on two of the chairs. 'Penny's coming round later. Are you home for the evening?'

'No, I'm off to see Maddie and Jade. I can't believe that I've finally met someone who's becoming more special to me every time I see her.'

'Jade still keen to come and see the pups?'

Freddie nodded. 'Yes.'

'How about one day next week? After-school tea?'

'Thanks, sis. I'll ask Maddie which day would be best.' Freddie flashed her a smile, went to say something and changed his mind.

'What?' Sasha said.

'We need to have a talk – nothing's wrong. Just that I need some sisterly advice.'

'Okay. Whenever you're ready.'

Sasha switched the oven on, ready to pop the pizza in, before putting plates, serviettes and glasses out on the table.

Penny appeared shortly after eight o'clock and the two of them enjoyed a glass of crémant sitting out on the terrace with the puppies playing around their feet, as they waited for the pizza to cook.

'You've done a brilliant job with the *trompe l'œils*,' Penny said. 'The wall looks beautiful. Mum and Dad are so thrilled with it – especially the middle one with Merlin looking out over his stable door towards the château.'

'I loved doing it. I was actually thinking of doing something on *this* wall,' Sasha said, pointing to the cottage. 'But we'll see. How is Ingrid? She seems to have stopped using her crutch these days, but I notice she's very careful.'

'She's still determined to work in the kitchen the evening of the wedding. Not sure how that's going to work out,' Penny said. 'It's going to be a bit of a madhouse getting the courses out quickly. So I've roped Jean-Paul in to help out in case Mum falls by the wayside – not literally of course, but you know what I mean. You are still happy to do waitressing duties with Alice and Lucas?' Penny looked relieved when Sasha nodded. 'If you and Alice take two tables each and Lucas does the head table, it shouldn't be too much to cope with. Dad is going to be in charge of the drinks.'

'What do you want Alice and me to wear? Don't think I've got anything formal.'

'A pretty summer dress will be fine. Stella insists she wants everything as informal as possible.'

'I can manage that,' Sasha said as the timer in the kitchen pinged. 'I'll fetch the pizza.'

As the two of them ate their slices of pizza and salads, Penny glanced at Sasha.

'Lucas asked me to have dinner with him.'

'I hope you said yes. Lucas is lovely,' Sasha said.

'I'm not sure I'm ready for another relationship yet,' Penny said quietly. 'I said no, but I did say he should ask me again after Stella's wedding.'

'Good. Go for dinner and tell him you'd like to be friends for a bit. That you're just out of a painful break-up and want to take things slowly,' Sasha said. 'I'm sure Lucas will understand.'

'Once this wedding is over, I'll definitely say yes,' Penny said. 'Did I hear Freddie has met someone?'

'Yes, Maddie lives in the next village and has a young daughter. He wants to bring them here for me to meet them properly. They're coming one day next week. I just wish I didn't have this funny feeling that it's all going to end in tears.'

Penny looked at her. 'Why would it?'

'My brother hasn't had much luck with women and I think he does really like Maddie. He said earlier that we needed to talk, he wants some sisterly advice. Which is worrying. But sorting his love life out is going to have to wait,' and Sasha and Penny looked at each other as they chorused together, 'until after the wedding,' before they both burst out laughing.

Just before ten o'clock, Penny stood up and pulled an envelope out of her jeans. 'I'd better get back. But I almost forgot to give you this. Mum said to say a big thank you for the *trompe l'œils*. They are truly special. She'll thank you in person the next time she sees you, but she wanted you to have this straight away.'

'I loved doing them,' Sasha said, taking the envelope and slipping it into her own jean pocket. 'Thank your mum for me.'

After Penny had left, Sasha cleared the table and had a quick tidy-up of the kitchen before taking the envelope out of her pocket and opening it. It was full of hundred-euro notes. Twenty of them. Sasha stared at them in disbelief. Had Ingrid really intended to pay her two thousand euros for her paintings? The note that was with the money confirmed it wasn't a mistake.

We can't thank you enough for your amazing trompe l'œils that have completely transformed the orangery. We hope that the enclosed 2K is enough to cover paint costs and also your time. L. Ingrid and Peter.

30

The day of the wedding began bright and sunny and Penny was up with the dawn chorus. Even though the wedding reception wasn't until late afternoon, she knew the day was likely to pass all too quickly.

Peter and Freddie had carried the five tables and thirty chairs through to the orangery the day before and placed them in a small horseshoe shape fanning out from the bride's table. A small round one had been placed in the middle of the space, ready for the wedding cake. An additional one had been placed in the corner for Peter to use as a bar. Currently, all the table-cloths and place settings were on it. Once the tables were set, Peter would transfer the champagne and white wine from the large fridge in the utility room to the smaller drinks fridge hidden under the bar.

The previous day, Penny had spent most of her time in the kitchen. The meat for the requested main course, boeuf bour-guignon, was cubed and marinating in red wine. Her first job this morning was to fry it off in butter before dividing it between two casserole dishes and slowly adding all the other ingredients, as per her favourite Julia Child's recipe. By nine o'clock, the two large casseroles would have been placed in the oven to cook the bourguignon slowly all day. The five dishes of dauphinoise potatoes to accompany the beef were prepared and ready to go in the oven.

Over thirty individual smoked salmon terrines for the first course were in the fridge, ready to be placed on a bed of cucumber and served with a light dill sauce, and the cheeses were in the old pantry in the utility room. The three desserts Stella had wanted were all ready: a creamy tiramisu, chocolate mousses and a lemon tart. Josette was bringing up a selection of freshly baked bread rolls this afternoon, along with some special petits fours to go with coffee.

Sasha and Ingrid were going to set the tables that morning and make sure everything was in place and looking as good as possible. The plants, a mixture of large and medium size, were all in good health; the two Grecian girl garden statues that Ingrid had found in the old out-of-town *pépinière* that was closing down, and which she had quickly snapped up, looked perfectly at home in amongst all the greenery. The chandeliers had arrived and been fitted, and the three hanging birdcages added an amusing touch. Both Penny and Sasha took photographs of the orangery set up for its first ever wedding reception.

Sasha, who'd offered to come and prep the green beans that were to accompany the boeuf bourguignon, arrived at eleven o'clock. There was no time for more than a quick 'Thank you so much for the money' to Ingrid, before she was caught up in the preparations.

When the wedding cake arrived, Penny took the baker into the orangery and showed her where to place it. The cake maker's exclamation as she walked in – 'What a wonderful venue for a wedding reception!' – made Penny's day. And when the woman insisted on giving her a business card and asked her to remember them for any future weddings, she smiled happily.

Everything was organised by five thirty – all they needed now was the newly married couple and their guests.

It was six o'clock when they all heard a loud cacophony of car horns approaching the château.

'Okay, everyone – action stations,' Penny said.

Three hours later, the food had been eaten, copious bottles of champagne and wine consumed, the cake had been cut and the speeches had everyone within earshot creasing up with laughter.

The only minor crisis occurred when Penny, plating up the main course, realised she'd forgotten about gravy boats. Although the bourguignon was going out with a normal amount of the rich red wine sauce, she always liked to send extra out for people who wanted to add more. 'We need five gravy boats.'

'Use the white china milk jugs,' Ingrid had said, moving across to the cupboard where they were stored. 'Don't point it out,' she instructed, 'and nobody will notice or care, the food is that good!' And so it proved.

Now the guests were ready to party...

* * *

In the kitchen, the pace had slowed down as everyone relaxed after a job well done and the clearing up was in full swing. Jean-Paul was reloading the dishwasher as Sasha carefully started to wash the vintage plates by hand. Within minutes, Jean-Paul joined her to wipe the plates and they worked in companionable silence. Alice and Lucas were back and forth from the orangery, helping Peter serve drinks as well as clearing tables of used crockery. As Ingrid, whose ankle was clearly aching if not actually hurting, sat down for the first time that evening, Penny threw an anxious glance in her direction.

'I'm fine,' Ingrid said in answer to the unspoken question. Peter, choosing that moment to appear, looked at her and she waved his look away too. 'What have you got there?'

'A bottle of champagne for you all to share as a thank you from Stella and Bastian for a wonderful evening and delicious food. You'll have to pour it yourself though, I have to get back to the bar. Lucas and Alice have theirs in the orangery.'

Minutes later, the four of them were raising their glasses in a toast to the happy couple and enjoying some leftover canapés.

Afterwards, Sasha and Jean-Paul packed the vintage plates away. As Sasha closed the cupboard door, she looked at Jean-Paul. 'Supper, *demain soir? Huit heures*?'

Jean-Paul smiled and nodded. '*Merci*. I see you at eight o'clock.'

Overhearing Jean-Paul speaking English, Penny gave Sasha a discreet thumbs up. They'd only met recently, but she liked Sasha a lot and had a feeling that they would easily become best friends the more time she, Penny, spent in France.

The low background sound of guitar music could be heard drifting out of the orangery. Lucas, bringing some dirty glasses through, said, 'I leave the door a bit open so you hear the next song, maybe have a look. Stella and Bastian are going to sing a duet, not have a first dance. Apparently, they are both professional cabaret singers – that how they meet.'

Hearing the first chords of 'Je t'aime... moi non plus', the song made famous by Serge Gainsbourg and Jane Birkin, they all moved closer to the door and slowly opened it fully to watch. Stella and Bastian were standing close together, gazing lovingly at each other, Bastian's eyes never leaving Stella's face as he strummed on his guitar. As they started to sing, everyone fell silent and, enraptured, watched as two people sang as if they were the only people there, leaving everyone who witnessed the performance in no doubt about how much in love with each other they were.

'Wow,' Penny murmured as they moved back and closed the connecting door. 'That was something else.'

Lucas moved to her side. 'A once-in-a-life sort of love, I think.'

'The kind of love everyone hopes for,' Penny said.

'You said to ask you out after the wedding,' Lucas said quietly. 'Have lunch with me one day soon?'

Penny turned to look at him. 'Thank you. That would be lovely.'

31

The next morning, after her usual dog walk to the boulangerie for breakfast croissants and baguettes, Sasha decided she'd spend the day quietly at the cottage and take Mimi and Mitzi for a walk at noon rather than wait until evening, then they could play in the garden. Alice had asked her if she could design and print out a dozen or so posters for the 14 July fete, so she'd spend time working on that. Then, this evening, Jean-Paul was coming for supper. Last night as she'd left the château kitchen, Penny had pressed a couple of plastic containers into her hands. 'For you and Jean-Paul to enjoy' – so supper was sorted. It felt a bit like cheating, but Sasha consoled herself with the thought that wedding leftovers were a definite step up from anything she could produce.

By midday she'd finished a simple design for the poster and emailed a photo of it to Alice. Clipping the puppies onto their leads, she started to walk down to the stables. There was no sign of Colette, so she made Mimi and Mitzi sit and stay while she stroked Starlight and fed her a carrot before giving both the dogs a small treat for being good.

Sasha strolled out through the main gates and turned right to walk the three hundred metres along the road to reach the back lane. Once she was several metres down the *route du galop* she let both Mimi and Mitzi off their leads and they raced backwards and forwards. Sasha smiled as she watched Mitzi stop and sniff a cabbage white butterfly resting on a blackberry bush leaf before gracefully flying away.

Sasha spent some of the afternoon pottering in the garden. It was a little breezy, but still warm in the sun. She loved how the two gardens were responding to her and Freddie's hard work although, to be fair, it was mostly down to Freddie's gardening experience and knowledge. She'd done little more than pull a few weeds, like she was doing now.

Making herself a cup of tea, she sat down on the terrace and opened the French lesson book she'd ignored for weeks. In truth, it was easier to use the app on her phone when she needed to say something, but she'd try to memorise a few phrases for tonight.

She peeled some potatoes, ready to boil later for mash to accompany the generous portions of boeuf bourguignon that Penny had given her, and she prepared the fresh green beans, ready to steam. She'd remembered to take both the brie and the camembert out of the fridge, and there was a bowl of green salad with olives to go with that course. Dessert – tiramisu – was again courtesy of Penny, and there were two petits fours each to go with coffee.

After her shower, Sasha set the terrace table and smiled to herself as she opened a bottle of red wine to breathe – that was something she'd learnt to do since moving to France.

The boeuf bourguignon was heating through gently in the oven and Sasha had just finished mashing the potatoes when she heard a car arriving. Quickly, she covered the potatoes to keep them warm, put the beans on to steam, and went out to greet Jean-Paul. Climbing out of his classic 2CV car, he greeted her with two cheek kisses and handed her a box of artisan chocolates.

'*Merci beaucoup*,' Sasha said. 'I love your car. It's such a French icon.' She realised Jean-Paul was looking at her and shaking his head, puzzled. '*J'adore votre voiture*,' she said slowly and carefully, remembering the word for car.

'*Ah, merci.* It belonged to my papa,' Jean-Paul said. 'I restore it.'

They were seated out on the terrace sipping a glass of wine and waiting for the beans to finish cooking when Jean-Paul smiled at her.

'I see the *trompe l'œils* you paint. *Tu as vraiment du talent.*'

'*Merci.* I loved painting them. Excuse me, I'll fetch supper.'

'I help you,' Jean-Paul said, instantly on his feet.

Between them, they took the food out to the table and settled down together to enjoy the meal.

'Freddie, he is not home tonight?' Jean-Paul asked.

'*Non.* I think he is seeing Maddie, his girlfriend. Do you know Maddie? Or her parents? They live in the village.'

There was a pause. 'Yes. I know Maddie; she has a little girl, Jade.'

Sasha noticed the pause and waited for him to say more, but he smiled at her and carried on eating. When he didn't add to the sentence, she decided the pause had been more of a hesitation because he'd spoken the sentence in English. They'd both placed their telephones on the table and Sasha picked hers up. She'd say something in French, Jean-Paul was trying so hard to speak English. She typed the sentence in and then struggled to pronounce one of the French words, so she held her phone out to Jean-Paul.

'*Avez-vous jamais eu envie de vivre ailleurs qu'en Bretagne?*'

'Live somewhere else? *Non.* I am happy here with the life I have on the farm. My parents couldn't wait to retirement and move to Bordeaux. *Peut-être* I feel the same when I am old,' and Jean-Paul laughed.

Sitting there enjoying Jean-Paul's company with both of them getting to know each other, Sasha realised how much she already liked him. Perhaps this was a friendship that could grow to be so much more.

It was late when Jean-Paul looked at his watch. 'I have to go. I have some late lambs expected and I need to check all is good.'

Sasha walked out to the car with him.

Jean-Paul turned to her. '*Merci.* I have a lovely evening with you. Next time I treat you.' Standing there, he gave her a gentle kiss before murmuring, '*Bonne nuit. À bientôt.*'

Sasha's heart skipped a beat. 'See you soon,' she said quietly, smiling at him as he got into his car.

About to close the door, he stopped and gave Sasha a serious look. 'I am sorry, *mais* I have to say something. I tell you this because I like you and your brother. Maddie is not good for Freddie. Please tell him be careful and not too quick to become involve. "*Il ne serait pas le premier et je doute qu'il soit le dernier.*"' And he closed the car door and drove away.

Thoughtfully, Sasha turned to go back into the cottage. Her French wasn't good enough for her to understand the last sentence he'd muttered, but she'd picked out a couple of the words – '*pas le premier*', which she translated as 'not the first', and then the final phrase '*qu'il soit le dernier*,' which she was fairly certain meant he wouldn't be the last either.

She poured the rest of the wine into her glass. What the hell did she do now?

32

Now that she was no longer up at the orangery every day and her time was once again her own, Sasha slipped back into a quieter routine but one which was no less busy, and the days began to speed by. Walking, playing and training Mimi and Mitzi took up a lot of her time, but she was determined to get on top of decorating the cottage, getting her workshop up and running properly, as well as the terrace and the garden. Sitting out on the terrace with Jean-Paul the other evening had been lovely. This summer, she planned on lots more al fresco occasions. First, though, she'd finish organising her workroom.

The small cupboard took the contents of several boxes of her craft things and paint supplies. Sasha set up her laptop and printer on the desk before emptying the two boxes of stationery into the eight drawers of the desk. She spent the rest of the day uploading the pictures of the *trompe l'œil* and updating her website and Etsy pages.

And all the time running through her mind was the problem of what to do about Freddie. If, in fact, she could or should do anything.

In the end, the decision was taken out of her hands.

Freddie brought Maddie and Jade for tea one afternoon. Jade stayed happily playing with Mimi and Mitzi in Sasha's garden while Freddie showed Maddie over his cottage.

'Mummy says when we get back to England I can have a puppy,' Jade said, gently stroking Mimi. 'But we aren't going back until August and I really, really, want one now.'

'You're going back to live in England?' Sasha said, startled.

Jade nodded. 'Granny and Grandad are going back to their old house and Mummy and me are going to live with them. It's all bloody Brexit's fault,' Jade said solemnly.

'I don't think you should swear like that,' Sasha said.

'Grandad says it all the time.'

'Maybe, but little girls shouldn't.'

'I don't think Grandad wants to leave France, but Granny says they have to.'

As much as she wanted to ask Jade more questions, Sasha didn't feel she could quiz the little girl about her family or her mummy. It was none of her business where they lived, but she had a horrible feeling that Freddie was going to end up being hurt.

'Shall we go and see if we can spot any dragonflies by the lake?' Sasha said. 'I'll have to put Mimi and Mitzi on their leads though, otherwise they'll be jumping in the water.'

Peter and Freddie had recently spent some time clearing the weeds away from the edge of the lake. Tall yellow irises were clustered in places and the huge plate-like pads of the pale pink water lily flowers were covering a large area of the surface. The nearby white buddleia bush was alive with butterflies and the long branches of the graceful willow dipped its fingers in the water.

Sasha couldn't see any dragonflies hovering over the water

lilies, but there was a 'plop' in the water and Jade looked at her, excited. 'Is that fish?'

'Might be,' Sasha said. 'Or possibly a frog.'

They both watched the water for a moment and were rewarded with a quick glimpse of several fish swimming slowly around. And then finally a dragonfly landed on one of the water lily pads, its wings fragile and translucent in the sun as Jade watched it, fascinated.

Freddie and Maddie joined them then, with Maddie telling Jade it was time to say thank you and go home.

'Thank you for tea,' Jade said dutifully. 'I love the puppies. Can I come again and play with them?'

'Of course you can. Thank you for coming,' Sasha said, wondering what the quick look she saw pass between Freddie and Maddie meant.

As Freddie turned to follow them to the car, he said quietly, 'Talk when I get back, okay?'

Sasha nodded, then sat out in the garden waiting for Freddie to return. She had a horrible feeling that what he wanted to talk about was not going to be good news.

A quarter of an hour later when he came back, she made them both a coffee.

'Jade told me that as a family they are returning to the UK soon,' she said as she handed him his mug.

Freddie nodded. 'Yep. Maddie's parents have decided to leave France and Maddie doesn't want to stay here without family support.' He took a sip of his coffee. 'She's been on at me about it every time we see each other.' Freddie took a deep breath. 'Maddie wants me to sell up and go back too so we can have a proper future together.' He shook his head and gave a long sigh. 'I don't know what to do. I like her a lot, but we don't know each other that well – we only met a couple of months ago – and now she's leaving, she's pushing me to do something I'm not sure I want to do. The thing is, I've only just arrived in France and so far, I'm loving it here. Things are working out great. Who knows, I might want to go back one day, but right now I don't.'

'Could you both settle for seeing each other every week or so? Either here or in the UK? I know long-distance relationships are difficult, but sometimes they work out.'

'I was hoping she'd stay and move in with me,' Freddie said quietly. 'Join her parents later if it didn't work out.'

'Is that why you were showing her the cottage?'

Freddie nodded. 'Turns out old cottages needing renovation on a private estate aren't her thing. So that's a no-no. Much better to sell up and buy something modern in England, I'm told.'

Sasha kept her thoughts about that to herself, but inwardly she was beginning to dislike Maddie intensely for the way she was pressurising Freddie. She knew instinctively that Maddie was definitely not the right person for her brother. But she couldn't say that out loud – yet.

Sasha sighed. 'You barely know each other. And there's also Jade to consider. If it worked out, you'd be her stepdad. It's not good for her to become attached to you and then you disappear out of her life. She seems to be fond of you already, so I think you have to ask yourself a question, or even a couple of questions, about how you truly feel about Maddie. Is she the love of your life? And can you bear the thought of her not being in your life?'

Selfishly, Sasha knew she didn't want him to go, but she couldn't voice her own feelings as it wouldn't be fair. Whatever he decided, she knew Maddie was going to hurt Freddie, whether they stayed together or parted. Freddie needed to talk to someone and with that thought, Sasha came to a decision.

'Will you do something for me please?'

Freddie looked at her. 'You know I always will if I can.'

'This isn't for me, it's for you. Will you please talk to Jean-Paul about what Maddie is suggesting you do?'

'Why? What does he know?'

'I don't know, but he's a local and he knows about things that happened before we arrived here.'

'Has he said something to you about me and Maddie?'

'He simply asked me to tell you to be careful,' Sasha confessed.

Freddie gave a deep sigh. 'And I thought it was all going so well. Okay, I'll talk to Jean-Paul in the bar tonight, but I can guess I'm not going to like what he tells me.'

33

Penny, although outwardly calm, was a bundle of nerves as she waited for Lucas to arrive and take her for the lunch she'd finally agreed to. She wasn't at all sure she was ready yet to let another man into her life. As a friend maybe, but what if he wanted more than friendship? What if he was another Rory? Charming in the beginning before he showed his true colours. No, deep down she sensed Lucas wasn't like that. Although she knew little about him, she could see by the way he treated Eliza and Alice that he was a decent man through and through. As she heard his car drive up and stop outside the château, Penny took a deep breath and decided she was in danger of over-thinking things. She'd simply make the most of a day away from the château and enjoy the company of a man she knew she was attracted to.

'Where are we going?' she asked as she settled into the passenger seat.

'One of my favourite places, Pont-Aven. Did you go there yet?'

Penny shook her head. 'No.'

'It's where the River Aven join the sea, so the town is on a tidal estuary. Very picturesque. It's only about an hour away. I book a table for one o'clock.'

As they travelled down the main road, they talked about how successful the wedding had been, how wonderful the orangery now looked, and how much Penny had enjoyed organising everything. When Lucas asked, 'Does that mean you maybe stay?' Penny simply shrugged and said, 'Who knows.'

It was less than an hour later when Lucas pulled into the town's car park.

'We got time for walking before lunch,' Lucas said. 'The tide is high, so you see the place at the best.'

Walking around the town with its footbridges festooned with flowers, stopping to admire the waterwheel on an old tidal mill building on the very edge of the river, and looking at the boats moored in the estuary, Penny smiled happily. 'It's such a pretty place, so many art shops. Sasha must visit, if she hasn't already. I'm sure as an artist, she'd love it too.'

'A lot of famous artist are inspired by this place through the years, Paul Gauguin included,' Lucas said. 'We better go to the restaurant now.'

Lucas had booked a table with a view of the river at one of its narrowest points. From their window table overlooking the water and one of the many bridges, Penny felt she could almost reach out and touch the bank on the opposite side. She watched as two swans glided serenely past on their way downriver, ignoring the impatient quacking of a crowd of ducks on the bank.

After handing them menus, the waitress fetched their drinks – a non-alcoholic beer for Lucas and a small carafe of rosé wine for Penny – before taking their food orders – a duck salad for Penny and moules and frites for Lucas.

Penny sipped her drink and looked around the busy restaurant before registering that Lucas was watching her with amusement. 'Why are you looking at me like that?'

'You're busy looking around and, I guess, as a professional caterer, you probably make mental note about all sort of things, from the decor to the food. I was just wondering if you actually enjoy eating out. Or if sometime you find it difficult to stop the working part of your brain?'

'I love eating out, and casing the joint for ideas is an occupational hazard,' Penny said laughing, before saying seriously, 'It's not something I have done much of in the recent past. Rory, my ex-boyfriend, wasn't great at trying different restaurants. He felt more comfortable going to a place he liked and where he was known.' Penny gently swirled her wine in the glass. 'His favourite was a place called Billy's Bistro. I was supposed to meet him there a few weeks ago but...' She hesitated and looked at Lucas. 'I stood him up and ran away to France instead. Not my proudest moment.' She took a sip of her wine. 'First time I've ever stood anyone up. It was a quite liberating feeling. I'm not sure why I've just told you that, it's not remotely interesting.'

To Penny's relief, the waitress arrived with their food before Lucas could respond. '*Bon appétit.*'

'I'm curious about what it is you do?' Penny asked, hoping to move the conversation away from herself. 'This duck is delicious, by the way.'

'Good. I was surprised to enjoy one of those liberating feeling a couple of month ago myself when I start this "sabbatical" which wasn't my choice,' Lucas said quietly. 'I tell you about it another day. I try to accept it and think what I do next. I give myself the summer at Grand-maman's to decide like where I go and what my next step are.'

'Much like me then,' Penny said. 'I have nothing to go back

to Bristol for, but I haven't got a clue where or what I'm going to do. Actually, that's not strictly true. I've realised I definitely do not want to return to Bristol to live, so I need to terminate the lease on my flat and make a quick visit to clear it, but what to do after that, who knows? Hey, I have an idea. Alice is jobless too, isn't she?'

Lucas nodded.

'The three of us could go travelling. I never did have a gap year.'

Planning an itinerary for their imaginary gap year kept them talking and laughing through to dessert and then coffee. It was gone three o'clock when they left the restaurant.

'Time to go home, I think. We do this again soon, yes?' Lucas said, staring intensely at Penny.

'Thank you for today. And yes, it would be lovely to do it again another time,' Penny said, feeling more and more drawn to Lucas. It was a shame that they were both only planning to stay in France for the summer so it could never be more than a holiday friendship because, she realised with a start, she liked Lucas a lot.

There was more traffic on the way back and Lucas needed to concentrate as he drove up the busy dual carriageway before turning onto the country lanes that led to the estate. Penny invited him in for a coffee as he pulled up outside the château, but he shook his head.

'Thanks, but I get back to check on Grand-maman, I'm not sure what Alice is doing this afternoon.' He leant across and kissed her cheek. 'I see you soon. À bientôt.'

Penny stared after his car for several seconds as it went down the drive. Why had he promised to tell her about quitting his job another day? Why hadn't he simply told her when it had come up in conversation? Was he hiding something?

* * *

Alice was in the kitchen making Eliza a pot of tea when Lucas got home and barged into the cottage.

'Did Penny tell you about her ex-boyfriend that night you travelled over together on the ferry?'

Startled, Alice looked at him. 'Why?'

'She talk about him a little today, but she use the phrase "I ran away", which worry me. Relationships end, you break up, but how often do you run away to end a relationship? Was he a bully? Or worse?'

Alice sighed. 'It's not for me to tell you about her past. Why not ask her?'

'Don't feel I know her well enough yet, and her past is not really my business. I'm more interested in her future. But I hate the thought of someone hurting her.' Lucas rubbed his face. 'We had a great time together today. I haven't met anyone like her before. She's different. She's—I suppose basically there is no fake in her.'

'You seriously like her, don't you?'

Lucas nodded ruefully. '*Oui*.'

'If it's any help, I think she likes you a lot too,' Alice said.

'Well, that something I suppose.'

'You'll just have to take it slowly, let her get over her bad relationship.'

Lucas nodded.

'In the meantime, brother dear, Grand-maman says you've quit your job, so how about telling me why? I thought you were on a sabbatical. You loved that job.'

Lucas shook his head. 'Not ready to talk about it yet. And if you know nothing, you can't go blabbing to Penny.'

'Blabbing! That's an outrageous thing to accuse me of,' Alice said, laughing. 'Seriously, you know you can talk to me. Grand-maman says you were a little preoccupied when you came back.'

'Preoccupied, yes,' Lucas said. 'Another week and it should be sorted, and then I can tell everyone what going on.'

'That sounds a bit ominous,' Alice said.

Lucas shrugged. 'It is what it is.'

34

Sasha looked around her studio with a happy smile on her face. At last it was ready. Everything was in its place. She could start to get serious about working from home and marketing her stuff. She quickly took a couple of photos for her website and Instagram account, knowing from experience the room wouldn't stay pristine for long once she started to work in there. Satisfied the photos she'd taken were good, she put the phone in her pocket. All she had to do now was to get rid of the empty boxes she'd thrown out onto the landing. They would be useful for packaging later, but she didn't want the clutter in her studio, so they could go up in the attic.

Freddie had discovered that the attic in his cottage had not only been floored, but that there were also a light and a fold-away ladder that came down to safely access it. Hopefully the same had been done in this cottage. Sasha took the pole with a hook she'd found in the small bedroom, slipped it into the ring in the ceiling trapdoor and pulled.

To her relief, it opened and dropped down, a dusty wooden foldaway ladder attached to it. Carefully, Sasha extended the ladder, placing its legs on the ground and making sure it was steady before she began to climb. As she reached the top, she saw a light cord on the right-hand side and gave it a gentle tug. A bulb hanging in the middle of the attic didn't instantly flood the place with light – it was more like a dim glow – but it was enough to see that the attic was floored and empty.

Except it wasn't.

On the left, a mere arm's length away from the opening, as if it had been flung there in haste just to get it out of the way, was a cardboard box. Sasha reached out and pulled it towards her, and brushed off the dust and cobwebs. The light was too dim to read the label, so she picked it up. Thankfully it wasn't too heavy, and she carefully descended the steps. She placed the box on the floor of the studio whilst she cleared the landing.

It took her two climbs up to throw the empty boxes into the attic before she pulled the light cord to switch the bulb off and went down for the final time. She slid the ladder up and pushed the trapdoor back into its place.

In the studio, she picked up the box, put it on the desk and studied it thoughtfully. It had clearly been sent through the post, but for some reason had never been opened by the recipient because the sealing wax was intact. The postmark had faded in places, but Sasha could just make out Mai 1965, although the name of the town it had been sent from, nearly sixty years ago, was illegible. The parcel, sent by registered post, was addressed to Madame Eliza Albertini, No. 1 Cottages du Lac, Château du Cheval. Finistère. No surprise there, Eliza had been living in the cottage then. The sender's name was written on the back: Maître Jocelyn Bellicam. *Notaire*. No address given here, just a *département* number that had been so smudged as to be unreadable.

So many questions began to tumble around in Sasha's mind.

Why had Eliza never opened the parcel? Had she put it in the loft herself, or did someone else hide it up there out of the way? Did Eliza even know about it? And what should she, Sasha, do now? She knew, of course, she should give it to Eliza straight away. Technically and morally, it did belong to her. But if she was the person who had placed it in the attic unopened all those years ago, would she find it any easier to open and see the contents now she was older?

Sasha took a photo of the parcel before placing it on the floor under the desk. Eliza had already had one major trip down memory lane with the contents of the box from the stable, a nostalgic trip she had clearly enjoyed. But what if the contents of the unopened box proved to be unhappy memories? Sasha didn't want to upset Eliza. The next time she saw Peter and Ingrid she'd mention finding the box and ask what they thought she should do with it.

* * *

Sasha clipped Mimi and Mitzi onto their leads and set off to the stables, hoping the walk and time spent talking to Starlight would clear her head and help her to think straight. Colette was just finishing saddling up her horse ready for a hack around the lanes when she got there.

'Enjoy,' Sasha said. 'Wish I were coming with you.'

Colette put her left foot in the stirrup, swung herself up and lowered herself gently onto Starlight's back before looking down at Sasha. 'Might have a proposition for you. A friend of mine has a Welsh Cob she adores and doesn't want to sell, but she urgently needs someone to take him on a permanent loan basis. She's pregnant with her second baby, so her time is going to be limited for several months at least. If you're interested, I

can give you her number. Think about it and let me know.'
Colette gently kicked Starlight into a walk and was gone.

Sasha watched until they'd disappeared, then she turned and walked back to the cottage. Having a horse on permanent loan was tempting, but would she really get to ride it that much? While she was trying to build up stock and do the marketing to generate an income with her art and craft work, her own time was going to be severely limited. Walking, playing and trying to train Mimi and Mitzi took up a lot of her spare time already. And the cottage renovations were by no means finished. But it would be lovely to have a horse in her life.

She'd ask Ingrid how much a DIY livery at the château would be, and add on the cost of hay, horse nuts, regular black-smith visits and possible vet charges. Even as she added it all up in her head, Sasha knew she was being unrealistically optimistic in thinking she could do it – wasn't she? The large amount of money Ingrid had paid her for the *trompe l'œils* had been unexpected, hadn't been included in her budget or allo-cated anywhere yet. Would it be terribly irresponsible of her to use that money to take on a horse?

* * *

Freddie was getting out of the van when Sasha got back to the cottage.

'You're home early. Or are you off again?' she asked.

'Determined to finish plumbing in my bathroom this evening,' Freddie said. 'Do you want me to cook supper first?'

'I was going to do a risotto,' Sasha said. 'Fancy a cup of tea in the garden right now?'

'Good idea. I've got some biscuits indoors.'

Five minutes later, they were sitting in Sasha's garden with mugs of tea and a packet of digestive biscuits on the table.

'Have you seen Jean-Paul recently?' Freddie asked.

'Not for a few days. Have you?'

Freddie nodded. 'Yep. I'm glad you told me to talk to him. He's a good bloke. Fond of you, I think.' He gave her a cheeky grin.

Sasha was not about to let the conversation be diverted to her. 'What did he tell you about Maddie?'

'Enough to make me realise that I was being foolish to even think about selling up and returning to the UK with her. I love it here, you're here, and I want to settle here, not throw in the towel after a few months.'

'Have you told Maddie you're definitely not leaving France with her?'

Freddie took a sip of his tea. 'Yes. I've also told her if she and Jade want to keep in touch, to come for a visit.' He glanced at Sasha. 'Ninety-nine percent certain that's not going to happen, for all her talk about how we clicked and how we could be happy together in England.'

'I'm sorry it didn't work out the way you hoped,' Sasha said quietly.

'Me too,' Freddie sighed. 'Anyway, I've stepped right back from her and Jade. It's for the best.'

35

'You know, I think this is rapidly becoming my favourite place in the château to sit in summer,' Ingrid said as she and Peter drank their morning coffee in the orangery. 'I think we could do with a few rattan chairs though, strategically placed.'

Peter nodded as he looked around. All three of the French doors were open, the muslin curtains were moving in the gentle breeze that was rustling the leaves of the plants, and the air was filled with the soft perfume of the three scented white rose bushes Penny had placed by each door. 'It's a delightful space, that's for sure. Those *trompe l'œils* of Sasha's are stunning; the citrus trees and the bamboo and the white rose bushes have all settled in their pots and look happy.'

'I've had several enquiries for wedding receptions since Stella's,' Ingrid said. 'The problem is that they're all for much larger weddings – one hundred guests is the smallest. The orangery isn't big enough for that number. And I'm not at all sure I could cope with such large numbers anyway. If I knew for sure that Penny was staying and would be in charge of the catering, I'd think about advertising it as an intimate, romantic venue but—' she shrugged.

'Alice has roped her in to help with the fete,' Peter said. 'So she'll be here for a couple more weeks at least. I was wondering whether tempting her with *La Maison du Jardinier* would be an incentive for her to stay?'

'It might. What might also work is if I step back from doing any catering here, other than breakfasts, and give her a sort of franchise to supply dinners for guests, and to be fully in charge of any wedding receptions in the orangery and in the château itself.'

Peter nodded thoughtfully. 'We could make her a partner in the business.'

'Of course, a certain Lucas might also play a part in convincing her to stay,' Ingrid said.

'Alice's brother?' Peter gave her a quizzical look. 'Have I missed something?'

'How many Lucases do you know? Yes, Alice's brother.'

'Talking of Alice,' Peter picked up the fete organising file that was on the small table beside him. 'You were right, we'd never have managed to organise this fete without her help. Far more complicated than I would ever have thought. Some of the forms made my eyes water and my brain close down. Alice took them in her stride. And she's an expert at getting people to donate prizes for the tombola and the lucky dip for the children.'

'Did she tell you that she's given me a list of events she thinks we could arrange?' Ingrid said. 'She reckons we could create a real hub in the community here in the château. Writers' and artists' retreats, antique fairs, day cookery courses, photography, even a local gymkhana is on the list. Maybe we should think about employing her as Events Manager for the château –

if we can afford her. The fete is for the village and she's happy to volunteer her expertise to help organise that, but for anything commercial, she'd need a salary.'

'Perhaps we should try to work out a package that would include both Penny and Alice,' Peter said thoughtfully. 'We certainly can't do those kinds of events without help.'

'I was wondering where you two were,' Penny said, appearing from the terrace and walking into the orangery. 'May I join you?'

'Of course,' Peter said. 'We were just saying how much we both love the way this orangery has evolved into something special, thanks to everyone's hard work.'

'Yes, I think once word gets out, people will be clamouring to come and stay here, simply to be able to sit in this special place,' Penny said.

'Bookings for the *chambres d'hôtes* are coming in and some are asking about evening meals,' Ingrid said. 'I know you said you'd stay until after the wedding, but how soon are you planning on leaving? We're not putting any pressure on you to either stay or leave. Obviously we'd love you to stay and help us to build up the business, but if you want to return to the UK, that's fine by us too. We'd just like to know so we can start to make our own plans.'

'There is one other thing,' Peter said. 'We were wondering how you'd feel, if you do decide to stay and make a life for yourself here in France, about moving into the old *Maison du Jardinier*? It would give you some independence and a place of your own.'

'Alice has asked me to help with organising the fete, so I'll be here for another few weeks. I haven't decided what to do after that, although I have to admit I've been thinking about staying here and working for you.'

Peter shook his head. 'We'd have to look into it, but we'd probably give you a franchise or make you a partner, so that you would be your own boss and responsible for all the catering business at the château.'

Penny looked at her parents, stunned. 'Okay. Lots to think about there. How about I commit to staying for the summer to help Mum with the catering and see how it works out? And I promise you I will seriously think about remaining here.'

'Thanks,' Peter said. 'Before I forget, Grandad phoned earlier. He and Granny are planning a visit soon. Probably around 14 July. I've already told them you'll still be here for that,' and Peter gave her an unrepentant smile.

Penny laughed and shook her head at him. 'Of course you have. I'll see you both later.'

* * *

After leaving her parents in the orangery, Penny went to the key rack hidden in a cupboard in the château kitchen. Taking the large old-fashioned key marked *La Maison du Jardinier*, she slipped it thoughtfully into her pocket. No time like the present to take a look.

It was a short walk down to the house and as Penny approached, she realised how secluded it was from the château. There was a well-established wisteria plant on the right-hand side of the house, its blossoms now faded and dropping, but there was no sign of an actual front garden. The lock on the heavy door clunked open and Penny turned the handle and pushed it inwards.

The wide hallway with its parquet flooring and the pale wooden staircase with its two small, rounded bottom stairs that started halfway down the hall gave a feeling of spaciousness.

Penny walked down along the side of the staircase; she stepped into a large, high-ceilinged room on the left with French doors that opened onto a terrace. A fireplace with a marble surround was at one end of the room. The kitchen at the end of the hallway, although not as big as the one in the château, was three times the size of the kitchen in her flat. There was a large range-type cooker still in situ and Penny moved to take a closer look, because surely it wasn't a vintage La Cornue stove... It was. In need of some tender loving care, but still a La Cornue.

Upstairs, as she wandered around, opening and closing bedroom doors, finding the antiquated bathroom with its claw-footed bath, she kept asking herself, 'Could I live here?' Standing on the landing, looking out over the view towards the village where she could just see the spire of the church, she nodded. Yes. She could live here. She could even see herself with children running in and out of the rooms. It would make a wonderful family home – and a good base for a catering business. She could run a cookery school from here alongside the job of cooking for the château guests.

She walked slowly back downstairs, deep in thought, and almost lost her footing when her mobile rang, shattering the peace of the house and making her jump. Emma.

'Hi. How are you?'

'I'm fine,' Emma answered. 'More to the point, how are you? No more trouble from Rory, I hope.'

'No. My dad warning him off seems to have done the trick, thankfully. Thanks again for your help there. How's business? Picking up as you hoped it would?'

'Yes, which is why I'm ringing. Are you planning on coming back any time soon? I've been offered a big outside catering contract and wondered if you were going to be available? If you are, I'd like to offer you a different contract – more secure, more money, and one that would involve you in the business more. Like a junior partner. We'd have to get together to thrash the finer details out. You don't have to give me your answer now but please think about it.'

Penny took a deep breath, remembering her thoughts and the excitement she'd felt just five minutes ago upstairs. Emma had been lovely to work for and by the sounds of it, the new contract would be one she'd have accepted without a moment's hesitation only a few months ago. She took a deep breath.

'Emma, I'm sorry but literally moments ago, I made the decision to stay in France. I'm going to work partly with my parents, but I'm also going to start my own catering business.'

'That's brilliant news. I've always thought you were too good to be working for other people, you're more than capable of being your own boss. I wish you all the luck in the world. But I'm sad too that I won't get to work with you again.'

'Thank you. I'll miss working with you too,' Penny said. 'Good luck with your new catering contract.'

After the call ended, she took one more look around the hallway before going out and locking the door behind her. One decision might have been made about her future, now she just had to get to grips with all the new questions it would inevitably raise.

36

Sasha parked in the village car park and got out of the van, locking it with the key fob. In the boulangerie, she bought a box of macaroons and carried them carefully down to Eliza's cottage. After mulling things over for several days, she'd gone up that morning to ask Peter and Ingrid what they thought she should do about the box. Penny was there on her own and said her parents had gone to Rennes for the day – Ingrid to shop, while Peter went to the big library there to see some microfilm copies of northern France newspapers from the early twentieth century.

'Not sure what he hopes to find, to be honest,' Penny had said. 'But searching for long-dead great-aunt Bernadette seems to keep him happy! They're treating themselves to lunch there so won't be home until late afternoon.' The château phone had rung then. 'I'd better answer it in case it's someone wanting to book a room,' and Sasha had quickly said goodbye and left.

Walking home, she'd come to the decision that the very least she should do was to tell Eliza about finding the box in the attic.

Now, knocking gently on the front door of Eliza's cottage, she hoped she was doing the right thing.

Eliza opened the door and gave Sasha a welcoming smile. 'How lovely to see you. Have you brought photos of the orangery all laid up for the wedding?'

'I do have a few on my phone if you'd like to see them,' Sasha said. 'I bought you these by way of a thank you for making the curtains and serviettes.'

'It was my pleasure. Come in and have a coffee.'

Over the next ten minutes, Sasha showed Eliza the photos of the orangery and her workshop.

'That's the middle bedroom, isn't it?' Eliza asked, peering at the screen. 'My daughter Claudia never kept the room as tidy as that!'

'I don't suppose I will either, once I start to get commissions,' Sasha said, laughing, before taking a deep breath. 'I was putting some things up in the attic recently and I found this box.' She held out the phone to Eliza. 'It's addressed to you but it's never been opened.' Mentally, Sasha crossed her fingers, hoping that Eliza would react in the same favourable way she had to the box of memorabilia from the stables.

Silently, Eliza glanced at the photo before looking up at Sasha. 'I didn't open it then and I don't want to open it now. I didn't need to know what was inside it fifty years ago, and I need that knowledge even less now. Times have changed. Thank you for telling me you found it. Please throw it away.'

'Doesn't the fact that it came from a *notaire* signify it might contain something important?' Sasha protested gently.

Eliza sighed. 'The box arrived a month after my daughter Claudia was born and a week after my mother Marie-Thérèse died. I just didn't have the energy – mental or otherwise – to deal with anything else. William put it up in the attic because it was in the way in the cottage and to be honest, I completely forgot about it. If it had been that important, somebody from the *notaire*'s office would have been in touch. Fifty years on, it's unlikely to have any relevance to my life these days. It's from another time. Let the past stay in the past. Put it back up in the attic or throw it away.'

Sasha put her phone back in her bag. 'Of course, if that's what you want. I hope I haven't upset you by showing you the photo, but I thought you ought to know I'd found it.'

'No, I'm not upset,' Eliza said. 'But I have no intention of dragging the past into my present. Your English author L. P. Hartley was right when he wrote, "The past is a foreign country." And I, for one, have no intention of travelling to it.'

* * *

Sasha drove back to the cottages on autopilot. She couldn't help but feel that Eliza was wrong not opening the box and at least checking the contents. But part of her could sympathise as well. From what Eliza had said, it had arrived at a time when she was feeling particularly low. Unwrapping it could possibly drag up feelings from fifty years ago which would not necessarily be a good thing. Sasha wished that Eliza hadn't given her the choice of putting it back in the attic or throwing it away. She definitely couldn't dispose of it as it was, but she couldn't rid herself of the fact that it wasn't hers to open. Simply putting it back in the attic unopened didn't feel right either.

Back in the cottage and deciding she'd like some female company, Sasha rang both Penny and Alice and invited them for a girly evening at the cottage rather than meeting in the bar. She walked Mimi and Mitzi into the village late afternoon for a couple of bottles of wine, ham and cheese, baguettes and some olives, crisps and nuts.

Penny was the first to arrive later that evening, walking through the château grounds and calling out '*Hello*' at the front door of the cottage. Alice opened the garden gate from the *route de galop* almost at the same time and Mimi and Mitzi went a little mad, barking and chasing back and forth, not knowing which of them to greet first. Once the three women were together on the terrace, the pups calmed down.

Freddie said '*Hi*' over the garden fence and declined the offer of joining them. 'I'm off to the bar to watch the sports with Jean-Paul. Have fun.'

Sasha poured everyone a drink before placing the sliced baguettes on the table, along with a round of brie, olives and some sliced ham, and emptying the crisps and nuts into bowls. '*Santé*,' she said, raising her glass of rosé. 'Sorry about the short notice, but it's great to see you both.'

'A girly evening is just what I need tonight,' Penny said. 'I haven't told Mum and Dad this yet, but my old boss Emma rang me earlier with a job offer. A better contract than I had before, more prospects and more pay.'

'How long did she give you to think about it?' Alice asked.

'I didn't need any time to think about it, I turned it down straight away because...' Penny took a sip of her wine. 'I'm not going back to Bristol. I'm staying here.'

'It's great news that you'll definitely be staying in the village,' Sasha said. 'What are you going to do for work though?'

'Mum and Dad have asked me to do the catering for the château as a partner with them but – and this is the wonderful part – they've offered me *La Maison du Jardinier* to live in. I can use the house to run a separate business of my own. A cookery school maybe. Or outside catering. I'm still processing it all. I'll talk it through with them tomorrow.'

'Exciting times,' Alice said. 'I keep thinking I'd like to stay and live here permanently, but apart from a job in the village bar, there isn't any work locally,' she shrugged. 'Grand-maman is a worry too. She's really perked up since Lucas and I have been back. If we both leave at the end of summer, I'm not sure how that will affect her.'

'Quimper is what, an hour's commute away,' Sasha said. 'Could you find something as an event manager there?'

'Possibly, I'll have to start to put some feelers out, see if there is anything.'

'So Lucas is definitely leaving at the end of summer as well?' Penny asked casually.

'I guess, but I really have no idea what my dear brother is doing. I didn't even know until recently that he was jobless.'

'What was his job anyway?' Penny asked.

'He's been working down on the Riviera recently for a private marine company. Usually he talks to me, but this time, nothing. I do remember there was a bit of a hiatus last year when the company were fined for bad working practices. No idea what, but I'm pretty sure Lucas wasn't involved in that.' Alice shrugged. 'He'll talk about it eventually. Grand-maman and I are wondering what he's going to do next.'

In the silence that followed, Sasha topped up their glasses. Alice was clearly cross with her brother and Penny... well, Penny obviously felt more for Lucas than she'd let on, judging from her quiet reaction to Lucas's possible departure.

'Jean-Paul rang before you two arrived. He's taking me to Châteauneuf-du-Faou tomorrow evening,' Sasha said into the silence.

'Hope you like jazz,' Alice said. 'The annual jazz festival in the town finished this week, but there are always a number of small bands who stay around throughout summer in the town and down by the canal.'

'How's your French?' Penny asked, grinning at her.

'Definitely improving. As is Jean-Paul's English,' Sasha said, smiling, knowing exactly what Penny was hinting at.

'Ooh, have you taken my advice already?' Penny said.

'No, it's too soon to be even thinking that. How was your grand-maman this evening?' Sasha asked, turning to Alice.

'Same as usual,' Alice said.

'She didn't mention I called in to see her today?'

Alice shook her head and looked at her curiously. 'No.'

'I was storing stuff up in the attic of the cottage and I found an unopened parcel from the sixties addressed to her. I showed her a photo of it on my phone. Eliza took one look and said to throw it away or put it back in the attic and wouldn't discuss it any further.'

'You haven't opened it?'

'No. I didn't think it was my place to do that. But I can't throw it away either. It was sent from a *notaire*. Maybe I'll just put it back in the attic. It's been up there for half a century, so a little more time won't make any difference. Everything in it is probably out of date now anyway.'

'I'll ask her when I get back this evening why she didn't open it all those years ago,' Alice said.

'No, please don't mention it to her,' Sasha begged. 'As far as she's concerned, she's told me what to do with it and there's little point in upsetting her again.' She turned to Penny. 'Your parents could have been the ones to find the parcel. If I bring it up to the château, d'you think they'd open it with me – be witnesses if you like, to what we find? You could be there too, Alice.' Sasha took a deep breath. 'And then if it's important, we can tell Eliza.'

37

When Sasha mentioned to Freddie at breakfast that she was going out with Jean-Paul that evening, he immediately said he'd walk Mimi and Mitzi and stay home with them. 'I'll look forward to it. I'll get to see how well you've trained them,' he said. 'It's not often I get them to myself,' he teased.

Sasha gave him a horrified look. 'You're not accusing me of hogging them, are you? It's just that I'm here most days and evenings, and you're out working.'

'No. Of course I'm not,' Freddie said. 'It's better for them to have a regular routine, which you've given them, than for them to be left alone in the cottage for hours at a time – which sadly they would be if it were just me.'

The cottage felt strangely empty to Sasha as she started getting ready for Jean-Paul. Freddie had taken the pups out as promised and she missed hearing the short barks they gave as they played with each other, and even their gentle snoring as they snuggled together in their basket. Freddie wasn't back when Jean-Paul arrived and Sasha had to leave without the usual fussing of the dogs, which was curiously upsetting.

On the short drive to Châteauneuf-du-Faou, Jean-Paul told her a little about where they were going – a walk along the canal and then a meal in a local restaurant. As he drove over the bridge down by the canal, Sasha said, 'What a beautiful place.'

'One day us and the dogs walk here *ensemble*,' Jean-Paul said, catching hold of her hand.

'Mimi and Mitzi would love it,' Sasha said quietly, her small hand nestled in the gentle but firm hold of Jean-Paul's.

As they strolled along the canal path, they met a couple of dog walkers and an elderly man striding out with his walking poles. For a few moments, they stood watching a pair of swans gliding gracefully down the canal, past a statue-like heron on the bank. He was so still, Sasha could barely believe he was real, until he took off and soared onto one of the tall trees overhanging the canal.

Jean-Paul glanced at his watch. 'I think we go to the restaurant now,' and they turned and began to make their way back towards the bridge.

Jazz began to drift on the air towards them as they neared the picturesque canal-side restaurant with its terrace overlooking the water. It was busy. Several people who were already seated smiled and waved at Jean-Paul as a waitress showed them to their own table. Looking around, Sasha saw the source of the jazz she could hear. A trio of musicians on a small, raised platform were softly playing 'C'est Magnifique' – one of her mother's favourite Cole Porter songs. Sasha swallowed the emotion that suddenly threatened to overwhelm her at the thought of her mum, how much she would have loved to talk to her about her new life in France, about Jean-Paul. Especially to talk about Jean-Paul, a man Sasha knew her mum would have liked.

'Are you okay?' Jean-Paul's anxious voice broke into her thoughts. 'You are quiet.'

'*Oui, merci.* I'm fine. This particular tune was a favourite of my mum's. It reminded me of her. In a good way.'

Before Jean-Paul could answer, the waiter arrived with the menus and asked if they would like to order drinks. 'I have the non-alcoholic beer tonight,' Jean-Paul said. 'Which wine you like?'

'A glass of rosé would be lovely,' Sasha said. 'It seems to have become my favourite summer drink.'

When the waiter returned with their wine and beer and asked for their food order, they'd both chosen the same things from the set menu. A selection of canapés, and a main course of chicken fricassee in a creamy white wine sauce served with roasted vegetables and a green salad on the side. Desserts would be chosen from the sweet trolley.

Relaxing and sitting there eating her favourite newly discovered canapé – green olive tapenade on toast – and sipping her wine, Sasha watched the evening activity on the canal coming to a close. Canoes and small rowing boats were navigating their way between ducks and swans towards the pontoon where they were tied up for the night. Swallows were dive-bombing off the surface of the canal and the moon was starting to show in the sky.

'It's beautiful here,' she said, smiling at Jean-Paul. 'Thank you for bringing me.'

They both agreed their chicken fricassee was delicious and Sasha resolved to try to find a recipe and make it at home. Maybe Penny would have a tried-and-tested one she would share with her.

Conversation between them was a mix of French and English, and not once did either of them resort to using the app on their phones. 'We help each other,' Jean-Paul said.

All too soon, the evening was over and Jean-Paul was driving her home. After pulling up in front of the Cottages du Lac, Jean-Paul got out of the car and opened Sasha's door for her.

'*Moi*, I enjoy *ce soir*. I hope you enjoy also?'

'*Merci*, I truly did,' Sasha said. 'It has been a perfect evening.'

'Next time, I think you come see where I live, no? You bring Mimi and Mitzi. I show you my farm.' Jean-Paul gave her an anxious look as if unsure she would like it.

'*Oui*. I'd love that,' Sasha said. 'Soon?' She smiled hopefully at him.

Jean-Paul nodded. 'Soon, but first we meet tomorrow evening.'

'Tomorrow evening?'

'It is book club night.'

'I'd forgotten,' Sasha said. 'See you then.'

Jean-Paul smiled before slowly leaning in and kissing her gently on the lips. '*Bonne nuit et fais de beaux rêves.*'

Watching Jean-Paul drive away, Sasha smiled happily to herself as she remembered something her mum had once told her: 'A slow burning romance that takes its time to ignite the flames is usually a long-lasting true love.' If that was what this relationship was, a slow burner to true love, she had the feeling that it could burst into flames at any moment in the future.

38

Ingrid and Peter had decided to hold the book club meeting in the orangery to give the members a chance to see it in all its newly acquired glory and hopefully spread the word. The *trompe l'œils* were admired by everyone and Sasha was overwhelmed by the praise when she arrived. Flustered and embarrassed by the attention, she sank gratefully down onto the chair Jean-Paul had saved for her next to him.

The book discussion when it began was lively. Everyone, it seemed, had views about *Tender Is the Night*.

'*J'adore*,' Josette said, and glared at Benjamin when Ingrid translated his words: 'The storyline was somewhat boring and out of touch.' Josette's audible mutter of '*Imbécile*' was heard by everyone and needed no translation.

Eliza too had found it 'a good read,' although the Americanisms were a bit confusing.

'The characters were so complex,' Sasha said. 'They stayed in my mind after I'd finished the book.'

After everyone had had their say, Ingrid held up their next read. 'This is the book chosen for our summer break. At over four hundred pages, it's longer than most of our usual novels, but you've got two months to get through it. *To My Daughter in France*, by Barbara and Stephanie Keating. It's not so well known as any of our other books, but it is one of my favourites – a story of impossible love, secrets, and families torn apart.' Ingrid smiled across at Benjamin. 'I hope you will like this one.'

'More wine or coffee, anyone?' Peter asked. When several people took him up on the offer, Sasha, realising that everyone was keen to stay longer this evening, made her way over to Colette.

'I've been thinking about the Welsh Cob you mentioned, and I'm definitely interested,' Sasha said. 'I haven't had a chance to ask Ingrid about the cost of having a DIY livery here yet, but equally important is, will he come with tack? I don't have any saddles or anything.'

'Definitely comes with tack,' Colette said. And she named a figure for the livery that Sasha knew was well within her means.

'I'll have to ask Ingrid before I ring your friend, but please may I have her telephone number?'

Colette and she quickly exchanged numbers.

'Before I forget, can you tell your mum that if she is still interested in a painting, I've got my workshop up and running now. But if she's changed her mind, that's fine.'

'She definitely wants you to do one for her. I expect she'll be in touch once I tell her you are ready for commissions.'

As Colette wandered across to talk to Eliza, Sasha made her way towards Ingrid and Peter. 'Can I ask you about renting one of the stables please? Colette has mentioned the possibility of the loan of a horse.'

Ingrid smiled. 'Of course you can. It will be lovely to have another horse back in the stables.'

'Thank you. There's something else I need to talk to you

about,' Sasha said. 'I found an old, sealed parcel in the attic.' She glanced quickly across at Eliza, hoping she couldn't hear the conversation. 'It was addressed to Eliza. When I went to see her about it, she told me to throw it away unopened.' Sasha shook her head. 'I really can't do that as it's from a *notaire*. Would you be witnesses and open it with me please?'

'Of course, Ingrid and I will happily be with you to open the box,' Peter said. 'Maybe we can try a bit of subterfuge and try to persuade Eliza to be here too? Offer her a champagne afternoon tea in the orangery as a thanks for all her help with the serviettes and the curtains.'

'I truly don't think she cares about the contents of the parcel after all these years,' Sasha said. 'But a champagne tea might do the trick.'

'I'll work out a suitable day,' Ingrid said.

'Thank you.' Sasha gave a grateful sigh.

As people began to leave, Ingrid called out, 'Enjoy summer and hope to see you all for the first meeting of autumn in September. And please don't forget to support the fete here on the afternoon of Bastille Day.'

Lucas joined Penny as she started to collect the dirty cups and glasses. 'Would you like spending an afternoon in the Valley of the Saints with me tomorrow?' he asked quietly. 'I need to talk to you.'

Penny nodded. 'Yes, I could fancy that if I knew what the Valley of the Saints was?'

'A special place across the border in Côtes-d'Armor. Wear walking shoes if you have some. I pick you up at two o'clock.'

39

The next afternoon, as Lucas drove them in the direction of Carnoët, just over the border from Finistère into Côtes-d'Armor, Penny said, 'I'm looking forward to seeing this Valley of the Saints. Creating half a dozen monumental granite statues every year seems an amazingly ambitious project to me.'

'You look it up then,' an amused Lucas said.

'Of course. I was intrigued. Have you often been?'

'Once or twice a year since they open it to the public,' Lucas said. 'There's something super special about the place. Not sure whether it's the knowledge that it has played a part in Breton culture for hundred of years, or the fact that there is a feudal mound on the chosen site, or...' He shrugged. 'I don't honestly know. But it's a great spot for walking and thinking. There's a lovely sixteen century chapel as well.'

After parking the car, the two of them set off to explore the area. With no official footpaths to follow, it was a case of meandering across the grass from one huge granite statue to another; they were all dotted about in the undulating open valley in any direction you looked.

Penny, catching her breath, looked around in amazement. 'I've never been to Easter Island, but I imagine this could be called Brittany's answer to it. I can't believe how tall they are.'

'Four metre,' Lucas said.

'There are so many of them,' Penny remarked. 'Each different and awe-inspiring, but all representing the founding saints of Brittany, according to the information I read last night.'

After Penny's initial excitement at seeing the site for the first time died down, the two of them walked slowly and companionably, absorbing the atmosphere around them.

'Thank you for bringing me here,' Penny said. 'I shall make sure every guest I cook breakfast for in the château knows to come and visit.'

'You sound like you are decide to stay here in Brittany,' Lucas said.

Penny turned to him. 'I have. I am. Didn't Alice tell you? I'm going to become a partner in the business, live in *La Maison du Jardinier* and start my own cookery school. I haven't decided exactly what that is going to entail yet, but I'm really excited. How about you? Have you made any plans yet?'

Lucas nodded slowly. 'A bit. This enforced time off make me realise I don't want to go back down to the Riviera.'

'What did you do down south?'

'I work for a private marine company with all sort of interests. My main job was oversee various boat-building projects, and also their small fleet of bulk carriers. Last year, I was going to be offered a bigger role in the company, but then there was a —' Lucas hesitated, '—an environmental problem on another of their projects that I wasn't involve with then, but I hear about it and I have to speak out. One of their bulk carriers en route from Africa plan to dump a load of toxic waste in the sea. Somehow the press hear about it, which I swear it wasn't through me, although I would have tell the media if they hadn't told me they were abandoning the plan. But suddenly I was *persona non grata*. I obviously didn't get the promotion – anyway, I didn't want it anymore – and the person who did suggest it would be a good idea for me to take a sabbatical, accept the redundancy package they propose and leave the industry.'

'You did the right thing calling them out on their awful plans,' Penny said. 'I admire you for that. But what will you do now?'

'Thank you. I have been thinking a lot about my future. Part of me want to work for me, but another part of me think I like to go back to college and do a degree in land management and conservation and stay in Brittany. I always loved it here.'

'The degree course sounds interesting.' Penny smiled.

'It is – especially now you definitely staying in France,' Lucas said. 'We can really get to know each other.'

Penny nodded thoughtfully. 'We can. We should take it slowly though, I think.'

'Why?'

'Because I'm not long out of a relationship, I'd like to take time and enjoy getting to know each other.'

'Oh, we will, no doubt about that. Any other reason you think we should take it slowly?' Lucas asked, a grin on his face.

'Well, I'm going to be busy with catering and renovating *La Maison du Jardinier* and you're going to be busy studying, so neither of us will have much time.'

'I'm excellent at renovating houses, so I can help you with that in between studying.'

Penny burst out laughing. 'How many houses have you renovated?'

'I admit I haven't actually renovate any house, but I'm a

quick learner. I'm sure I can help you.' The smile he gave her made Penny's pulse race.

'I might let you paint a wall or two then. Come on, let's look at some more statues.'

This time as they wandered around, Lucas put his arm around Penny's shoulders and pulled her close in a hug. 'My future have definitely improve this afternoon; I hope you feel you too,' he said, planting a gentle kiss on her temple. 'I will thank the saints of Brittany when we visit the chapel.'

Both were lost in their own thoughts as Lucas drove them home later. Penny, thinking about the way they had bonded back in the Valley of the Saints, was happy to sit and let her impressions wash over her. She knew it was early days but taking the decision to stay in France had, it seemed, kick-started a new life for her in several directions. New home, new business and now a new boyfriend. Lucas too, it seemed, was feeling happy and carefree judging by the way he kept giving her quick, almost conspiratorial glances.

As they drove through the village towards the château, Penny caught him giving her another sideways happy smile.

'I can see you,' she said, laughing. 'Please stop looking so pleased with yourself. People are going to wonder why you're grinning like a Cheshire cat.'

'I not care. I want people to know I got the most beautiful girlfriend,' Lucas said.

'Ah. Remember what I said earlier about taking it slowly? Can we keep it to ourselves for a bit?' Penny said quietly.

'Why? I want people to know about us. Don't you?'

'It's not that I don't want people knowing, it's just that—' she hesitated, '—I like the idea of you and me being a secret with nobody knowing about us for a little while.'

'Again, why?'

'I need to get used to the idea of you and me being a couple.' She didn't add that part of her was afraid of being hurt by him, even though she knew in her heart that Lucas was a totally different kind of man to Rory.

Lucas sighed as he turned the car onto the château drive. 'Okay, I agree. But do you have any idea how long it will take you to get use to the idea of us?'

Penny shook her head. 'No. I just—Oh my God.' She stared, frozen, at the car parked in front of the château and at the man gesturing at, and clearly arguing with, her parents.

'What the matter?' Lucas asked, his gaze following hers.

'Please stop the car and let me out, and then you should leave. I don't want you getting involved in this,' Penny said.

'It's Rory, isn't it?'

Penny nodded miserably.

'I'm not going anywhere,' Lucas said, and deliberately putting his foot down harder on the accelerator, he drew up alongside the parked car in a flurry of flying gravel. 'Come on. Let's get rid of him forever.' Lucas got out and slammed the car door behind him. Penny took a deep breath, tried to stop shaking, failed, and got out slowly.

Rory turned and swore at Lucas. 'What the hell were you thinking, driving up like that? If that gravel has damaged my car, you'll pay.' His eyes widened as Penny appeared at Lucas's side. 'Penny – what on earth is going on? What are you doing with this... this... creature?' and Rory brandished his hand in the air irritably in Lucas's direction.

'What are you doing here, Rory?' Penny said through gritted teeth.

'I've come to see you of course. You are my girlfriend.'

'No, I'm not. We were finished the night you assaulted me.'

'But you know I didn't mean it. I've come all this way to

apologise and to make things right between us so we can start again. Yes?' The smile he gave her faltered as Penny stared at him without answering.

'You heard her – she is no longer your girlfriend,' Peter said. 'I've already warned you once to stay away from my daughter. I suggest you leave now before I call the gendarmes to have you thrown off my property.'

'I'm quite happy to do that right now,' Lucas said, taking a step forward.

Rory glared at him. 'What's it got to do with you?'

'I believe any man who assault a woman is not a nice man,' Lucas said dispassionately. 'Beside,' he continued, his voice taking on a hard tone, 'I am very fond of Penny and the thought of you hurting her make me extremely angry.' As he was speaking, he took a couple of steps towards Rory's car and opened the driver's door. 'As Peter say, it is time for you to leave and remember, nobody here ever want to see or hear from you again.'

'What if I don't want to go?'

Lucas gave a deep sigh. 'But you do want to go. Only a very stupid person would stay here and wait for the gendarmes to arrive when Penny she tell them about how you assault her.'

Several seconds passed before Rory finally got in his car and Lucas slammed the door shut and stood back. Nobody expected what happened next. After starting the engine, Rory reversed back until he had enough space to suddenly turn and drive forcibly into the side of Lucas's car, before accelerating away down the drive with his arm out of the car window and making a rude sign at everyone.

'Oh, Lucas, I'm so sorry about your car,' Penny said, nearly in tears.

'Not as sorry as Rory will be,' Lucas said, pulling out his

phone and quickly pressing a number. A rapid-fire conversation in French followed. '*Merci beaucoup, André.*'

As the call ended, Peter looked at Lucas. 'Friends in high places?'

Lucas grinned. 'Not in very high places, just the local gendarmerie who are going to make a certain Englishman life a little difficult for the next few hours when they stop him on the autoroute.'

40

'You didn't tell me that Sasha came to see you about a box she found in the attic at your old cottage,' Alice said, looking at Eliza.

'I didn't see the necessity of mentioning it. I told Sasha to either throw it away or put it back in the attic. I hope she did one of those things,' Eliza said.

'Sasha was worried about throwing it away unopened and asked Peter and Ingrid what they thought she should do, as it wasn't truly her property to dispose of and she didn't feel happy with the responsibility.'

'If she doesn't want to throw it away, she can simply put it back in the attic.'

'Do you have any idea what's in the box?' Alice asked.

'No. And I honestly don't want to know or to see what it contains all these years later. I'm too old for it to make any difference to me now.'

Alice gave her grand-maman an exasperated look. 'Anyway, when Sasha mentioned your unopened box to them, they agreed with her and so do I – the contents should be looked at before it's thrown away. Just in case there is anything important in it. So she's asked them and me to be with her when she opens the box. They would like you to be there too.'

'Why would they want that?'

'Because it's your box. And as it's come from a *notaire*, there could possibly be legal papers inside?'

Eliza shook her head. 'I doubt that there will be anything like that in it. The *notaires* would have contacted me when I didn't reply if it was anything of significance. And they never did.'

Alice shrugged. 'We have been invited to a champagne afternoon tea at the château in two days' time, as a thank you for all your help with the curtains and serviettes for the orangery; and afterwards, the plan is to open the box and then you can decide to throw or not to throw the contents away.'

'Thought I'd already decided that,' Eliza muttered. 'All this fuss over a box that I simply wanted thrown away. Well, *you* can go, and tell me about it afterwards. The date they've suggested isn't convenient. I already have a rendez-vous in the village.' The look she gave Alice dared her to question that statement, even if she realised it was not true.

* * *

Late the next afternoon, Alice was in the kitchen with Peter going through the fete plans for Bastille Day when Penny walked into the kitchen. 'How's it all going?' she asked.

'Coming together well, thanks to Alice, who is an organizer par excellence,' Peter said. 'She's a stickler for detail and making sure everything is covered.'

'I've enjoyed it,' Alice said. 'Although it's made me realise how much I miss organising events and that I'm going to have to start looking for another job soon. I can't be a lady of leisure forever.'

'Have you ever thought of going freelance?' Penny asked.

'Fleetingly. I could start small with just my laptop, but I'd really need a business address to look professional for the upmarket events and I don't have the funds.' Alice stood up. 'Right, I think we're finished here for now, so I'll be off. See you soon.'

Penny followed Alice out. 'I'm off to *La Maison du Jardinier* for another look around. Are you in a rush? Or would you like to see it too? Maybe even give me some ideas.'

'Love too,' Alice said, and the two of them strolled through the grounds towards the house. She glanced at Penny. 'Lucas told me what happened when Rory turned up. Are you okay?'

Penny nodded. 'Yes, thanks.' She hesitated. 'Your brother is something else. Did he tell you how he stood up to Rory?'

Alice nodded. 'Your knight in shining armour, I gather?'

Penny laughed. 'That's one way of putting it. I feel guilty about his car though.'

Alice waved the comment away. 'Superficial damage, nothing major.'

Just then Sasha, walking Mimi and Mitzi down to the stables, waved to them from the footpath.

'Come and join us and have a look around my new home,' Penny called.

'I'd love to but better not,' Sasha said. 'I know the house is empty, but I wouldn't want the pups to be naughty in there. Another time maybe?'

'Definitely,' Penny answered.

'Wow,' Alice said as they walked into the large kitchen a few moments later. 'This is a wonderful space. You'll cook up a storm in here.'

'Come upstairs, I want to show you something.'

'How many bedrooms has the house got?' Alice asked.

'Four, but I think one could be used as an office.' Penny glanced at her friend as she opened the door of one of the rooms. 'If I start doing outside catering as well as opening a small cookery school, I'm going to need an assistant for the admin and the marketing, as well as organising some events in the château. To start with I can only afford a part-time assistant – or a freelance one who uses this as her office for her own business as well. Would you be interested?'

There was a short silence as Alice looked at her. 'Are you serious?'

'I wouldn't have mentioned it otherwise. Of course, there's the small question of renovating the place, but Lucas is keen to help with that.' Penny gave Alice a mischievous grin. 'If we start with the kitchen and this room, we can both be up and running at the same time.'

'I'll need to pay rent,' Alice said. 'And we'll have to draw up a proper agreement for both our sakes.'

'We can sort all the paperwork no problem, if you think it's a good idea?'

Alice nodded. 'I think it's a great idea. Thank you.'

After Alice had left, Penny walked back to the château and found Ingrid and Peter in the sitting room about to have aperitifs before supper. Penny accepted the gin and tonic her father poured for her and raised her glass as they all said 'Santé'.

'I know you're on tenterhooks about me staying or not staying so...' She took a deep breath. 'I'd love to stay here with you and accept your generous offer of both *La Maison du Jardinier* and taking over the catering for the château.'

Ingrid tried to wipe her happy tears away unseen as Peter said, 'Good. We hoped you would.'

'There is one other thing. Alice is going to start a freelance events business, working from one of the rooms in *La Maison du Jardinier*. She is also going to do my admin and organise events here at the château. I think we all agree that is good news.' And Penny raised her glass in a toast. 'To Alice.'

41

Ingrid was in the château's entrance hall the next day polishing Merlin and keeping an ear out for Peter's parents arriving. As soon as she heard their car, she called out to Penny who was in the kitchen, 'Granny and Grandad are here,' before she opened the heavy oak front door. She knew Victoria, her mother-in-law, would take delight in walking in through that entrance rather than the back door. Penny quickly joined her and the two of them went down the steps to greet Edward and Victoria Chevalier.

After taking her grandparents' cases upstairs, Penny joined them and Ingrid in the kitchen where coffee and fresh patisseries were being enjoyed. 'Where's Dad?'

'He'll be back soon. Just popped into the village for something,' Ingrid said. 'Before I forget, will you tell Sasha about postponing the champagne tea, please.'

'I'll wander down after coffee and one of these delicious almond slices,' Penny said. 'I know the four of you will have a lot of catching up to do.'

Peter was back before Penny made her excuses and left to find Sasha.

Walking down towards the cottage, Penny saw Sasha disappearing in the direction of the old chapel. She called out, 'Sasha, wait for me,' as she started to follow her.

Sasha turned at the sound of her voice; she stopped when she saw Penny and waited for her. 'Hi. Something wrong?'

Penny shook her head. 'Not really, but my grandparents have arrived and with Eliza refusing outright to come for the champagne tea, Mum thought we'd be better off postponing it for a few more days.'

'I'm not surprised Eliza said no, to be honest,' Sasha said. 'I don't suppose another few days' delay will make any difference after all this time.' She turned to carry on walking. 'Freddie's working in the chapel and I thought I'd have a quick look.'

'Mind if I join you? I'd like another look inside.'

'I heard all about the trouble with your ex turning up, but how was your actual date with Lucas?' Sasha asked.

'Good – no, better than that. It was lovely,' Penny said, feeling herself starting to blush. 'I've finally admitted to myself how much I like Lucas and he seems to like me too. We're going to take things slowly, but as we're both staying in France now, we have time.'

'What about his job?'

'He's looking for a change of direction,' Penny said, feeling it wasn't her place to tell anyone about why Lucas had quit his job.

The door of the chapel was ajar when they reached it and Sasha pushed it open. Freddie was on his knees repairing the wooden steps leading to the round granite pulpit and raised his hand in greeting. The rostrum was attached to the wall at the side of the undressed altar table with its cross on the stones behind. An uneven slate floor, several memorial plaques screwed in place on otherwise plain white surfaces and two small beautiful, stained-glass windows across from the pulpit were the only decorative items.

'It's strange how these small, empty churches or chapels always give off an air of peace – the feeling that somehow, bygone worshippers' hymns are still lingering in the air,' Sasha said quietly. 'Even when they've not been used for years.'

She wandered over to look at the memorial plaques. Names of local men lost in both world wars, buried who knew where, but remembered on the estate. She glanced at the pulpit. There must have been countless weddings and christenings performed here during happier times. She hoped – as Freddie said they were – that Peter and Ingrid were indeed planning to use the renovated chapel to hold marriage blessings for couples after the legal civil ceremony in the *mairie*. As unadorned as the building was, the peaceful ambiance within its walls would be perfect for such functions.

A fleeting vision of herself standing in front of the altar, her bridegroom at her side as the priest blessed their marriage, brought a smile to her face. She could only hope that perhaps one day the dream would come true.

42

It was another few days before Penny finally set up the champagne afternoon tea in the orangery. Alice had already apologised for failing to get Eliza to change her mind about declining the invitation, but Ingrid and Peter said they'd open the box with Sasha as planned after the thank you tea with Alice and Lucas. Peter's parents would be sitting in on the occasion too. Freddie had been asked to join them, but he had a gardening job on the other side of the village which he was unable to change.

'This all looks delicious,' Sasha said, arriving with the box and looking at the scones, jam and cream on the table, alongside a three-tiered gateau stand full of tempting fruitcake, strawberry tartlets, eclairs and slices of carrot cake. 'Now you're staying, you can advertise afternoon teas.'

Penny smiled. 'Alice has given Mum so many ideas for moneymaking events, offering cream teas is just one of them. If we were to do everything she suggests, I'd never get a day off!'

'There are eight of us for tea today, is that right?' Sasha said, placing plates around the table. 'I do wish Alice had been able to persuade Eliza to come, it is her box after all.'

Just then, Peter, his parents, Ingrid, Lucas and Alice arrived and within minutes, Ingrid was urging everyone to sit down and 'tuck in' as she poured the champagne. It was nearly an hour later before Penny and Ingrid cleared the table of dirty plates and cups and the few remaining cakes, and Sasha placed the box on the table in front of Peter. They all watched as he carefully cut through the string and unfolded the thick brown paper used to parcel it up to reveal an old-fashioned square tin.

The lid came off easily and Peter set it to one side as everyone leant forward to peer into it. A sealed envelope with the word *Confidentiel* and Eliza written across it was on the very top. Peter took it out and laid it on the table before he continued to lift out unsealed envelopes containing black and white photos, marriage and birth certificates and various other pieces of paper. A ring box was tucked into a corner at the bottom and Peter removed it, putting it unopened on the table as he picked up several loose photos from the bottom of the tin.

One of the photos, a portrait of a woman with a baby on her lap, slipped through his fingers. As he picked it up and saw it properly, the colour drained from his face. Silently, he handed it to Edward. Surprised, he too glanced at the photo, giving a visible start before he handed it back to Peter, his eyes wide open and a questioning look on his face.

'Alice, Lucas, I think it's important that your grandmother is here before we go any further,' Peter said quietly, picking up the lid and placing it back on the tin.

'Why?' Alice asked. 'She's said we can tell her about the contents of the box if they're important – she just doesn't want to see them.'

'I'm sorry, but that is no longer possible. She has to see

them. She needs to be here because I think she is possibly the only person still alive who can explain this photo and the rest of the contents of this tin,' and Peter handed the photo to Alice.

'I've never seen a photo of a woman like this in any of the photo albums Eliza has,' Alice said, staring at it before handing it to Lucas and looking up uncertainly at Peter. 'I'm not sure Eliza will even know who this person is.'

'Maybe not,' Peter said. 'But I, on the other hand, suspect I know who she is. I think my father, from the look on his face, also suspects who she is.' He took a deep breath.

'Eliza needs to come and try to explain to us how a photograph of my great-aunt Bernadette, who vanished from our family records at the beginning of the twentieth century, came to be in a tin sent to your grandmother over fifty years ago.'

'Grand-maman, you have to come up to the château with us right now,' Alice said, running into Eliza's cottage. 'They've just opened the box Sasha found in the attic and Peter wants you there before they go any further.'

Eliza sighed. 'I've told you I'm not interested.'

'I'm not taking no for an answer, Grand-maman. Lucas has the car waiting outside. You. Have. To. Come,' Alice begged. 'It's important. They're waiting for you before they take anything else out of the box.'

Eliza tutted, but finally got to her feet and followed Alice out to the car.

* * *

When Eliza walked into the orangery, Peter stood up and took her by the arm. 'Eliza, I am so pleased you've joined us. Please come with me, I'd like to show you a painting hanging in the château before we look at the contents of your box together.'

In the dining room, Peter led her over to the family portrait.

'This is my great-grandfather Edward, his brother Charles and their sister Bernadette. It was painted just before the brothers left to fight in the First World War. Sadly, Charles never came back. The ring Bernadette is wearing is rather beautiful, don't you think?'

Eliza peered at the picture. 'I suppose it is. But why are you showing me this?'

'Let's go back to the orangery and the others, and I'll tell you why I've shown you this family portrait and in return, I hope you can explain some things to me.'

Eliza gave him a sharp look. 'I don't know why you should think that. I know nothing about your family.'

Back in the orangery, Alice pulled out a chair for Eliza and took hold of her hand.

'It's going to be all right,' Alice said as reassuringly as she could.

Peter handed Eliza the black and white photo before opening the ring box and silently pushing it towards her 'You've just seen my great-aunt Bernadette in the old family painting wearing both a ring that is identical to the one in this jewel box, and a dress that looks to be the same one she is wearing in the photo. The baby on her lap is presumably hers.' Peter swallowed hard. 'Eliza, I sincerely believe that this all points to the lady in the photo being Bernadette Chevalier – and the baby on her lap is your mother. Which makes Bernadette your grand-maman as well as my great-aunt which in turn, makes you and me related.'

Eliza, visibly shocked, looked at him. 'I've never heard the name Bernadette Chevalier before, and this afternoon is the first time I've ever seen a portrait or a photo of her. All I know about my grand-maman is that her name was Bernadette Gilet.'

'Then you need to go through the papers in this tin and see if you can piece together how your family history is linked to mine.' Peter gave a soft sigh. 'My father and I are happy to help you. The last thing anyone wants is to upset you or to cause you pain. With that in mind, I want to say to you that if any wrongs were committed by the Chevaliers to your close family a hundred years ago, then this generation of the family will do everything in their power to make amends. We can't change history, but we can definitely make a difference in the present.'

Eliza trembled. 'Thank you.'

Peter picked up the envelope marked Eliza and handed it to her. 'Perhaps the contents of this will explain.'

Eliza's fingers were shaking as she carefully opened it and drew out several pieces of paper with old-fashioned French handwriting. One was a letter addressed to Eliza from her mother, Marie-Thérèse, and the other one bearing the signature Bernadette Gilet (née Chevalier) was addressed to Marie-Thérèse. Eliza began to read the letter from her mother to her.

43

My darling daughter Eliza,

I am so sorry not to have met my first grandchild, Claudia. You know I have not been in the best of health for the past few years, and now you are reading this you will have received the news that I have passed.

The parcel this letter will have been placed in contains all that is left of my maternal family.

Both you and I have had a better life than my maman, Bernadette Chevalier. We married men that we loved rather than being forced, not into an arranged marriage exactly, but to accept a marriage of convenience like she did. I know you and William are truly happy together and with the arrival of Claudia, you are now a family.

I regret not giving you the enclosed ring when you reached your majority, but I simply couldn't face all the questions you would ask and I knew some of your questions would be difficult, if not impossible, to answer truthfully. I think the enclosed letter from your grandmother explains the family rift and why you have never met any of your maternal relatives. Perhaps one day you will – the world is shrinking, it seems to me, with people travelling more and more.

Your loving mother,

Marie-Thérèse.

* * *

Dear Marie-Thérèse,

I know you always felt that I did not love you, that I was cold and distant with you. I have to admit that I was, because for many years I blamed you for ruining my life. It took me a long time to admit that the only person who had ruined my life was me. By then, it was too late to repair our relationship; you were grown, married, and living far from home.

I never told you about the life I lived before you were born. There was little point in you knowing about that life because it was as if it had happened to a stranger. Telling you about it would only have brought up memories for me that I couldn't bear to remember. But I do have a duty to tell you who your ancestors are.

So, briefly, my early years, until I was twenty, were spent happily in the family home in the countryside near Rouen, with my brothers Edward and Charles, both of whom I adored. There were soirées, entertainments and dances year-round. I had no expectation that my adult life would be any different. I would naturally marry someone of my own class and have a comfortable house with servants to oversee.

Charles dying in the war was something my parents never recovered from. Neither did I. I was heartbroken at the loss of my brother. The truth is, I found solace in the arms of an unsuitable man and to the horror of my parents, I became pregnant with you out of wedlock.

I married Alphonse Gilet, a Huguenot priest, before you were born. He was not your father, but when he realised my situation, he offered me a form of respectability and I took it gratefully. Afterwards, though, the family disowned me and you. Marrying Alphonse was as bad as becoming pregnant before marriage to my family of staunch Catholics. They completely cut us off. My older brother Edward was forbidden to contact me. I was forbidden to contact him.

Once I was married, I never heard from the Chevalier family again. Alphonse was basically a good man, although he was a man of his time both morally and... well, let's say life wasn't always easy with him; he did care for you even though you were not his.

I did try once, and once only, to introduce you to your grandparents. They refused to see or acknowledge either of us.

I trust your marriage is a happy one and that you will continue to have a good life. I hope and pray that you and Eliza are close, as mothers and daughters should be.

I have very few material possessions, but the enclosed ring belonged to my mother before me, and I would like you to give it to Eliza to pass on to any daughters or grand-daughters she may have. I would like it to stay in the new branch of my family. No longer Chevaliers by name, but they still own their lineage of several generations through me. That is something nobody can deny them.

With sincere and loving thoughts, your mother,
Bernadette Gilet (née Chevalier).

With tears streaming down her face, Eliza looked at Peter and held the letters out to him. 'You need to read these letters. You were right. We are related,' and she gave him and his father a tremulous smile. 'So much to take in. I think I'd like to go home now if you don't mind.'

Both Alice and Lucas leapt to their feet and were at her side instantly, helping her up.

'Do you want to take the box with you? It is legally yours,' Peter said quietly.

Eliza shook her head. 'No, not right now. Alice will take me home. Lucas can stay and go through it with you and work it all out. Then we will decide what to do with the contents.'

After Eliza and Alice had left, Penny insisted she would do the clearing away, leaving Lucas and everyone else to carefully go through the contents of the box. Sasha, feeling that she didn't have the right to be there now it was clearly a family affair, offered to help.

'Thanks, but there's no need. You get off home,' Penny said, her mind whirling with what had happened. She wanted some time to think through the implications of the family link that had been discovered. Once the dishwasher was working and she'd wiped down the work surfaces, she took *La Maison du Jardinier* key off its hook. She'd get the privacy she wanted there.

Once safely inside, she closed the door behind her and slumped back against it. She'd have to step away from Lucas now they were related; it might be only distantly, but she didn't feel comfortable about it. She suspected just being friends was going to be difficult for both of them. It would have to be a real break-up. No keeping in touch. To think she'd been almost floating with happiness after their visit to the Valley of the Saints. The way Lucas had defended her from Rory. And now the future she'd envisaged with him had been taken away from her. If only Sasha had thrown Eliza's box away.

No, she couldn't think that. Peter and Grandad Edward, as well as Eliza, were thrilled to finally know their family history. I wasn't their fault that discovering the family connection was going to have such a negative impact on her own life.

44

It was two days before Bastille Day when Jean-Paul took Sasha, together with the pups, to show her his farm. About a kilometre from the château in the opposite direction of the village and down a long, gated rough track, the traditional granite stone *mas* nestled in a valley. Looking at the house, Sasha's fingers itched to create a painting of it. With its faded red shutters opened flat against the walls, pale blue wisteria framing the front door and Viking asleep on the doorstep, it was picture-perfect.

She turned to Jean-Paul. 'You leave Viking out when you're not here?'

'Sometimes, if I have the need. The yard gates are closed, the land around is mine and Viking, he never leave. I bring him with me most times, but today, with Mimi and Mitzi, there was no room in the car.'

Viking stood up and lazily stretched as Jean-Paul opened the car door and Mimi and Mitzi bounded out straight for him.

'Come in,' Jean-Paul said, leading the way. 'I confess I do very little to the house since my parents leave.'

Sasha gazed around at the kitchen with its beams and red tiles on the floor, a large, battered table standing in the centre of the room, half a dozen chairs scattered around it. Although old-fashioned in style without built-in units, alongside the large dresser with its display of Bretagne pottery, it did have a modern stove and a dishwasher. Sasha thought it was the perfect-sized kitchen for feeding a family and entertaining friends. A picture window above the sink gave a view out over an orchard of apple and plum trees. Several chickens were scratching at the ground, while a few were enjoying dust baths in the loose soil they'd already scratched up.

'They are not suppose to be in there,' Jean-Paul said, laughing. 'Their run is the other side of the fence. I give you some eggs when you leave if you like. Come see the rest.'

The sitting room alongside the kitchen had a wood burner fitted into the inglenook fireplace, two comfortable-looking settees, rugs on the tiled floor and bookcases lining two out of three walls. 'You've got a proper library here,' Sasha said.

Jean-Paul smiled. 'My parents, they always read a lot and me the same. Some books are from my grandparents' time.' Mimi and Mitzi ran into the room at that moment and skidded to a halt, scattering the rugs. Jean-Paul laughed. 'We let them run outside?'

'Good idea,' Sasha said.

Out in the farmyard, Viking lay stretched out in the sunshine again and warned the pups off with a short growl when they tried to ambush him into playing.

'The sheep and most lambs are out in the fields,' Jean-Paul said. 'But the couple of late ones are still in this barn,' and he took her over to the half-door of a small building.

Peering over, Sasha saw two ewes standing there contentedly chewing some hay whilst their lambs headbutted each other in play.

'They join the flock out in the field later this week, I hope, when the weather is better,' Jean-Paul said.

'So sweet,' Sasha said, quietly watching them.

'Come on. I make some coffee and you can tell me what happening up at the château.'

As they turned to make their way back into the farmhouse, Sasha's mobile rang. Jean-Paul gestured to her to answer. 'It is perhaps important.'

Sasha recognised the number as the one Colette had given her, which she'd rung a couple of days ago to ask about the loan of the Welsh Cob, leaving a message. 'I have been waiting for this call,' she admitted as she pressed the button. 'Hello?'

It was a few minutes later when she said, 'Thank you for letting me know. If it doesn't work out, please feel free to give me a call.' Sasha sighed as she followed Jean-Paul back into the kitchen. 'I thought I was in with a chance of having a horse on loan, but the owner has already found a new home for him. Probably just as well. I've got enough going on without adding a horse into the mix. One day the time will be right and I will have one,' she said, smiling at him.

'It is a pity this time it not work out but I hope you have your own horse one day in future,' Jean-Paul said.

Five minutes later the two of them were sitting at a tiled table in a small garden at the side of the farmhouse, Viking and the two puppies under the table at their feet. Jean-Paul had placed coffee and two delicious-looking raspberry and cream tarts on the table before opening a large parasol to provide some shade from the heat of the sun.

Sasha bit into her tart and gave a little moan of delight. 'This tastes even better than it looked.' Jean-Paul, eating his own tart, nodded his head in agreement.

After she'd finished eating and could speak again, Sasha looked at Jean-Paul. 'I need to thank you for talking to Freddie.'

'I feel bad I interfere, but it would be a mistake for him to be involve with Maddie not knowing the truth,' Jean-Paul said.

'Don't think of it as interfering,' Sasha said. 'You simply told Freddie something important and he made up his own mind, thankfully.'

Jean-Paul nodded. 'It is better to think that.'

Sasha sipped her coffee. 'If anybody can be accused of meddling in someone else's business, it's probably me, not throwing Eliza's box away as she told me to.'

'*Mais non*. It was a good thing to not do. You make several people happy. If you are finish, we walk and I show you some of the land, yes?' Jean-Paul stood up and held out his hand. 'There is a little river at the bottom of my valley; you like to see? The dogs they can play in the water.'

'Sounds fun,' and Sasha sprang up from her chair.

Walking down the side of a flower meadow full of poppies and wildflowers, with her hand enclosed in Jean-Paul's work-roughened one, she felt a surge of happiness flood through her body. Being with this man felt so right.

The stream, when they reached it, was an idyllic spot. Fresh clear water trickled over pebbles and small rocks and gurgled its way around larger boulders, creating several pools in the process. 'What a beautiful place,' Sasha said watching the dogs splashing around in the shallows. A willow-tree dipped its branches in the water and they both saw a flash of blue flying out of its protection.

'Was that a kingfisher? I've never seen one before,' Sasha said.

Jean-Paul nodded. 'Yes. We are lucky to see it.'

Sasha gave a contented sigh and looked at Jean-Paul. 'I understand why you've never wanted to leave the farm, you have everything you need here.'

'I am proud to be the fifth generation of my family to work this land, to live in the farmhouse. I accept my destiny happily.' Jean-Paul smiled at her. 'My papa, he teach me well in the ways of country life. You like the French countryside?'

'I love it. The countryside is my happy place.'

'That is good for me to hear,' Jean-Paul said quietly. 'The farming life is not for everyone.' He paused for several seconds, leaving Sasha anxiously wondering what he was going to say.

'I meet you and my heart begin to sing. Life, it take on a different vibration. Something special happen. I start to wonder.' He hesitated, staring down at the water gurgling over the rocks before looking up at her. 'But it is difficult when the language is not the same to know if the other person feel the same.' Jean-Paul gazed at Sasha, his expression full of hope, his body tense as he waited for her reply to the question he was about to ask. He caught hold of both her hands. 'Do you?'

'Do I what?' Sasha asked quietly.

'Do you have the feeling for me I have for you?'

There was a split second of silence as Sasha looked at him with a big smile on her face as she nodded. 'Of course I do.'

With a deep sigh, Jean-Paul pulled her close and enveloped her in a tight hug before giving her a kiss that left neither of them in any doubt about how the other one felt about them.

45

The day before Bastille Day, Eliza accepted an invitation from Peter to go up to the château for lunch with him, his parent and Ingrid. 'Alice and Lucas have both got a rendez-vous in Quimper, but Lucas has said he'll drop you off here first and Alice will collect you later. So it will be just us oldies to talk things through and show you the family bible, and for you to go through the contents of the box.'

Penny cooked and served lunch for them but declined to join them, laughingly saying, 'You're all guests today.' She'd been relieved when she'd learnt that Lucas wasn't staying for lunch. She'd managed to avoid him ever since the afternoon when opening the box had changed things for them both.

When she saw the family bible with Bernadette Chevalier's name scratched out, Eliza's eyes filled with tears. 'That poor woman. One cannot begin to comprehend what she went through. Such a different world in those days. No wonder she was unable to bond with her daughter.'

Edward Chevalier nodded. 'We need to reinstate her name

add in her marriage to Alphonse Gilet and continue the family tree with her descendants. Set the family history straight.'

'Thank you,' Eliza said. 'Until I read those two letters, I had no idea of what had happened in my family in the past. It seems Bernadette was a very unhappy woman for most of her adult life. The only grandparents I ever knew were my father's parents and they died when I was quite young. Growing up, although my mother and I were close, I accepted without question that she never talked about her own mother. I remember when I was about ten, I think, I asked did she think her mother ever thought about her? She gave a shrug and said, "I doubt it. She wasn't a maternal sort of woman".' Eliza gave a sniff. 'Bernadette's letter shows the real reasons.'

After lunch, Peter placed the contents of the box on the table. The mixture of old photos, letters, and birth and marriage certificates had been tidily sorted into date order as far as possible. Eliza picked out a letter to read, from Charles to 'Bernadette, my dearest sister,' when he had first enlisted, and she was still clearly living at home. Thanking her for the last letter that had finally reached him, he told her how much he missed home and her, and how he detested being a soldier. He couldn't wait to be back and go walking the dogs with her in the countryside. Replacing it in the pile, Eliza saw a framed sketch of a large country house and picked it up.

'Our family home near Rouen,' Edward said.

'It looks a substantial *maison de maître* for a successful family. Does a Chevalier still own it?' Eliza asked.

'Sadly no,' Edward answered. 'My father had to sell it in the forties after the war when we moved to England. He hated doing it but basically, a problem with inheritance tax and no money in the bank after the war gave him no choice. I've driven past it on a couple of occasions when we've been in France and dream of buying it back. Not likely to happen.'

Eliza picked up the ring box and, opening it, stared at its contents sitting on the velvet cushion. 'It's beautiful.'

'Try it on,' Ingrid said.

Eliza shook her head. 'No. It won't fit over my arthritic knuckles.'

'That's a shame,' Ingrid said. 'Put it somewhere safe when you get home then.'

Eliza smiled. 'Definitely.' She looked at the family history in front of her and shook her head in disbelief. 'I find it hard to take in that I now have relatives. I always longed to have at least an aunt and a cousin; now I have...' She stopped. 'What do I have exactly?'

Peter took her hand. 'You have a whole family of new relations. We'll work out all the family links later, but you and I are definitely related.'

Alice arrived shortly afterwards to take Eliza home. As Peter walked her to the car, he mentioned the fete.

'Tomorrow's the village fete. You are coming, aren't you? Good,' he said when Eliza nodded. 'And in the evening, we're having a private party for family and friends in the orangery, to which you are naturally invited. So we'll see you again tomorrow, cousin.' And Peter leant in and kissed her cheek.

46

Alice, as organizer-in-chief of the fete, had taken the decision to keep all the events close to the main entrance. 'Easier for people to see everything and not have to walk too far through the estate, especially if it rains.' She'd worked out a plan of where each stall or event would go and pinned it to a makeshift sandwich board by the tarmacked area where cars would park. Peter and Penny were primed to stand by to show people where to place their stands and equipment and to generally help them to get organised.

Thankfully, the early morning clouds had disappeared and the sun was high in the sky by midday, most of the stalls were in place and the frantic feelings of 'will we ever be ready' had been dispelled. As Alice walked slowly around the stalls checking everything was in order, Freddie was 'testing, testing' the sound system he'd set up, ready for the vicar to officially open the fete at two o'clock prompt.

The first visitors started to appear before two o'clock and happily paid their one euro entrance fee. By the time the vicar had arrived and given his welcoming speech, all the stalls had people eager to either buy what was on offer, play boules or take part in the lucky dip. The trio with their Celtic music and songs entertained visitors all afternoon and the ice cream van had a queue from the moment it parked on the drive.

Sasha, in a quiet moment at the tombola stall, watched as Maddie and Jade stopped to talk to Freddie, who was again adjusting something on the sound system. Sasha saw him pick up Jade and swing her around, before gently setting her back down. Maddie seemed intent on saying something to Freddie and Sasha saw him smile before he answered Maddie, ruffled Jade's hair and walked away. She'd ask him what was going on later.

'Sasha, I'd like you to meet Dawn who saved my life a few months ago,' Penny said, appearing with a tall dark-haired woman in front of the stall.

'Well, somebody had to rescue you from you know who,' Dawn said.

'Lovely to meet you,' Sasha said. 'Have you come to stay?'

'No. I had a few days' holiday due and I thought I'd surprise Penny and see how she was. I miss her. I needed to make sure she was okay. I'm staying at—'

'Here, at least for the night,' Penny interrupted. 'We're having a family party this evening and I insist you stay. Your help was crucial to me escaping from an unpleasant situation and a certain person. I can never thank you enough. And I know Mum and Dad will want to thank you too.'

Dawn looked uncertain. Sasha, sensing that Penny really wanted her friend to stay, said, 'You can't possibly turn down the offer of staying in the château. It's amazing.'

'Yes,' Penny laughed. 'The next time you come, you'll be roughing it in the old *Maison du Jardinier* with me.'

'In that case, I give in,' Dawn said, laughing. 'Thank you. I'd love to stay tonight.'

It was gone six o'clock when the vicar thanked everyone for coming and spending money to help the church, wished them a good evening at the fireworks in Carhaix if they were going, and told them the fete was now officially closed.

As she and Freddie helped clear rubbish away, Sasha said, 'I saw you with Jade and Maddie earlier. Are you okay? Maddie wasn't pressuring you to change your mind or anything?'

Freddie gave a rueful smile. 'How did you guess? But don't worry. My mind is not for changing.'

* * *

Lucas, who had been wanting to talk to Penny all day, finally managed to track her down as she and Dawn stacked some chairs near the orangery for later in the evening, ready for their own family and friends' Bastille Day party.

'There you are,' Lucas said. 'I am looking everywhere for you.'

'And now you've found me,' Penny said, her voice flat.

Dawn looked from one to the other, not sure what was going on but deciding the two of them didn't need an audience. 'I'll go and see if I can help anyone else,' Dawn said and quickly walked away from them.

'Why do I get the feeling you avoid me since our afternoon in the Valley of the Saints?' Lucas said.

'Because I *have* been avoiding you. Avoiding having this conversation. A conversation I have no desire to have,' Penny said, close to tears now the moment had come. 'You have to realise we cannot have a future together other than as friends,' she said quietly.

'Why? I don't understand. I thought after the Valley of the Saints...' His voice trailed away.

'Oh, come on, Lucas, you were there when the box was opened and your grandmother's family history was discovered.'

'Yes, I was there, but I don't see how or why it affect us?'

'How can you say that? Of course it affects us. We are related. It might be distantly, but we are both in the same family tree.'

Lucas shook his head. 'But we're not related.'

Penny gave him an exasperated look. 'You and Alice are brother and sister and the three of us are Chevalier cousins. We have a great-great-relative in common – your great-great-grand maman is my great-great aunt. I know it's a distant connection but a cousin is a cousin.'

Smiling, Lucas caught hold of her hand. 'We aren't cousins. You and Alice are cousins,' he said quietly. 'Legally, Alice and me are brother and sister, but we are not blood relation. Alice is my stepsister, not even my half-sister.'

Penny stared at him in disbelief, shaking her head. 'What?'

'You didn't realise?'

'No. You call each other brother and sister, Eliza calls you her grandson.'

'We grew up together. Alice was about four and I was just three and a few months I think when Claudia and my papa married. They did all the legal thing necessary to make us a proper family because they didn't plan on having children together, but they want us to be brother and sister. It's simple as that.'

'So just to confirm the facts, you and I are not even distantly related?' Penny said.

'No. But I would very much like to be in a relationship with you for the rest of my life,' Lucas said.

Penny gave him a shaky smile as she moved into his arms. 'Sounds good to me.'

After the bulk of the clearing up had been done and all the visitors and stallholders had left, everybody disappeared for an hour or two, glad of a breather before meeting up at eight thirty for supper in the orangery.

Dawn was helping Freddie arrange the small tables and chairs on the terrace in front of it whilst inside, Sasha helped Penny put several platters of finger food on the big table alongside plates, serviettes and champagne glasses.

When Alice, Lucas and Eliza returned, the doors were open, and the muslin curtains were blowing in the balmy evening breeze. Penny had switched on the fairy lights and the LED candles that were hidden in the plant pots and in the three big moonlike orbs that she'd recently found in a garden centre and placed by each French door.

At Eliza's request, Peter poured two glasses of champagne, placed them on a small table as Eliza sat in one of the comfortable Lloyd Loom chairs, and called Sasha over.

'Eliza would like to talk to you,' he said.

Looking at Sasha, Eliza raised her glass. '*Santé* and *merci beaucoup*. I am so happy you did not throw my box away. I would have lost something precious that I didn't even realise I had. *Merci*.'

'I was so worried about upsetting you,' Sasha said. 'I'm happy for you and relieved.' And the two of them clinked glasses in the time-honoured fashion.

Penny was standing with her parents and Lucas when Alice approached her and quietly drew her away.

'Grand-maman gave me the ring tonight,' and she held out her hand for Penny to see.

'It's beautiful and it truly suits your hand,' Penny said.

'I love it,' Alice said. 'But I can't help feeling it really belongs to your side of the family – to you, to be precise.'

'No.' Penny shook her head. 'Your great-great-grandmother was very definite in her letter, wanting her own side of the family to have the ring as an heirloom. It's yours, no question of that. Wear it and enjoy it – cousin!'

It was eleven o'clock when Peter tapped the champagne glass he was holding.

'Very last minute, but I managed to find a few fireworks – nothing to rival Carhaix's display and not noisy because of the dogs and other animals around, but hopefully you'll enjoy them.'

Sasha, standing with Jean-Paul's arm around her shoulders and Freddie and Dawn on her other side, watching the colourful starbursts in the sky, gave a deep sigh of happiness. Everything had changed so much for her and Freddie in the last three months or so. Losing their mum last year had been hard, but the decision to move to France together had been a good one. The people around her oohing and aahing at the fireworks overhead were her friends, good friends, that she knew would now always have a place in her life. Especially Jean-Paul. She couldn't truly imagine being without him now.

She wasn't naive enough to expect everything to go completely to plan. Circumstances had thrown enough problems at her in the past and would inevitably throw up more in the future. Some would be unexpected, some would be seen coming from miles away, perhaps because of mistakes she'd made. Sometimes, though, for a short while like right now, her mum's favourite expression was singing in her head: 'Everything in the garden is coming up roses.'

EPILOGUE

A YEAR LATER

Sasha has settled well in France and can't imagine ever returning to England. The cottage still requires some work, but her Etsy business is starting to thrive. She is still hoping to have a horse sometime in the future, but for now she's enjoying living in the countryside and having Mimi and Mitzi. But most of all she is happy to have Jean-Paul in her life, and knows that her dream of standing in the château chapel with him at her side, having their marriage blessed, will be more than just a dream in the near future.

Freddie has built up a successful garden business. Dawn has been a regular visitor since they met last Bastille Day, and he is starting to hope she may turn out be the one for him, if only he can persuade her to move to France.

Ingrid and Peter have been busy with guests and wedding receptions during the summer season. In winter, the château hosted several private events, vintage car shows and a small music festival, all organised by their events manager, Alice. With the château at the heart of village life now, hosting several community events as well as the book club, Peter and Ingrid annot imagine ever leaving their dream home, the Château du Cheval.

Penny and Lucas are living together in the old *Maison du Jardinier*, which Lucas is helping to renovate – and turning into their forever home. Penny is busy with her cookery school and Lucas has started his degree in conservation and environmental management.

Alice is living with Eliza in her cottage and is busy with the marketing of events for the château, and working from the office in the *Maison du Jardinier* on her own small business. She's slowly built up a reliable team of people, including a new team member, Marc, an ex-maître d' with considerable experience in hotels around the world.

Eliza is happy to be related to the Chevaliers and talks proudly about her relatives up at the Château du Cheval. She can often be found enjoying an afternoon tea in the orangery.

Once again, there is a true community living, loving and adding to the long history of the Château du Cheval.

ACKNOWLEDGEMENTS

Once again, my heartfelt thanks must go to 'Team Boldwood' who deserve my unreserved gratitude for every book I write. Especially Caroline, my editor; Jade, the copy editor; Christina, the proofreader, and of course Claire and the marketing team. Thanks to Rachel Gilbey and all the bloggers, the book groups – especially 'The Friendly Book Community' and 'Riveting Reads and Vintage Vibes'– all of whom are amazingly supportive.

And of course, huge thanks to all my readers without whom I couldn't do the job I love most in the world.

Love to you all.

Jennie xxx

ABOUT THE AUTHOR

Jennifer Bohnet is the bestselling author of over 14 women's fiction titles, including *Villa of Sun and Secrets* and *A Riviera Retreat*. She is originally from the West Country but now lives in the wilds of rural Brittany, France.

Sign up to Jennifer Bohnet's mailing list here for news, competitions and updates on future books.

Visit Jennifer's website: www.jenniferbohnet.com

Follow Jennifer on social media:

facebook.com/Jennifer-Bohnet-170217789709356

x.com/jenniewriter

instagram.com/jenniewriter

bookbub.com/authors/jennifer-bohnet

ALSO BY JENNIFER BOHNET

Villa of Sun and Secrets

A Riviera Retreat

Rendez-Vous in Cannes

A French Affair

One Summer in Monte Carlo

Summer at the Château

Falling for a French Dream

Villa of Second Chances

Christmas on the Riviera

Making Waves at River View Cottage

Summer on the French Riviera

High Tides and Summer Skies

A French Adventure

A French Country Escape

LOVE NOTES

LOVE IN EVERY CHAPTER

WHERE ALL YOUR ROMANCE
DREAMS COME TRUE!

THE HOME OF BESTSELLING
ROMANCE AND WOMEN'S
FICTION

 WARNING:
MAY CONTAIN SPICE

SIGN UP TO OUR
NEWSLETTER

https://bit.ly/Lovenotesnews

Boldwood

Boldwood Books is an award-winning fiction publishing company seeking out the best stories from around the world.

Find out more at www.boldwoodbooks.com

Join our reader community for brilliant books, competitions and offers!

Follow us
@BoldwoodBooks
@TheBoldBookClub

Sign up to our weekly deals newsletter

https://bit.ly/BoldwoodBNewsletter

Printed in Great Britain
by Amazon

50059183R00155